Milkmaids,
Meadows,
Boys Called Peter

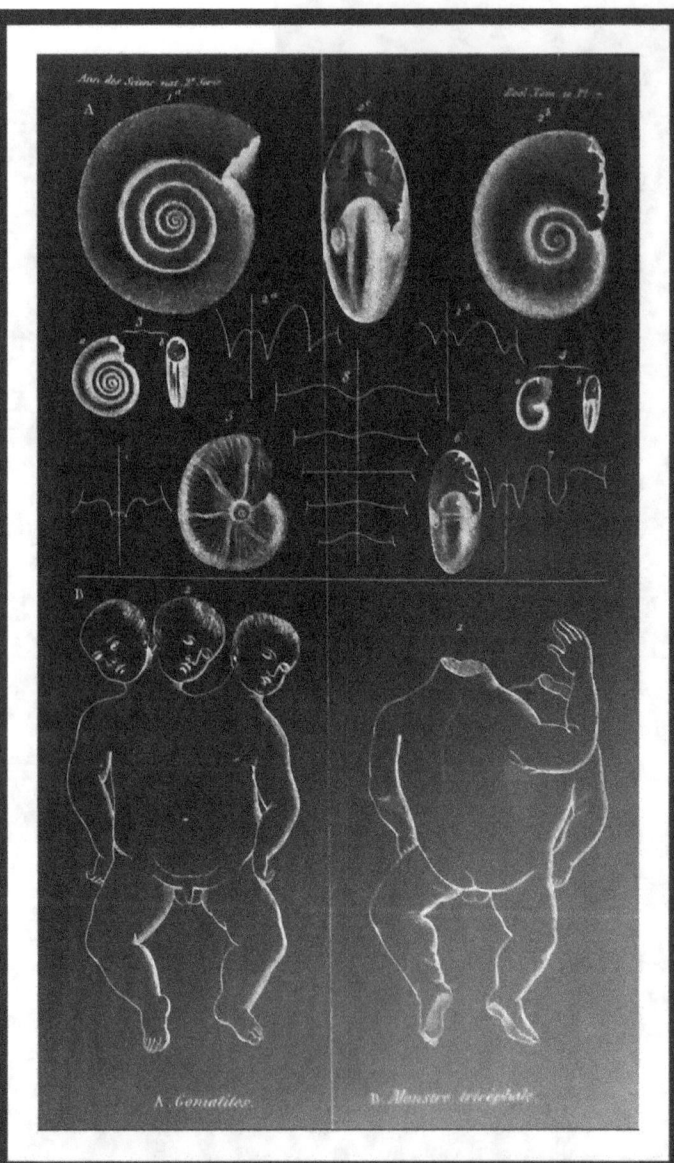

A . *Cornalites.*   B . *Monstre tricéphale.*

Milkmaids, Meadows, Boys Called Peter

A Pseudo-Fairy Tale
Set in a World of Science rather than Magic

A. N. Schweitzer

Blue Lias Press

This Blue Lias Press edition June 2019

For postdocs past, present and future

and

for my family

ONCE UPON A TIME, in the mid-1990s, when few people carried cell phones and the internet was in its dawn…

Part I

Exposure and Infection

Chapter One

ALICE WAS NOT YET used to this dazzling light. If she had still been in Britain and had not felt the instant chill, it could have been the start of a fine summer's day. But this was not Britain, it was New England at the end of January. Hauling out her scuffed red bicycle, she hoisted it onto one shoulder, closed the door and climbed the steps. The twelve-speed racer was an unexpected perk of the otherwise modest apartment, left behind by a former tenant. "Another visiting scientist, just like you!" her wizened landlord had said with disproportionate delight. It was slightly too large, with a rock-solid seat, but saved fifteen minutes each way on her daily commute—when the tires were not flat, that is. Today the front wheel landed like a deadweight on the flagstones of the garden path.

Alice groaned. She had been making such good time. Besides, last night the tire was fine—though all she remembered of her way home from the lab was her delight at the freshly broken news that her sister was engaged. Even if the blacktop had been glittering with glass shards, the sparkling would simply have resonated with her celebratory mood. Actually, the force of her own elation had surprised her far more than Ian's proposal, which was long overdue. The exuberance with which Diane had described the moment, and her childlike euphoria and blatant relief, must have been infectious over the phone.

This morning, however, Alice's excitement about the wedding had deflated too. As she lugged the bicycle back down the damp sunken stairwell and in through her front door, she acknowledged the likely reality of that pending day in August: the furtive glances cast her way as relatives and friends shared trite family clichés. *Poor Alice, stuck in her ivory tower with no time for romance; Alice: the eternal student, footloose and fancy free; or Diane's the practical one, and Alice the dreamer with her head in the clouds*. None of it, she would have to tell them, was remotely true.

For a start, she thought, pulling off her gloves, she might work in academia, but she was a scientist and science was practical in the extreme. And she hardly lived in an ivory tower in her basement abode. Removing her helmet and opening her coat, she released the front wheel, pried off the tire and freed the tube. In little more time than it took for the vulcanizing fluid to dry, she had patched up the hole. Before she tucked back the tube and replaced the tire, she used the tweezers from an old dissection kit to extract the glass sliver she found lodged in the worn tread. And she really did feel happy for Diane, she affirmed and jammed the axel back. Even if Diane was younger by three years.

As she zippered her coat again and rewound her scarf, another cliché tolled: *Diane has the looks and Alice the brains*. That one might even be true, she thought, sweeping back her hair—now unfamiliarly long after six months of near-neglect—and holding it in place with her helmet. Then again, she observed, it hardly explained the fact that most of her peers in academia, whether beautiful or not—though plenty of them were—had paired up and settled down like anyone else. Who could blame her, or even those friends and relatives, for wondering why she had not?

A SHORT AND CHILLY bike ride later, Alice hurried inside and took the stairs up to her floor. In the otherwise empty lab, a small yellow Post-it note brightened the desk in the dead end of her bay. "Missed call from a fellow countryman @ 8:25 am," Sage had written in red pen, double-circling the *man*. Today of all days, Alice thought. It was now eight fifty-five. Any other day and she would have been there for the call. Immediately she backtracked to the coffee room, and checked the small computer lab, but Sage had disappeared. Back at her desk, she finally set down her helmet and took off her coat. Examining the half-baked hint again, her wishful brain swiftly magnified a pinprick of hope and her enforced trip home for the wedding became a journey of possibility and even necessity that had nothing to do with Diane. Was her own happy ending finally in sight?

But she was getting ahead of herself. Peeling the note from last night's scatter plots—which looked no more promising in the light of day—she added it to the patchwork of other memos lining the window by her desk. Down below, in the narrow U-shaped parking lot still folded in her building's shadow, her bicycle remained alone in the bike rack, although the well-wrapped attendant was already opening out the sandwich board marking the parking lot as full. A car drove up and the attendant leaned toward its wound-down window, waving directions with a thick black glove. The car pulled away and turned into the stream of traffic separating the parking lot from the medical school quad.

"Alice?"

Alice jumped at the sound of Helen's voice. "I was just looking for an elastic," she said, instantly gathering her hair with one hand—her helmet did not fit over the ponytail she wore at work to comply with lab safety rules.

"And I'm just looking for my graduate student," Helen said from Sage's bay, peering through the open shelving and pulling on an auburn curl as if pulling rank—Alice's hair had tarnished during childhood from golden to mouse-brown and despite the bread crusts she had devoured was still dead straight.

"He was here earlier," Alice said, thinking of the Post-it note—and trying to remind herself that it was probably just Richard or one of his new postdocs calling to ask where something obvious was. It was all Richard's fault anyway for forcing her to leave. Having mentored her doctorate in Cambridge and then dragged her off to London when he transferred his lab—where she had overseen the move and trained an army of new recruits while he dealt with bureaucracy and four spoiled teenage sons—he had rewarded her unswerving loyalty by sending her away. True, he had offered her a lectureship when she returned, but only if she went away first and came back with a few good publications and some novel expertise. And even that might have been all very well, except that—

"Well, he's not here now," Helen said, circling into Alice's bay. "But you are. So tell me: How did it go last night?"

I could ask you the same thing, Alice thought, lapped by tendrils of perfume—always a sure sign, Sage had told her, that one of Helen's many 'gentleman friends' was in town. Instead Alice looked at the evidence strewn on her bench: the rack of used pellucid tubes, the empty boxes of pipette tips and still-pristine polystyrene box in which a blue lid floated in some erstwhile ice. "Same again," she said. "As inert as the untouched controls."

Alice wished she could blame her data on Diane, who had phoned just before she harvested her T-cells, the tiny white blood cells she had spent much of the previous week purifying and culturing in yet another attempt to outwit nature in a dish.

The first time Alice ran the experiment—a series of complex manipulations that she now knew by heart—the response had been momentous, beyond Helen's wildest dreams. If she had let a step run for too long during the phone call, or lost her focus in the aftermath, she might almost have been glad. But she knew the nuances of this assay like the back of her hand, and knew it had gone according to plan last night; the phone call had changed nothing.

"And I've been thinking," she added before Helen spoke. "I've repeated the procedure eleven times now and never seen the effect again. Don't you think it's possible—"

"It's too good a result to lose. If you've seen it once, you'll see it again. Think—*think*, Alice—what you could be doing wrong."

Or what I could be doing right, Alice thought, squeezing her fistful of hair. For almost six months she had been trying to stay positive, but was starting to wonder how anyone could become so fixated on what was obviously a one-off mistake.

"This is our key to the Sharden's grant," Helen reminded her needlessly. Sharden's was a poorly understood syndrome that had recently been renamed for a moderately well-known actor who had just been diagnosed. According to Helen, the resulting media coverage had worked wonders for philanthropy, and the newly formed Sharden's Syndrome Foundation was offering several large grants to attract new minds to the cause. Helen wished to be one such new mind, and had enlisted Alice to help formulate her pitch.

"I could give it another try tonight," Alice said doubtfully.

"Why not give it a try now?"

"I'd like to catch the seminar at noon."

"Ah. In that case you can head off to the library meanwhile.

As far as I'm aware, the proposal's still lacking published precedents to bolster our case."

"About that," Alice said, trying to sound meek. "What I've noticed is that there are more Sharden's papers hinting that it's caused by microbes, or even immunodeficiency, than by auto-immunity."

Helen's long-time focus was autoimmune disease, caused when the immune response, which evolved to attack invading pathogens, mistakenly attacks itself. As a result, she needed evidence tying Sharden's to some—or any—kind of autoimmune activity in order to justify the relevance of her approach.

"Don't waste your time on microbes," Helen said with supreme confidence. "As you say, they're all merely hints. No one has proof of anything yet, and that's because no one's looked yet in the right way. You've checked that citation I gave you?"

"Yes. But it's the same: all speculation with no evidence.

"Well, keep plugging away. It's a lucrative syndrome and we have to cash in on every option we can. As for your data, that's top of the list, and not only for the grant. That result has profound implications for autoimmune disease in general," she repeated for the thousandth time. "Quite apart from calling Hollhausen's bluff."

Alice murmured assent. Hollhausen—arguably one of the grandfathers of immunology—had claimed that not only was the assay in question technically impossible, but would show nothing new. Helen's delight had been palpable when Alice's first attempt had seemed to overthrow both claims. And despite her misgivings at Helen's combative tone, Alice had been happy, too—and not only with the science. Just as she sought context for her data in the scientific literature, she sought context for her actions in the not-so-scientific literature. Surely her immediate and antagonistic success was like Dorothy squashing the Witch of the East when she landed in Oz: this was the first step to publication, and Richard had made it quite clear that timely publication was one major factor that might hasten her return. Except that despite the hurricane that had been forecast at the time—which Alice had confused at first with a tornado—she had still found no metaphorical yellow brick road, no Emerald City, and certainly no silver shoes or ruby slippers that would take her back home.

"Well, I'll keep my fingers crossed," Alice said.

"Whatever it takes." Helen frowned and nodded at Alice's fingers, which were not crossed at all but buried in her hair. "You should try braiding it," she said.

"It doesn't stay," Alice explained. Because while Diane had spent hours trying out hairstyles with her childhood friends, Alice had not. Few people had lived in their small village, and fewer still with children, and none Alice's age. Fate, and her natural inclination, had led Alice to spend her youth wandering the clifftop trails lost in daydreams and thought instead of learning to braid hair. She began to demonstrate.

"No, not like that," Helen snapped. "Here, let me." Wreathing Alice now in cloying perfume, she moved in behind her. "The trick is to gather up the sides first," she explained before Alice realized what was happening, "and trap them here, like so…" Helen's fingers moved fast, her tone transitioning as she worked from mild irritation to near-camaraderie. "Stick to those few rules," she said, transferring the braid to Alice's raised palm, "and it'll stay in all day—even maybe under that thing," she added, nodding at the helmet lying upturned on the desk.

Taken aback, Alice thanked her profusely. With her free hand, she groped in her drawer for a hair elastic and wrapped it around the end. There was more end than braid by the time she was done, but she liked the way the it felt; and she liked the way *she* felt, as if she had crossed a threshold with Helen, been elevated to a new level of kinship. And maybe—just maybe—this meant she could now speak frankly to her boss. "About my project—" she started to say.

But Helen was already walking away. "Seriously," she called from the sink, at which she had stopped to wash her hands, "do you know where Sage keeps his results? I can't wait all day."

"Have you tried the binder on his shelf?" Alice was surprised by her light tone.

"I've looked in every damned binder I can find."

"In that case, I'm afraid I've no idea—but I'll ask him if I see him," she assured her retreating boss, and then dropped into her chair. She could have told Helen that she would have known exactly where those results were if the project was hers. Because it should have been hers. Sage's project was why she had chosen Helen's lab, and—she had thought—why Helen had chosen her. The fact was that even after Alice gave in to Richard and started looking for positions, she had been bound by inertia, by the arbitrary list of places advertising openings for postdocs. She had no preference among any of those jobs, so why should any of those prospective employers prefer her? Only then she met Helen in a crowded restroom at a big symposium, and everything had changed. Helen had heard Alice's talk, she said, and as they inched past the mirrors, claimed she needed someone just like her to jump-start a new project for which she had funds. Alice had been flattered and intrigued, and by the time they reached the grey-walled stalls where their ways diverged, Helen had promised her a two-year fellowship and a place in her lab.

Unlike those arbitrary advertisements, Helen's offer was to

Alice alone. Besides, everyone had heard of Helen Jonas, who was lively and smart and had a reputation for looking like an aging fashion icon in her well-cut clothes and Italian shoes. In fact, Helen was so at odds with the clichéd stereotype of the female scientist that Alice had seen her as the perfect role model. Admittedly Helen's sartorial style was firmly out of bounds of a postdoc salary; but then rustling raw silk, flowing scarves and teetering heels were impractical anyway for hands-on research. Most importantly, though, Helen had been excited by Alice's work with parasitic worms that dampen their hosts' immune system in order to co-exist; she had confided her plan to transpose this concept—using a far simpler viral microbe—to find signals that would dampen an over-active *auto*immune response and restore healthy self-tolerance. Sensing the hand of fate at play, Alice had accepted on the spot, only later suspecting and subsequently confirming that fate had been helped along by Richard; he and Helen were old friends. Still, all parties had been content—except for the minor problem that by the time Alice finally arrived in Helen's cutting-edge lab after many months of misdirected paperwork, the project in question had been given to Sage.

Nevertheless, Alice had decided not to mind. She was using Helen for the furtherance of her career and in return should not ask for too much. And she liked Sage. Having realized he was unaware of her prior claim, she had done nothing to enlighten him. It was hardly his fault, and he was having enough trouble with the project as it was. In any case, it was common knowledge that at the forefront of science priorities changed fast; if you wanted to survive you had to adapt.

In her accommodating way, Alice had adapted. After all, she liked life at the bench in its own right. She liked formulating questions, designing and performing experiments, even carrying out the mundane tasks of an active laboratory. However, on a day like today she had to admit that, despite her diligence and dedication, she had lost the joy in science she had known as a child.

Back then, in her out-of-the-way village on the coast of South Wales, science had seemed almost magical. The village nestled around a castle: a real Medieval castle with gargoyles and grand halls, arrow-slit slashed walls and a long-dry moat. Before Alice was born, the castle's once-formidable defenses had been annexed by the university in the nearest town and turned into a field station for littoral studies—literally studies of the shore—and although the knights in armor were long gone, the moat's grassy slopes were strewn with peace-loving students softly strumming guitars; the battlements that had protected feudal lords now housed classrooms and laboratories, and wafts of brine and formaldehyde mingled with whatever ghosts still roamed the corridors. Alice had roamed those corridors too, led most often by her grandmother, who had taught biology at a small London school and read books on the psyche and the soul and came to live with them when she retired. When Grandma was not probing out-of-date ideas in a borrowed corner of a friend's laboratory, she had told Alice stories about the evolution of life and thought, and adaptation to place and time, letting her in on the secret that science strips myth from reality to reveal more wonder rather than less.

Alice knew her grasp of that wonder had failed. She had first noticed one day in Cambridge, soon after she met Ben. That morning, she had run into him on her way to the lab, and he had dragged her on a detour to look for his lost pen. He had led her down a narrow alleyway and into a dark chamber, a small archive of some kind, and then left her alone. She had waited in the gloom between two walls of washed-out tomes, and soon found herself imbued with the same quiet reverence she had felt as a child wandering among the tombs and headstones by the old village church. She had liked to read their well-worn epitaphs— the poignant quotes and summarized lives, even names and dates alone that said so much about too many infant deaths, deaths in the prime of life, lineages that had thrived and then ceased—hoping that her effort might revive the essence of those once beloved. And there, in that out-of-the-way library, she had opened up one of the volumes, a long-outdated *Journal of Experimental Medicine*, hoping that laying her eyes on its obsolete wisdom might likewise resurrect the spirit of antiquated thought. Immediately she had come upon the words, "*...the simple shifting of a lighted candle from the normal atmosphere into one of oxygen.*" This simple phrase—actually describing the physiological benefits of exercise—had induced such a pang of longing and loss that tears had filled her eyes. She had not mentioned it to Ben when he came back. But ever since, a copy of the article went everywhere with her, in an old dog-eared folder, like a talisman or tribute to the poetry of science, along with the conviction that poetry had been lost from more than the language in which science was framed.

Now she pulled that same manila folder from her bag, wondering if the magic would come back if she reproduced her one-off result. More likely, she thought, she would need magic in the first place to bring that about. What she really longed for was to work on Sage's project. She had been so excited about it before she arrived—excited enough that she had almost not minded putting her life on hold. She had taken it for granted that she would have no problem rounding out her resume with good publications and novel expertise—surely more than enough to satisfy Richard, because what could possibly go wrong? Before she left, she had taken every opportunity to read around the subject and familiarize herself with its subtleties and avant-garde goals. But that project was not hers; and the one she had was going nowhere fast, and along with it the grant proposal for which she had yet to find one concrete piece of supporting evidence. Was it too much to ask that *something* would work out? She was starting to feel trapped, held captive in this state-of-the-art laboratory by bad timing and bad luck. There was no obvious way out—except to keep on trying, to set up another assay tonight as she had just promised Helen, and meanwhile waste even more time over in the library scouring ever-lower quality journals for non-existent precedents.

Slipping her shrinking list of articles-to-find into the folder, she returned it to her bag. Outside, the shadow had fallen from the building opposite, unveiling its smooth sun-splashed ocher façade. Ocher like the crumbling cliffs of South Wales, she thought, except that this stonework's even regularity was a far cry from the stratified chaos of that rain-washed limestone shale. And along with the sharp memory of her primordial rocky coastline came a heartfelt surge of childlike yearning for whatever it was she lacked. "Please, just for once," she whispered to fate or destiny or luck, "let me find what I need." Then, although she dropped back down to earth the moment her fingers touched the Post-it note, added, "And please let that countryman be Ben."

Bundling up again, she fastened her coat, not sure what to do with her new braid. In the end, she tucked it in around her collar. Shouldering her bag, she was about to follow in the faint miasma left by Helen when her eyes fell again on last night's debris: she had meant to clean it up first thing. On the other hand, she thought, surely those microscopic lymphocytes could dry out for a few hours longer at the bottom of each tube, testament to her technical success—even if all she had done was highlight the difference between an assay that works and a result worth pursuing. As a concession, she reached over for the icebox, fished out the floating blue lid and tipped the water into the sink.

Chapter Two

HIGH ABOVE the reference desk, smoked glass windows silhouetted railings and volume-filled shelves. Figures milled among the first floor stacks, or strode across the pale blue carpet, some in white coats or scrubs, some in regular clothes. A muffled hush prevailed. Like a place of worship, Alice thought and held toward the guard the institutional ID card she wore on a thin metal chain around her neck.

"Just a second," the guard barked, frowning at a man who had stormed past behind Alice. The detained man retraced his steps. Alice stood aside. The man's tension chafed at her, was almost physically abrasive. She watched him extract his billfold and thrust it at the guard while he glared at the floor, his features set in the perpendicular—in fact so perpendicular that he looked almost comically determined and fraught. And then it occurred to Alice that he looked fraught and determined because something was wrong. She felt an overwhelming impulse to take him in her arms—which was patently ridiculous, especially for her; she never initiated physical contact, even with friends. The guard nodded to the man, who snapped his wallet shut and dragged away his fretful emanations, along with Alice's tangential gaze.

"Sorry about that."

Alice snapped her attention back. "That's OK," she said, mirroring the guard's genial smile. And she was instantly aware of the gulf between her reflected gesture and the unrestrained anguish of the man she had just seen. The guard waved her on.

She continued to look out for those perpendicular features as she zigzagged through the stacks, but saw only a young man in a lab coat with his face averted, journal tucked beneath his arm like an oversized hymnal. Like a place of worship indeed, she thought with less awe, and bean searching through the reams of information within which she hoped and yet doubted she would find sustenance today.

"Hey, Alice!"

Alice almost dropped the huge volume she was carrying as Sage, with his short bleached hair and anxious eyes, leapt straight into her path.

"Off to read more on Sharden's and its synonyms?" he asked, squinting at the volume's spine. "Ah. The so-called *Journal of Excess and Redundancy*. You must be desperate…though to be honest, I'd be glad to publish anywhere myself. You saw my note?"

"Richard?"

"Not lah-de-dah enough. Youngish sounding."

Maybe it really was Ben. "Any message?"

"Just that it didn't matter."

"Well I guess it doesn't then." Even if it was—and it probably was not, since he had not even sent her an e-mail since she left— he was sure to have an ulterior motive and she had had enough of those. "Nice jacket," she told Sage.

He held out a fringed arm. "Seven ninety-nine at Goodwill— and real suede, too! But hey, what's with the hair?"

Alice untucked the skein. "Helen's idea," she said, suddenly self-conscious. "She even braided it herself."

"Whoa, she's really taking it to the next level with you!" He laughed. His poor relationship with Helen was a running joke on the fifth floor. But Alice had liked him ever since the day she arrived straight from the airport with her two large suitcases and a cardboard box tied up with string, and found him waiting for her outside the building while a woman with a snake tattoo read his outstretched palm. "Well, according to this," the woman was saying, "you don't have a flair for science." "Told you so," Sage had said, withdrawing his hand with an ambiguous grin. That first week Alice had stayed in his apartment while she looked for her own place. Every evening, after a hearty home-cooked dinner, he and Bill—a deep-voiced Adonis who taught art to disadvantaged kids—had left her browsing his vast array of books and memorabilia of the Old Wild West and gone off to Bill's place for the night. So it had come as a shock to discover that Sage was the one working on the project that should have been hers.

"Speaking of Helen," Alice said, "she's looking for you and she doesn't seem pleased."

"Damn, I'd best get going then. See you at the seminar," he called back, fringes already swinging to the rhythm of his gait.

Alice checked her watch. Today's visiting speaker was Melvin E. Rollins—or Mel, as he had urged her to call him in Aberdeen at the same fateful symposium at which she had first met Helen. She was planning to arrive early and say hello, but still had two useful hours. Without further ado, she hurried down to the lowest floor of the stacks. This was where the pre-1980 journals had been compactly consigned—as if the past had been cleft from the present in 1980 and petrified, she always felt—and few people went down there except in search of peace and quiet. At her favorite desk along one windowless wall, she set the volume down, took off her coat and laid the contents of her bag along one edge. She opened up the tome—and confirmed, and not for the first time, that science was no more immune to spin than anything else.

It was always the same. Too many times she had followed up on a reference and discovered that while the citing authors had not strictly lied, they had lifted the supposed evidence out of context, or massaged it with careful wording into compliance, or even paraphrased a citation without checking its source. This time she had been led to believe she would find copious primary data that might—if she was lucky—be open to interpretation in the context of her needs. Instead she found a consolidation of studies she had already seen, none of which had been consistent with Helen's hypothesis in isolation, and they were no more consistent—with Helen's or anyone else's theories—when analyzed *en masse*.

Which, Alice reminded herself, did not have to mean that Helen was wrong—as Helen was always pointing out. Maybe it was true that no one had looked yet in the right way. Alice sat back and stretched, wondering what the right way might be and how they would ever make their case—and froze, staring in near-disbelief at the author of the next article on the facing page: Melvin E. Rollins.

Alice had always liked coincidences; they seemed laden with potential meaning and intent. True, she had not especially liked Mel, but she did give him credit for showing interest in her work. He had cornered her after the session in Aberdeen at which she had given a talk, already known her name—although not from her talk, since he had been for a run, he explained, and lost track of the time and had only just come back. "Which is really too bad," he had said, stroking his damp hair, "because my good friend Bob Walsh tells me you have some super-cool results." Alice had wondered about that. Bob Walsh had been Richard's long-time postdoc when she started her doctorate, and had degenerated from easy-going confidant to bitter antagonist by the time he moved on. He was also a practitioner of the knife-edged joke with a penchant for bets, and in fact she had seen him that day at breakfast talking to Mel, making a bet then too judging from the way they'd shaken hands. So when Mel begged her to fill him in sometime—That very evening, perhaps? Over a drink?—she had happily agreed, fully expecting to have to defend herself against whatever Bob had actually said. In the end, they had sat and talked for several hours in the conference bar and barely touched on her results at all—though she had seen Rollins sign thumbs down to Bob across a crowded seminar room the next morning, whatever that might mean.

Since she was seeing Mel soon, she skimmed his paper. The data were clean, the study was convincing and well-presented but…disappointing? Like the man himself, she thought, her eyes glazing on the final paragraph as she remembered their exchange. Because the closest they had come to talking about her work was when, after he had referenced his running habit for the third or fourth time, she had made the mistake of showing him her old photocopy the physiological benefits of exercise— then, as always, safe and sound in the folder in her bag. She had thought he might appreciate the author's sentiment, if not the lyrical prose. He had just stared at the page, not seeing her point. "Man, those idiots got sidetracked by ludicrous ideas," he had said, shaking his head. Worse still, she had laughingly concurred.

Angry now for not staying her ground, she rose from her seat. Who was Mel to judge, after all? She laid a protective hand on the nearest row of spines. For all he knew, his own work might seem ludicrous one day. Moving between the looming stacks, she wondered how many cutting edge discoveries had been seeded by ideas that seemed laughable now, concepts that had grown and branched and merged, and been shaped beyond recognition as they were honed and applied. And for each seminal insight that broke fresh ground, how many good ideas had never taken root—not because they were dead ends, but because they were too original, or too thoroughly disguised by misinterpretation, or simply not seen by the right person at the time? Even Helen knew you had to look in the right way. Alice imagined laying her eyes on a long-forgotten treatise that, once revived and viewed in the context of what has come since, would take on new meaning and fill unforeseen gaps in understanding, enlightening and transforming thought—surely every scientist's dream…

She had reached the furthest corner of the stacks where the alphabet began. *Annales des Sciences Naturelles*, she read, the words embossed in flaking gold on each replicated spine. Annals of the Natural Sciences. The title alone was like a breath of fresh air, she thought, the composite, natural sciences, so much more wholesome—so much more creative and free—than its carved out components. Physics, chemistry, biology, geology and astronomy: they all seemed so…so disciplined. Following the gilded dates through paling shades of blue and into earnest well-worn brown, her fingers came to rest on 1838. Easing out the desiccated volume, she cradled it reverently in one elbow and turned the freckled pages. And her quest for new meaning was instantly forgotten as an illustration caught her eye: a drawing of a baby—or rather babies—with three heads, two torsos, one pair of legs.

This *monstre*, she extracted from the French, had been the fruit of the first pregnancy of a young woman of lymphatic temperament—*une jeune femme de tempérament lymphatique*—whose mother had eighteen children over thirty-six years. Lymphatic— lacking energy and vitality?—with an especially productive mother. So poetic, she thought. So quaintly irrelevant—and yet was it really so ludicrous to think a woman's lassitude and family history of fecundity might contribute to something like this? She read on. Four days of unsuccessful labor and then, too late, after thinking it was merely twins or a two-headed *monstre*, the realization of a third head. Suffice to say, one of the heads was already deprived of life; this one was amputated. The so-called monstrous being was finally delivered but not without further—and fatal—mutilation. As she read, Alice pictured the doctor's frantic efforts at delivery, and sensed how his anxiety had changed as hope waned, channeled into a thirst to examine, classify, define; because at the end, as if it—they—were a newly discovered species, he had proposed a generic name: *ileo-costo-tricéphale*.

This had to be preserved. Hurrying upstairs, she waited in line for the one functioning copy machine, still captivated by the sketch of three babies tapering to one. She noticed that each face had its own distinct expression—one resigned, one sorrowful, one at peace. This sharp reminder of their humanity made her sad. But they were all at peace now, she supposed. And at least each had been given his own personality for all posterity. Her fondness for the authors grew. It was almost as if they had drawn a visual epitaph for each deceased babe. Alice thought about the churchyard epitaphs back home, how some had been written in a script where *s* looked more like *f*; and how those seeming errors had made her laugh with naïve condescension when she first learned how to read, before she understood that they had simply used the old long s—the integral symbol of calculus—following the mores of the day, as with their phrases: *Here lieth the body*—

And she felt again the impact of discovering the headstone of the nameless drowned youth—on the same day, by memorable coincidence, that a real-life boy had almost drowned; another boy about whom she knew little except that for the briefest moment he had looked up at her, she was sure he was the one.

It was a cold windy Saturday soon after Grandma died. The low rushing clouds promised rain, but Diane and her friends had been getting on her nerves at home and so she had gone down to the church. She had not gone there to visit Grandma's grave, because Grandma had no grave. Unlike Alice's father's parents, Oma and Opa, who lay beneath small granite squares in a cemetery in Kent, Grandma was not buried anywhere. She had insisted that her ashes be scattered from the cliff-top promontory and blown out to sea; she had wanted no memorial. Alice, however, liked memorials, and it bothered her as she walked among the tombs that Grandma had left no epitaph—no prompt with which to be recalled. Then again, Alice knew she had not always understood the idiosyncratic insights Grandma had tried to share before she died, let alone why someone so self-contained in life had been so eager to become one with the wind and waves in death.

It was while she was contemplating this paradox that she came across the weathered slab. She had never noticed it before, perhaps because it had been hidden by the bed of stinging nettles, now a swathe of fresh stubble, that used to line the western wall. *Here lieth the body of a youth,* it said, *washed ashore in the fearful storm of June 1804. May he rest in peace.*

Poor boy, Alice had thought, picturing his corpse pale and

tragically beautiful, draped on the rocks without identity or life. How romantic; how desolate and terrible. And not only because he had died, but because no one had known who he was: a fate worse than death alone. Grandma had disappeared by choice, but this nameless youth had had his anonymity thrust upon him and literally set in stone. Someone somewhere must have missed him and awaited his return, never knowing he was just another washed-up body, found and dutifully buried, and then forgotten in an obscure village on the coast of Wales. Now that she had found him, the least she could do was mourn for him, even without his name. Or better yet, she thought, why not daydream about him, give him a persona, even if it were made up? And that was what she had done, though in the interest of efficiency she allowed him to merge with the handsome stranger she had already conceived.

How her stranger would be handsome she had not yet worked out. But he was quiet and thoughtful, quite unlike the boys she knew, who called her names like Too-clever-by-half. And unlike the heartthrobs of her school friends, who were always agreed upon by popular vote, her quiet stranger was someone she alone would fall in love with, and he would fall in love with her alone. So after laying claim to her long-forgotten specter, she had left the churchyard and headed for the cliff-top, where she often went to think up passionate fantasies of coming across her handsome stranger in dire need of help—lost or trapped or fighting for life on that briar-lined trail along which, in truth, she rarely saw anyone.

By the time she reached the elevated promontory of Grandma's scattering, a fine drizzle had taken hold. The lush late-spring foliage that had been lining the trail gave way to short tufted grass. On the far side of the Bristol Channel the coast of

Devon had almost disappeared, sea and sky seeming to fuse. Down below, whitecaps flecked the ripening swell that rolled in systematically with deliberate restraint. Surf burst against the headlands and frothed in the coves, and filled the deep dark tidal cave in which a legendary pirate may have been buried alive. Beyond the cave, Alice could just make out the crenellated parapet that spanned a dip in the cliffs. Behind it, tiers of belvederes and well-kept topiary ascended to the castle, although the castle, its gardens and the village in which she lived were hidden from where she stood by an intervening wood.

On her other side the path dropped down into a recessed bay. When she turned that way, hair whipped across her eyes and she raised a hand to hold it back, remembering Grandma's small dry palm doing the same not long before. "What are you trying to hide?" Grandma had said, and Alice still wondered what she had meant, what was wrong with the straggling fringe, and might have gone on wondering if not for the breakers tugging at the huge high-tide boulders and exploding like wet fireworks on the low bluff beyond. In fact, the rapidly darkening sky and flailing trees, and the wind-borne roar of an evidently swollen tide, seemed about to recreate the fearful storm of her tragic youth's demise. This is perfect, she thought with a passion nourished by the cold wind-swept rain. Perfect for a true-to-life dream of rescuing my ghost from the furious swell.

And then she noticed the real boy. He was standing on the rocks that encircled the bay, braced against the wind like a mythic hero, a teenage god. She had never seen him before—but knew at once that his barely distinct features filled her abstract ideal of what handsome must mean. My living breathing stranger, she thought. My solitary youth.

Even as she watched, however, a small car laden with kayaks

pulled up on the gravel behind him with a crunch she could hear. Two older girls from school—notorious flirts—jumped out and made a beeline for the boy. Except that—yes!—he had turned away from them, averted his face as if looking up at her instead. She felt tethered by fate, as if he had stepped out of a memory not yet formed—until the girls converged on him and he was theirs. And from the way he walked between them, helped them lift the kayaks from the car and haul them to the water's edge, she could tell that he knew those girls well.

A burst of laughter ricocheted below. Fools, Alice thought, looking down at them. Couldn't they see the swell? Anyone who had grown up around there knew about the rip tide, knew how easy it was to get caught in the undertow and swept out to sea. People did drown. Idiots, she hissed to the wind. Still, it was their life, not hers. Turning her back on them, she started to retrace her steps.

Soon the castle's battlements rose beyond the treetops, like a fairytale palace lost within the woods. Alice walked on. It was raining in earnest now. The castle disappeared again. The coastline snaked; the parapet vanished too. When she rounded the next bend, she looked for the rocky outcrop that had always been a welcome landmark on long family walks. All she saw was a smooth telltale plane and the next retreating wave revealed, directly beneath it, a pile of loose rubble. Like a monumental cairn, she thought, worrying again about Grandma's posterity until she remembered how excited Grandma would have been at the prospect of a treasure-trove of fossils down there when the tide turned. She could almost hear Grandma guessing which varieties they would find, which vein of the past had been opened this time.

However, the tide had not yet turned and the breakers were

still wild. Alice could feel their slow beat against the cliff-face, hear the rumble of submerged boulders being rocked by the swell. It should have been easy to imagine her nameless youth down there, about to meet the tragic fate from which she alone could rescue him. Only she kept picturing the boy on the rocks. She should have warned him, told him to watch out—regardless of those girls; maybe even because of those girls. Then again, who was she to interfere? Especially with the wind gusts tearing at her hair and the volleys of cold raindrops now hammering her face. She pulled up her hood. And then, amidst the tangle of brambles that stretched like coils of barbed wire between the path and the precipice, she saw the red bricks of a gun emplacement left behind from World War II. Soon she was skidding down the muddy incline toward its dark unbarred door.

She stepped across the earthy threshold. And forgot all about saving either her drowned ghost or the boy on the beach. Instead, a pair of flesh-and-blood lips touched hers for the first time in a kiss.

Alice knew she should not have gone inside. Her parents had always told her never to go near the gun emplacements teetering at intervals along the crumbling coast. But that early-summer's day when the rain was falling in sheets, there had been nowhere else to go. All she had wanted was to go on dreaming of her spectral youth, of saving her quiet stranger from the vast and grasping waves. She had not forgotten that in *The Little Mermaid* the rescued prince had never understood; she knew this was different, she was different, this was real life; her handsome youth would know she was the only one for him.

Anyway, this gun emplacement looked safe; there was a wide band of scrub between it and the edge. Clusters of pink-edged white blossom softened the tangle of thorns almost covering its walls. The path down to its entrance was lined with buttercups, red campion and blue forget-me-nots. It was just a low hexagonal hut of old red bricks. Besides, she was starting to get wet—and perhaps deep inside she still cherished childish notions of secret doors into magical kingdoms, new worlds waiting to be found.

Up close, it was squat and crumbling and desolate. The sunken doorway was a gaping black hole beyond a trickle of stone-strewn earth. It would only be for a few minutes while the storm passed. So she slipped down the last part of the incline and took a step inside.

Immediately she was met by an overpowering stench of urine and stale beer. Impenetrable darkness. Then an arm from the side, like a tentacle, pulled her over and around and held her tight. She was held against a body clad in leather reeking of nicotine and oil. And in the terror of the moment, before she could think, her mouth was stopped with flaccid warm wet flesh. Stopped. Her romantic, childish dreams stopped. The words *mucous membranes* filled her mind instead. She had been learning about mucous membranes in biology class at school.

And just as suddenly she was released and a hand pushed back her hood. Another pulled her by the elbow to the door. "Crikey, I thought you were someone else," said a gruff embarrassed voice, and she saw a face she vaguely recognized. For a moment that seemed an awful lot longer she stood where she was. Then the man-boy merged again with the darkness—and Alice was back in the rain, pulling herself up the bank, fending off the niggling thorns that kept springing across her way. She returned to the well-worn path flanked by clinging weeds. Back to where she had been. Only something—everything—had changed. The world had lost its smooth oneness. Every object, every sense, every sensation, was discrete and disconnected, the mere sum of its parts, and the saturating vividness that once pervaded her existence had drained through the rifts.

The path was now a sticky muddy ditch. Leaves adhered to her calves and she stooped to brush them off. When she looked up again, someone was coming toward her, hurrying through the rain beneath a turquoise umbrella. She stepped aside to make way for the girl, who held up her umbrella—briefly sheltering Alice—as she squeezed by. Alice knew exactly where that girl was going and who was waiting for her there. At that moment she became aware of a delayed sensation blossoming on her lips. It was overridden straight away by the knowledge that it was not meant for her. She had no right to that budding response. There was no point in feeling anything from that kiss.

The rain fell on, unabating. But the wind dropped as Alice turned inland. She passed through a dense copse of sycamore trees whose lower boughs dripped slow syncopation to the patter of rain above. On the other side of the kissing-gate into the lane, a brand new motorbike was parked. Just then an ambulance wailed past in bleak alarm on its way to the cove. That evening word spread through the village that a teenage boy had almost drowned in the bay.

If she had only gone down and warned him that day, Alice thought now as she stood in line, she could have saved an actual life. Or at least saved him from needing to be saved. Instead, she had been busy saving specters on the cliff-top—until…until she was kissed by mistake and turned into a young woman of lymphatic temperament?

That sentence had seemed to complete itself. Lymphatic: lacking energy and vitality—*like a lighted candle that needs oxygen*, it struck her with catalytic force. Was it true? She had always though the nostalgia linked to the phrase was for the author's extinct style. Now she wondered if it touched a more private longing, a more personal loss. It all began to connect—

"All yours," a woman called cheerily, closing the copier lid. The impact of the fusion passed. Alice thanked her and took her place. The copy machine whirred and clicked; a duplicate slid out. *Lymphatic*: also a vessel that conveys lymph, she thought. Made up of lymphocytes, the core of immunology. Here she was, back on track, brought full circle against all the odds. Another duplicate emerged. Back on track, she thought, on the straight and narrow track of modern science, of impersonal terseness and adherence to the point.

Gathering the still-warm reproductions from the rack of the machine, she set off back downstairs. As she rounded the final corner to her desk, she saw a man leaning up against her chair. One of his hands resting on the journal she had left open there. Ordinarily she would have felt indignant, even violated, but she felt nothing of the sort. Instead, she gazed at the hand: a lean, perfectly proportioned hand that she wanted to touch—and she wondered again what was wrong with her today. At that moment the sleeve of the man's shirt slipped down, covering his wrist. Absently, he pushed it to his elbow, neatly rolling up the plaid; and as he did so he looked up, bringing Alice face to face with the suffering man. Only he was no longer suffering. His perpendicular features had undergone a transformation and were sweetly softened now, and they collapsed at the sight of her into a warm boyish smile—a smile in which she caught a glimpse of sharply pointed canine teeth that flew like arrows to her heart. He is handsome, she thought and smiled back.

"Sorry, I couldn't help noticing the paper," he said. "I didn't mean to—"

Past, present and future merged as Alice drowned in his eyes. "That's OK," she said, floating nonetheless. "I've finished with it." For here, in his luminescent gaze, was her own private oxygen, the substance of her need. Tea-without-milk, she thought. His eyes were the color of tea without milk. And from the depths of delight, she felt compelled to add, just to keep him standing there: "It wasn't useful anyway—I'd seen it all before." As if that mattered to him.

Apparently it did matter. His gaze lost its glow and the softness drained from his face. He looked aside—and revealed to her a profile so elegantly Romanesque that she heard herself gasp. "Haven't they all," she thought she heard him say—to the page and not to her—with his features locked in angular distress. He slammed the journal shut. And then he looked up, straight into her eyes. For a moment he just stood there frozen like a deer caught in headlights, about to be run down. The tension drained.

"And he's done it again," he muttered, backing away with his shapely hands raised. And before Alice could straighten out her thoughts, he had turned on the heel of his hiking boot and disappeared among the walls of fact and artifact.

Chapter Three

THE LIGHTS in the auditorium dimmed; the murmur of the audience died; heads turned toward the podium. Alice was confused: the man from the library was not there. She had been scanning the tiers around her ever since she sat down, and would have seen him if he was. And he should have been there. Moments after he disappeared, she had realized she had last been looking at Rollin's paper, whereas when she came back she had had Sharden's on her mind. So her stupid comment had not even been relevant, which made it all the more mortifying that she had clearly hit a raw nerve with her mindless blind precision. If she could only find him and explain, she thought, she might see his geometric features realign and relax, and once more she would float and…then again, if he was really so invested in that Rollins's paper, why was he not here at the seminar? Something did not add up.

Alice turned her attention to Rollins in the flesh—she no longer wished to think of him as Mel. He was standing in the spotlight up front, being introduced in glowing terms. His behavior just now also made no sense. He had been leaning on the podium when she walked in, shuffling index cards and looking bored.

"Hi," she had said. And when he looked up, she had seen his pupils shrink to pinpricks and then dart toward his host, the illustrious Professor Wharton, who had been waylaid near the back. "I don't know if you remember me," she had offered to help him out. "We met in Aberdeen two years ago."

"Aberdeen." A deep crimson blush had risen from his tight white collar and through his neatly combed blond hair.

Nodding expectantly, and wishing herself away, she had saved him further embarrassment by telling him outright: "I'm Alice—Alice Gaines. I used to work with Richard Webb."

"But of course, that little British Society meeting!" Rollins was suddenly avuncular, although the tight folds of his smile had looked all wrong on someone so young—and entirely at odds with how he had been in Aberdeen.

The doors to the left of the podium splayed and heads turned toward the light. The fleeting outline that appeared there could only belong to Tom Dannet, with whom Alice had just had lunch—yet another thing that made no sense. He passed within a few feet of her on his way up the steps without as much as a glance, although admittedly it was dark. According to Sage, behind whom she now sat down, he did the rounds of all the weekly seminars in order to play devil's advocate. He always sat somewhere near the back, in stark contrast to the local elite to which on scientific merit he could easily have belonged, whose polished members always occupied the front row, saving seats for one another, patting one another's back. In fact, Alice had assumed that Helen was one of them, but now she was not so sure. Helen had breezed in a little earlier and stretched her lipsticked smile at the front-row dignitaries, but she had had to ask several times before she found a vacant seat. And as soon as she had laid her coat on that seat and rushed to greet her old friend Mel, the far-too-suave Professor Wharton had stepped between the two of them and made some kind of joke—a joke that made Helen glare at the oblivious Wharton and retreat to her seat while the two men heartily guffawed.

Unlike Helen, however, Tom Dannet did not even try—although Alice wondered if he went out of his way to look quite so unkempt. He always wore a creased khaki shirt and scruffy chinos, and his lank grey-white hair was either overgrown or crudely cropped. It was crudely cropped now, as she had noticed in the cafeteria checkout line on her way over to the seminar—not noticing much else while she replayed obsessively the conversation in the stacks, thinking of all the things she could have said instead or in the moment afterwards if she had thought of them in time, until he had turned around and grinned.

"We come face to face at last," he had observed.

Still distracted, she had smiled. At last? How did he know who she was?

"How do you like our food?" he had asked, staring at her takeout bagel. "Me, I prefer the more exotic dishes." He had held up his plate. "This one's not bad—chicken in a Thai sauce."

She had smiled again and wordlessly exclaimed; he had mumbled a dead-pan witticism she did not catch, but she had laughed anyway. Just before he took his turn at the checkout, he had asked if she had time to join him; he had some questions about her work. "That would be lovely," she had said, although she had planned to eat her bagel on the go.

But when she met him on the other side, his features had slackened. "You have an *English* accent," he had said as if accusing her.

"I do," she had replied amiably. "I'm from Britain."

"Huh. I could have sworn…" He had not explained what he

could have sworn. And by then it was too late anyway. He had already made his invitation, and Alice had fairly jumped at it, not least because she always hoped that in the presence of a brilliant mind, some of that brilliance might seep into her. So even though she was well aware that she was not whoever he had thought she was, she had gladly trailed him through the seated diners to a table by some large dark ferns on the far side of the room. Besides, she was taking consolation in his clumsy effort to hide his mistake. At first, that is. All too soon she was frantically on guard, fending off his pointed questions about her research, struggling not to feed him the foolish answers he seemed eager to provoke. Moreover, his criticism of Helen had awakened a latent and intriguing loyalty and, without lying outright, she had mentioned her one-off result and its possible significance if it held up, as if she really thought it might. However, when he started to speculate, and scrutinize the implications with perceptive—but ultimately futile—insight, she had given in and confessed that it had not held up so far and she doubted it would. And in the end she had been the one set him free in her great haste to catch Mel Rollins, naïve fool that she had been.

Puzzled, she looked down at Rollins in his tight white collar and wondered what had made him squirm. For pity's sake, she thought, all they had done that night was talk. She could only imagine that, like Tom Dannet, he had confused her with someone else—someone he had reason to want to avoid. All the same, she could not help wondering what Bob had said about her that day in Aberdeen, and why Rollins had lied—though she doubted Rollins ever said what he meant. "It's been a pleasure," he had said down by the podium when she said she should find a seat. "A pleasure for me too," she had answered like a parrot, well aware that neither he nor she had thought it pleasurable at all.

TOWARD THE MIDDLE of the talk Tom Dannet interrupted. "Tell me," he said. "When are you going to show us something new?"

Alice came back down to earth. Was Rollins was being ridiculed? Had her wish come true so soon? People shifted in their seats or sighed and rolled their eyes, as often happened when Dannet spoke. Alice wished she knew whether his comment was justified, but she had been lost in her own thoughts for she knew not how long. And despite herself, she felt sorry for Rollins, standing there in the spotlight facing his denouement. Because, like a movie villain whose humanity is revealed too late, he had shown a new side of himself in his first few of slides, the only ones that she could now recall. To her surprise, he had started out by referencing the past, with a contemporary painting of Edward Jenner, one-time British Physician who, in 1796, performed the first experimental vaccination against smallpox. Instead of ridiculing Jenner or his work, Rollins's next slide had been a sketch of a milkmaid sitting on a stool beside a cow, captioned by the words from the nursery rhyme: *My face is my fortune, sir, she said.* For Jenner deduced, Rollins had explained, that milkmaids were not disfigured by smallpox because they were already immune to the cowpox they contracted from their cows.

As Rollins went on to explain that *vacca*—as in vaccination—was Latin for cow, Alice had drifted off into a different past: her childhood in Wales when she had thought milkmaids were make-believe, created solely for the sake of rhymes—and all because one day she had asked the wife of the farmer from whom they bought their fresh-laid eggs how many milkmaids they had.

The woman had shrieked with delight, taken Alice by the hand and shown her their milking machines milking, a clamor of cows, tubes, udders, rhythmic noise. It had seemed only natural to conclude that if the idea of milkmaids was so laughable, they could not be real.

Meanwhile, Dannet was on a roll. "This is yet another example of using cutting edge techniques to restate the obvious," he told the mute audience. "All we're being shown is prettier versions of old truths." As Rollins began to reply, Dannet stood up, snorting like a carthorse, and left with noisy undisguised disdain.

In the surge of clapping at the end of the seminar someone scooted up behind Alice. Someone, a man, leaned up close. "Hi," he whispered in her ear.

Alice turned around. Hoping, longing against the odds.

"Oh. I thought you were someone else," said a man with a smirk. Alice wanted to scream—though all he had done, she supposed, was mirror her own thought when she saw his glasses, grey eyes and his salt-and-pepper hair.

"Seriously, you look a whole lot like my friend Petra," the smooth voice intoned.

"Well I'm afraid I'm not." Alice forced a cool smile. She was willing to bet that this Petra had a mouse-brown braid.

"Why be afraid?" The stranger's smirk broadened and he drew away as if to better see. The tinted ovals of his glasses had slipped down his nose; he gazed above the thin metallic rims. Then he seemed to have seen someone near the exit: his attention quivered between Alice and the door. "Well," he said. "I hope we'll meet again." He squeezed her for the briefest moment on the shoulder and then vaulted over several rows of seat backs before dissolving into the crowd.

Three times, Alice thought as she stood to leave. Three times today I've been mistaken for someone else. How strange. Didn't bad luck come in threes? But *third time lucky*, she countered optimistically. It didn't really help. She could still feel the impression where the man's hand had touched her, but she could also feel her vain desire for a different man whose hand she longed to touch.

Chapter Four

PETER STOPPED at his bench and picked up the tube he had been labeling when he left. His pen had disappeared. And his thoughts were pounding, knocking up against one another—until he realized that the room was pounding, the stereo in the main lab blasting out a bass beat that was making the glassware on his shelves vibrate. Charging back along the corridor, he plunged into the jungle of noise next door and turned the stereo off.

"That's my frigging demo tape," Stace yelled from her bench.

Damn, Peter thought. "Yes, well…it was still way too loud." He knew he should have said something first. Then again, Stace—a dictatorial technician who fronted a rock band—would have taken it wrong whatever he had said.

"You ordered those reagents yet?" she called after him.

"Yes, and they're backordered by two weeks."

"Shit," he heard her reply.

Back at his bench, at which he should have been half way through today's experiment by now, he heard her yell into the hallway that they were heading out for lunch. The call was not meant for him. He had brought his own lunch anyway. And he preferred eating alone. Over the years, his social energy had faded as his friends dispersed worldwide to positions across the globe. They had left him enough mismatched furniture and crockery to last more than a lifetime, and even a live pet; he only wished he had also inherited their luck with professorial jobs.

He dropped the tube again. In two short strides he was in his small office where the latest evidence that he had not lay face up on the desk. Sitting down, he opened his lunchbox and read over the letter as he scooped up forkfuls of rice. He had stopped reading earlier at the word *However*, which was all he had needed to know—though the mere fact of it being a letter and not a phone call said enough. At the time, he had not even cared, had not especially liked the place, and had set to work labeling his first batch of tubes in the solitary lab he had inherited when the previous senior postdoc left. That lab with its small corner office was intended as a haven during the arduous business of applying for jobs, especially on days like today when he was tossed back among the swollen ranks of overqualified contenders for the mere handful of tenure-track positions and was best left alone. Except that this morning he had not been left alone.

"Two seconds," Stace had said from the doorway. "Our fume hood's a mess, and we have to get this done, and you're clearly not using yours." And in she had come, followed by the newest postdoc, Lou—who wore the biggest diamond Peter had ever seen on her left hand, which was always ripping her latex gloves—and without missing a beat, Lou had resumed: "…and he has this huge lab, and super-generous start-up funds, but he has to teach undergrads this *entire* semester, which is really such a drag—"

"Seriously?"

Both women had turned to look at Peter.

"Why does no one ever want to teach? Where would any of us be if no one wanted to teach?"

They had continued to stare.

"Well, it's true," he had said.

Stace had rolled her eyes. "He's always like that," she had whispered to Lou and they had turned back to the hood.

There had been no point in saying anything more. When he joined the lab, it had been full of postdocs, students and technicians who had gotten along well. They had hung out, discussed life and the universe, worrying the truth—to the point of tedium sometimes, but always with goodwill. And then Stace was hired. Slowly and systematically she had worked her charisma on each new person who arrived, and meanwhile shared her dislike of him. Now he felt like an outcast. Not that he cared. All the same, he did not need to sit there and put up with them. "I'll be back," he had muttered, slamming down his pen and exiting the lab as if he had some place else to be.

Though maybe they were right, he had thought half way down the corridor. Maybe we would be fine if no one wanted to teach, and what mattered was whether a student wanted to learn. Maybe no one else did want to teach. But *I* want to teach, he had affirmed. Never mind about anyone else. He stepped out of the building, and was hit by a blast of cold air at the top of the steps—and acknowledged the real issue: It did not matter how much he wanted to teach, or whether he did or did not want that job, if no search committee wanted him.

The sky was mockingly blue. He had left the shadow of the parking lot and crossed the sunlit road, wondering why they even interviewed him when the problem was already obvious on his otherwise decent resume: that two-year hiatus from science about which everyone asked with a look of concern. It was also obvious, he had observed he skirted the quad, that he was bitterly cold—he had not thought to grab his coat. Not in the mood for turning back, he had taken advantage of the library, the womb-like warmth of its archives where the pungent aroma always smote him at first breath with a sharp sweet nostalgia for the cluttered used bookstore in which he had spent those fateful two years.

Two calm and pleasant years away from science, he had reminded himself deep within the temperate maze. Far away from scientists, too. Moving through a book-lined aisle, he had thought about how no two used copies of a given edition felt alike—and not only from distinct wear and tear, but as if each owner processed what they read and gave something intangible back. At the far end, he had been about to U-turn into the next aisle, when he noticed the layout on the pages lying open on a desk against the wall. In a state of near-disbelief, he had stopped to look, and indeed there was his name, his science, his very own paper; and the very paper in which he had published the hypothesis he should have been testing at that very moment; and not on any old desk, but the desk of...

Midway to his mouth his hand stopped. If she had already finished reading, it would have been open on the last and not the first page of the article.

"I'm an idiot," he said and bit down on the fork. She had not even been talking about his work. He cursed his knee-jerk reaction, the reaction of a jerk. Dropping his fork, he pushed his lunchbox aside and pressed his head onto the desk. He had been caught off guard. Because when he saw his paper there, defying the laws of probability, he had ignored his distrust of coincidence, the sense that one of life's dimensions had been lost, pathetically flattered by the seeming evidence of someone's interest in his overlooked work—someone who, when she appeared, had caused *all* of life's dimensions to collapse, and in the best possible way, joining up loose ends and at the same time weirdly freeing him—until synchronicity, or whatever it was, had gone too far.

I'd seen it all before, she had said. Past and present had collided and normality crashed back. *We've seen it all before*, someone had written in a scathing editorial when that paper first came out, because—for reasons that had nothing to do with synchronicity and everything to do with antagonism—another far-too-similar study had just stolen what little glory should have been his. Similar, but hardly the same, though few people saw the difference and fewer still cared; after all, the work was mathematical and few biologists care for math. If they had only looked a little closer, they would have seen that, unlike the contrived complexities of his competitor's model, his simple equations served to clarify rather than confuse.

He sat up and rubbed his face with both hands. None of that had been her fault. And it was not her fault that he was doomed to display every private thought and feeling on his features for all the world to see. And by the time he had caught himself it was too late. She had seen it all—seen him for the monster he was, and so he had run off through the stacks before he made it any worse.

"Well, at least someone's still around," Tom said, ambling in. "The main lab's like a goddamned grave."

"They've gone out to lunch," Peter said through his palms.

"They're always out to frigging lunch. But *you* rarely skip the Friday seminar."

Peter dropped his hands. "Damn. It totally slipped my mind."

"No great loss. Anyhow, I came to show you this." Barely missing the lunchbox, Tom emptied out the envelope he had brought in with him. "It's from my old friend Joe," he said. "Did I ever tell you about Joe?"

"Yep." Tom had told him more than once how Joe gave an annual undergraduate lecture about his almost-but-ultimately-not-at-all ground breaking studies because it seemed a shame to waste the lesson he had learned. Poor guy: according to Tom, he had been happily churning out data supporting his hypothesis, and publishing in high profile journals, until he reached the grand finale of the discovery of a single wrong assumption he'd been making all along, without which his whole theory collapsed.

"Good old Joe," Tom said. "Hates to waste a thing—especially when it comes to data. Which is why," he added, spreading out the pages he had just tipped out, "he sent me this. Says he can't use it himself, but take a look!"

Peter stared at a bar graph sketched in haste, by hand, on an old-style turquoise grid. No one plotted graphs by hand these days. "What am I seeing here?" he asked.

"Inflammation," Tom said with satisfaction. "In the goddamn gut."

"I thought Joe worked on the brain."

"Read the label on the other axis."

"NGF—Nerve Growth Factor. So?"

"So it turns out that *nerve* growth factor receptors show up on more than just nerves."

"You mean on…" Peter lifted up a grainy photograph and squinted at the magnified tissue section, torn between curiosity and the prospect of being lured into something new when he had too much else to do.

"Yes, lymphocytes. The gut immune system. Apparently Joe was seeing if NGF— What, another rejection?" Tom reached for the letter that was now streaked with olive oil.

"California." Peter folded it closed.

"Darn. Another wasted trip. What, seven down now? What about Schofield's department?"

"Interviewing in a couple of weeks. But—"

"Peter my boy. The big one! Go for it!" Tom slapped Peter's back. "I knew it'd come through in the end."

"It's only a first interview." He had had plenty of those.

"Yes, but you'll have your results by then. Wow them with the story from abstract prediction to hard and fast evidence. They'll be begging you to come! I mean, you make the shortlist every goddam time." Tom perched on the window sill, jostling Peter's mug.

"And never get the job," Peter said, grabbing his mug. *Hard to choose between so many strong candidates*, they wrote without fail. *Our decision was subjective.*

"Well, at worst there's BLAI."

"I wouldn't be so sure." BLAI—Boston Liberal Arts Institute—was a newly founded center for interdisciplinary teaching and research with no reputation yet, not even locally. "No word since the second interview," he said.

"Man, that was weeks ago. Hmmm. I really thought…."

"Me too." Peter had thought he was a prime example of blurring boundaries between disciplines. How picky could they be?

"Well, don't let it get to you," Tom said. "They're still novices. Let's see what Schofield thinks after he's seen your new results!"

Peter laughed. "Let's see what we think, too, when they finally exist." He had high hopes, however. The big experiment he was setting up—would set up after lunch—was the moment of truth for his mathematical model. He needed something big, something truly exciting to bridge that two-year chasm in his resume. Leaning back, he looked up at the framed print he had hung above his desk: an illustration of thistle varieties salvaged from a flood-damaged field guide he had found in the 'discard' pile at the back of the store. At the time he thought he had left science forever, and had been genuinely content cataloguing cast-off books and attending to discerning customers in cordial anonymity. But he had not bargained on Tom, who one quiet afternoon walked up to the counter and asked for him by name.

Peter had nodded, instantly alert.

"So…Manny Hall's big disappointment in the flesh," Tom had said. Ignoring Peter's affirmation—part groan, part whimper—he had gone on to explain that Manny was telling anyone who'd listen that his one-time prodigy had dropped out of science all because he was scooped on some hypothetical sideline that he shouldn't have been wasting time on in the first place. "Calls your theory intellectual masturbation," Tom had added with a grin. "Leastways that's what he would've said if he'd gotten his tongue around the words. I'm Tom Dannet, by the way," he had said, holding out a hand. "Evolution of virulence and—"

"—and obligate pathogens." Peter had come across Tom's latest review in a copy of Nature at the public library—obligate pathogens being infectious microbes that can't survive without the hosts they infect because, as Tom had variously illustrated, they've spent so many generations scrounging the ready-made products of their hosts that their own genes encoding those same products have degenerated—mutated, or even disappeared—due to long lack of use.

"Ha! So you *are* still keeping up," Tom had said.

"Look, whatever Manny told you, it was way more complicated—"

"Of course it was. Look, hear me out. You see, I'm a big fan of catastrophes, ha, ha!"

Peter had half-smiled. He knew Tom meant the mathematical 'catastrophe theory' that drove his model's predictions—the mechanism by which his abstract medical interventions cured his hypothetical infections—rather than its catastrophic effect on his career. With just a few simple equations Peter had defined pivotal points of sensitivity—or instability—in the race between rapidly dividing lymphocytes and the pathogens they were trying to kill. These points of instability corresponded to specific biological processes that if disrupted even very slightly could have a drastic effect on the outcome, and would be ideal targets for as-yet-undiscovered treatments that, instead of being proportionally more effective as the dose increased, might even at a low dose flip the switch from a raging infection to protective immunity. Only no one had wanted to know.

"So what I suggest," Tom had said, "is that you drop all this here, come work in my lab and see your model redeemed."

Peter had just finished reading a Joseph Conrad novel that quiet afternoon, in which the protagonist died in the process of redemption. Redemption and catastrophe, he thought, straightening out the sign that said *Sorry, No Returns*—and then laying it face down on the counter, concluding that perhaps his mind had been deprived of science for too long. That same day, over mugs of tea in the back room of the store, Tom had reminded Peter that his model could be a powerful tool for identifying new drugs and vaccines, but only if it was verified. "And the same goes for your competitor's model," he had added. "Sure, it caused a big fuss at the time, but even that's gone by the wayside now. Let's face it, no one was ever going to pay attention to either one for long without some actual data."

Peter had been well aware of this. Each model was supported by circumstantial evidence alone, and that was never enough. What he needed was a clean and quantifiable microbe with which he could test the robustness of his math. And Tom was offering him exactly that: an easy to measure and manipulate virus that triggered an easy to measure immune response—with the added bonus of not causing pathology since they had knocked out all the symptom-causing genes in order to prove which ones they were. "A few more simple manipulations," Tom had said, "and you'll have a perfect set of variants for definitive trials." Here was the key to the difference between good and brilliant; between a mediocre future and a place among the stars.

All Tom had asked in return was that he work on at least one other project of Tom's choosing. Since then Peter had built a solid reputation on the basis of three other projects—for which he felt Tom had given him more credit than he deserved. All the while, though, he had persevered what had proven to be a set of none-too-simple manipulations. Finally, after several years of trial and error at the bench, and countless late nights trouble-shooting dead-ends over mugs of strong black tea, he was ready to put his model to the test.

"So where do we stand?" Tom asked Peter now.

"I'll infect the first set of mice this afternoon and start analyzing them...probably a week Monday." In good time for the interview, he thought. "And I'll start another batch to check a few days after that. Six time points each at pre-set intervals, so we'll have the full picture by the middle of March."

"Excellent. I reckon we'll show that bastard. Intellectual masturbation, eh? Well, this is the flesh and blood intercourse."

Peter winced.

"OK, so not quite the real thing yet, but say…safe se—"

"Tom? I thought I heard your voice." Tom's portly secretary, Elaine, came hurrying through the lab. "Marion called, I said didn't know where you were—and don't forget we have a recommendation to write first."

Tom grabbed Peter's wrist by the watchstrap. "Hell, I'll bet Marion called. We have to be at Logan by two."

"You're off somewhere?"

"Not me—just Marion. Off to see Jody, who's just gone into labor…but hey, can you get over that, me about to be a grandfather?"

"Congratulations!"

"Yeah, well, the kid's hardly my doing. Anyhow, Marion has to make the afternoon flight to Heathrow. Speaking of which, I met this British girl today."

Me too, Peter thought, cradling his mug.

"Mistook her for the new German postdoc in Wharton's lab, matched his description to a T—but then maybe everyone just looks the same these days."

No, Peter thought. The woman in the library had looked different—clear and distinct from anyone else, standing out against the book-lined backdrop like the vivid subject of a Renoir painting, looking straight at him, and into him and only him.

"But get this," Tom was saying. "She's come all this way to work with Helen Jonas. Who, incidentally, has just trashed Mike Burns's latest grant proposal. Remember Mike Burns?"

"Mike Burns?"

"Before your time, I guess. Too bad, you'd have gotten along well. Mike said Jonas's name appeared on the list of reviewers at the eleventh hour like the angel of death. I told him to appeal, explain to them what happened—"

Peter did remember Mike; they had overlapped for a couple of months. Mike had given him some old cooking pans when he left.

"—Ha! More a matter of what didn't happen. Truth is, I had him collaborate with Jonas for a while—though nothing came of it. But when he married his out of town girlfriend, Jonas told him to his face that she gave his marriage seven years. Like a curse, goddamnit! What does she think she is—a frigging witch? Though I guess she's been like that ever since she was swept off her feet by what's-his-name—you know, big shot in cell bio-chem—or leastways ever since she found out that the bastard kept a tally of his student conquests; she's well rid of him. But hey, any idea what Mueller's postdoc does look like? Finally I hear about someone with a background in yeast genetics and I can't pin her down."

"Uh, Tom," Elaine said, tapping her wrist.

"We'll talk more about all this when I get back," Tom said over his shoulder and followed Elaine out.

"Sure," Peter called after Tom and then stared at the thistles. His favorite, a subtype to the left of center, had no prickles. *MELANCHOLY THISTLE* was written in pale uppercase beside it. Peter wished he knew who the woman in the library was. If he knew, he could find her and apologize and start over again.

Chapter Five

On HER WAY BACK from the cafeteria, Alice told herself that she was full, that her lingering discontent was with the blandness of the food, or the hasty way she had wolfed it down since she was eating alone. The Friday night ambience seemed devoid of something, too. Tiny snowflakes hovered in the desiccated air as if not sure whether to fall. A woman across the street bade the man with her a great weekend and he wished her the same, their farewells isolated, crisp. The man mounted his bicycle and rode away. Alice waited as a group of young people, most likely graduate students, walked clamorously past, talking about where to go—all of them talking but one, a mild looking woman in a skirt, who was listening with an eager smile. Alice remembered Friday nights like that in Cambridge. She would have been the one in the skirt, never minding where they went but still wishing they would ask her. Life had been spontaneous back then, she reminisced. Whereas nights out in London had been far more constrained, planned out in advance, albeit usually with one or two of those same Cambridge friends. Friends that had included Ben, she thought. If she could call Ben a friend.

The nature of Alice's connection to Ben had always defied words. That was why it had been so hard to argue with Richard when he urged her to leave. "Experience," he had said. "You need more experience." Obviously he had meant the acquisition of credentials, the gathering of useful skills, but Alice had thought of the kind that touches heart and soul, the kind that Ben had seemed to offer, at least sometimes. She had been almost thirty by then and did not want to miss her chance, but how could she use that as an excuse? Richard had extolled the better pay in the States, the tax emption if you stayed less than two years, which was how he had come back with a down-payment for a house. Did he not see, though? He already had a wife and child when he did his postdoc in New York. Even the prospect of that lectureship when she returned had not quite tipped the balance for Alice. "Think about it," Richard had said. "Especially now, when I understand there's no one holding you back." Though he understood nothing, all she could think was *touché*. At that point, what could she do but agree?

Slipping through a gap in the traffic, she skirted the almost empty parking lot. Ben had not held her back and that was fine. In a way, he had done her a favor—had been doing so all along. Because until she met him, she had been drifting on the path of least resistance—not sure, in fact, how she had managed to come so far. He, by contrast, had been driven since birth. By the time their paths crossed, he was laden with accolades and scholarships and, most significantly, a critical mind. He had raised the bar for her, sharpened her faculties, forced her to try. If it had not been for Ben, she might never have impressed Richard, who would not have kept her on, or recommended her to Helen; she might never have come over here, and being over here was an experience whichever way you looked at it. Ben—like Richard—thought experience was key. This might yet be for the best.

With one last breath of cold crisp air, she hurried up the

steps, squeezed through the doors of the glass-clad vestibule and into the bright foyer. The sudden warmth lured the blood back to her cheeks—and she found herself longing with stringent urgency to see the man with tea-brown eyes.

Alice stopped in her tracks, awed by the galvanizing power of desire—and the lasting impact of a total stranger's glance. Something momentous had happened in the stacks! But even as she basked in a hurried flashback of his smile, she thought of what had happened next. She walked on, squeezing her gloves into her bag and mentally planning out the evening ahead. Alice liked working late, and at weekends—a habit she had picked up from Ben. She was, in any case, more efficient when the others, except sometimes for Sage, had packed up and gone home. There was no need for sign-up sheets, no waiting in line for the centrifuges, hoods or PCR machines and she could spread herself out.

On her way past the restrooms at the end of the hallway, she stopped again. Something had changed. There was an odd chemical tang in the air. Coming from the labs to her right, she surmised, glad that she was turning left—until she veered toward the elevators on her way to the stairs, and met a strengthening of the odor and a barricade of chairs.

"Sorry, ma'am, we're waxing the floors tonight," a small man intoned.

"But I have to go up, I'm in the middle of—"

"There's a stairwell—fire escape—through those double doors to the right," he said as if not for the first time. "Red door—about half way down."

Alice thanked him, noticing the sparkling sheen where the wax had been applied—and also the large detour arrow taped to the wall. She made her way, as instructed, through the double doors to the right and found herself in a corridor of labs almost exactly like the one on which she worked four floors above. But subtle differences in furnishing, background noise and aroma produced an otherworldly feel such as found in a dream, of familiarity awry. The way was ominously quiet. She glanced repeatedly from side to side as she passed one darkened lab interior after another. She felt conspicuous, like an imposter on the verge of being found out.

And then her attention snagged. The light was on beyond a glass-paneled door. And not only that; framed within that patch of light was the man she had just been thinking about—and in glorious profile, too. She felt replete again, the world set to rights; this had to have been meant. He was seated at a bench, eyebrows drawn in that straight frown beneath thick neatly cropped brown hair. Once again the sleeves of his plaid shirt were pushed up to his elbows, though his memorable hands were obscured by latex gloves. Between the thumb and index finger of one hand he held a microfuge tube; with the other he worked a micropipette. As Alice watched, he pressed the tube into a rack, laid the pipette on the bench and started to peel off his thin gloves. Alice's viscera yearned.

Here was her chance to set things right. Impulsively, she reached for the door handle, planning to walk in and say…say what? She should apologize first. For saying the wrong thing. Provided that he recognized her. Maybe she should introduce herself, explain who she was. And she should probably knock, she thought. Give him time to register, and maybe remember. Raising her knuckles, she hesitated just a moment and—and in that brief moment he happened to move. And Alice saw Dee. On the far side of him, sidling up close, was the dreamy undergraduate who helped Sage in the lab. And, as if he had been waiting for Alice's undivided attention, the man reached for Dee's hand with impetuous passion.

What kind of cruel joke was this? What kind of horrible farce? And not just any woman either; it had to be Dee. Reeling beneath the insult to her sensibilities, Alice shot a silent curse his way. And as if in response, he swung around toward the door with that startled deer-like expression already carved on his face. His eyes locked with hers in paralytic recognition. Burning with humiliation, Alice ripped herself away and positively charged for the blood red fire-escape door.

THE LIGHTS WERE still on in the lab but no one was around. Alice supposed Sage had left for the movie he was planning to see with Bill. When she went off to eat, he had been giving hurried instructions to a flustered and reluctant Dee, who was whining that she would end up being late for her date. Not too late, it seemed. For a while Alice sat at her desk, staring out beyond the quad at the nighttime pattern of illuminated wards spread in punctuated rows beneath the tall dark column of the incinerator chimney. Crown by its four red pulsating beacons, the windowless tower seemed to rise above the place of healing like a somber landlocked buoy.

A timer beeped on Sage's desk. Alice pulled herself together and rushed over to turn it off and leave a note to say that she had. Then she went to fetch the boxes of pipette tips she had left sterilizing in the autoclave. From the coffee room at the far end of the corridor she heard music and laughter. The weekly Friday social—salsa and chips at four o'clock—was dragging on it seemed, most likely fueled by wine or beer. Alice was not enticed. Back in the lab she began preparing cells. Again and again, she tried to pry her mind from the look in those penetrating eyes—What did he think, that she was spying on them?—and that horrifying image of his hand clamped on Dee's.

Alice had never cared much for Dee. Even the mention of Dee's name set her on edge. Only that afternoon, Sage had come bounding in while Alice was busy at her bench—laboriously filling perforated racks with new pipette tips from a large plastic bag, ninety-six tips to each rack. "Get Dee to help," he had said. "That's what she's here for." Alice had told him she was fine, it helped focus the mind—but her rhythm had been lost. Dee was just an undergraduate, but she always made Alice feel insecure with her blatant self-confidence, and Alice could never tell whether her compliments were genuine. Had she really thought Alice was cool for wearing a skirt on her first day? Alice had not worn one since—though that was more out of convenience when biking into work. And did Dee really like Alice's earrings—one of her few concessions to adornment—even after Alice said she made them herself? Maybe she did. Alice had chastised herself for her irrational dislike of the girl who, to be honest, had never done her any harm. Well, not entirely irrational: Dee always managed to turn those compliments back on herself, wondering if the admired item would look good on her, or if she could get away without make-up, as she claimed Alice could. Dee thought the world revolved around her, was so…so indiscriminately sensual, always thought she was being watched by men and who knew, maybe she was, Alice hadn't seen why she should care. Only now she did see—she cared and it hurt. And there was no way she was ever going to ask Dee for help. Angrily she labeled sterile tubes with black indelible words and let the roar of the hood's extractor fan drown out her pain.

"You really don't give yourself a break," Sage said, making her jump. "Come along to the party—the guys from the fourth floor have joined us and brought some beer."

"Not tonight. I called in before I went to eat." The party had been quiet then, mostly married-with-children faculty making a token appearance before hurrying home. Opening a still warm rack of pipette tips behind the Perspex of the hood, she dispensed red media into a tube. Not that the experiment she was doing really mattered, she was well aware of that.

"Anyway, I thought you'd already left," she said presently to Sage, who had moved off to his bench.

"Bill had a crisis with one of his kids, so we're aiming for the next showing. *Casablanca*—did I tell you? They're doing Bogart reruns at the—wait one second, I have to stop a gel that's running across the hall…

"By the way, sorry if I upset you earlier," he said when he returned. He sat down on the chair at the neighboring hood.

"You didn't." Alice managed to smile. She felt desolate but it was not because of him. He had chastised her good-naturedly when she said she would be working that weekend. "Loosen up!" he had said. "Take off and explore. If it wasn't for Bill I'd be out of here, weekend or not." Alice had pointed out that he always worked weekends when Bill was not around, and he had let the matter rest.

"Still, I was being tactless," he said now. "Of course it can't have been easy coming over on your own like that. You must miss your old life back home."

Alice had made a vague sound, and acknowledged the reality of her old life back home. True, she had spent many a good hour in Leicester Square and Covent Garden and the bookshops on Tottenham Court Road; she knew Hyde Park and Kensington Gardens like the back of her hand; she had been to plays and movies and diners at enticing restaurants. And too many nights she had ridden home on the Tube alone among the many other solitary bedsit-dwellers just like her—though not really just like her, since not one of them had ever looked her way, at least none worth a second glance because no second glance of hers had ever lived up to the first. And although those dinner dates had been pleasant enough, they were dates on which she realized from the start—except when she was with Ben—that she and the person with whom she dined had little more in common than a mutual past. "Part of the circuit yet?" one of her single friends had asked. Alice supposed she had indeed become part of the circuit, always available to dine, to be a complimenting companion time and time again on each sequential revolution that was not revolutionary at all, merely repetitive. She stared unseeing at the fraying lace of Sage's shoe.

"By the way," Sage said, tucking in the cord. "I saw you talking to Rollins. Do you know him from before?"

"Sort of." Alice turned back to the hood and began resuspending lymphocytes in fading red fluid. "Actually," she added, "I think he mistook me for someone else. Everyone's been doing that today."

"It's the braid," Sage said. "I hardly recognized you myself."

"But this different." Alice dropped the used pipette into the biohazard bag. "More than not recognizing. Each of them actually seemed to think I was someone else."

"Maybe you are."

"I'm serious."

"Sorry. But hey, maybe it's because you're out of context here," Sage offered. "Like a bit of data you come across in isolation, the way it can mean just about anything without its proper reference points."

Or nothing, Alice said to herself, thinking of her own stupid mistake, the smile in the library that might have meant so much but did not. Still, it boiled down to the same thing, to the fact that she was an alien, and aliens can't interpret the obvious. Except for Rollins's discomfort in the auditorium…only then it dawned on her: Rollins had recognized her all along. He had never cared about her data, and nor had Bob—Bob, who had liked her so much once, more than she had wanted to acknowledge, even subconsciously—and the bet that Rollins had lost to Bob had been all about her, about getting her into bed.

"Don't worry," Sage consoled through her disgust. "I like that idea—being judged out of context. Isn't it kind of liberating? Exempting yourself from all that typecasting, all those labels and constraints imposed by so-called society. That's why so many people headed out West, way back when…"

"Exempting?" Alice roused herself. She had barely been listening, too busy contrasting her obliviousness to Rollins's motives with the way she had read too much in a momentary glance. But Sage was already walking off again, leaving Alice to accept that it had been no different back home. She had been just as confused, just as much an alien there. The only difference was that back home she had had no excuse. Everywhere it was the same old charade—one to which she did not know the answer though she played along as if she did. Only with Ben had it ever felt different. It had always felt different with Ben.

Except that Ben was always in pursuit of someone else. She had only to think of the last time she had seen him. He had called her one evening the previous June to say that he had tickets for a dinner-dance at a hotel along the Thames, and would she like to come along? For a careless moment she thought he had changed. "It's tomorrow night," he added with a weakened laugh. "A—uh—a sudden cancellation if you know what I mean, no questions asked. I'd be awfully grateful." And she had gone along and why not? She had nothing better to do, and knew he probably knew that, too. She had told herself that it was flattering he would ask, would know she would not take offense, would know he could depend on her. She had asked no questions in perfect keeping with his trust, and played along with exquisite manners and grace. Ben had sat morosely at a table while she maintained the tactful distance she assumed he would wish, passing most of the evening with a nice young man from Camden who was there with his brother who was friendly with Ben. She no longer remembered either brother's name.

No, it was not easy coming here alone. No easier than extracting herself from quicksand, it occurred to her unbidden, and the tube of fresh new cells she had been holding slipped and fell. Cloudy red fluid flowed, amoeboid, from its mouth. She cursed and bit down on her lip. She watched the puddle spread—thin, even, unrestrained. Eventually she shrouded it with paper towels to soak up the spill.

"Valuable cells?" Sage had come back.

"No." Alice wiped her eyes with her forearm and removed her latex gloves. She wondered why she even tried. She knew the assay would have shown nothing useful, however clean the data looked. But you had to keep searching, grasping at straws, hoping that the next time something meaningful would bloom. Like that moment in the library? What a fool she had been.

"Something's wrong, isn't it?"

Alice shook her head and tried to smile.

Sage tightened the lid on the bottle of culture medium and took it to the fridge. "I'm sure this can wait," he said. Then, gently, he raised Alice by the elbow and led her down the hall to where the music played.

Chapter Six

THE COFFEE-ROOM pounded with a bass beat, the lights had been turned down. Manic laughter erupted and then died.

"Relax," Sage said, holding open the door.

Alice steeled herself against the ambient mood and followed him in.

"Well, well. If it isn't Petra!"

A barricade of bodies peeled away, and there he was: the man with salt-and-pepper hair. He was smirking, leaning back in a chair balanced only on its hind legs; one of his long narrow shoes rested on a large red pail of ice. His eyes were hidden by tinted glass.

"Hi," Alice said, feeling conspicuous.

"Hey, man! Haven't seen you in months," Sage said, crossing her line of sight to lock hands with him, and looking askance at her. "You two know each other?" He seemed surprised.

"In a manner of speaking," the smirking man said, his veiled gaze resting on Alice. "I don't think we exchanged our real names, though." He shot her a sly smile and then, righting his chair, reached across and squeezed her hand.

"I'm Dan," he said, grinning and still watching her.

Daniel. Well, at least she liked his name.

"Short for Danson," he said. "Name's Matthew Danson, Matthew L. Danson—maybe you've come across it either at work or play—but to my friends I'm just plain Dan."

Alice cringed, but maintained a friendly smile. "I'm Alice," she said. "Alice Gaines."

"Pleased to meet you, Alice Gaines." Dan's dry hand retained hers for too long, and his eyes stayed on her face even after he dropped her hand. Alice looked away, mildly impatient. Sage was talking to someone else. Dan previous company had re-congealed of to one side.

"How about a drink, Alice Gaines? You look as if you need one."

Alice turned back to him. Maybe he was right. On the conference table pushed against the wall she saw two empty wine bottles among a scattering of clear plastic cups lined with gold or ruby dregs.

"Here," Dan said, digging in the ice at his feet and grabbing the neck of a bottle of beer. "How about one of these?"

"Sure," Alice said, though she rarely drank beer. Then, again, tonight was a last resort in every way.

"Wait…" Dan snatched the bottle back and rolled its top against his tightly closed eye. "Du-nuh!" He lifted off the cap.

Alice exclaimed, though she had seen the trick before.

"Screw cap," Dan confided. "Alice Gaines, you should have seen your face!" She laughed and pressed the cold glass to her lips. The beer was unexpectedly good—mild, refreshing and cool. She took another swig and pulled up a chair. She supposed that laughter did, indeed, help.

"So, Alice Gaines. I'd never seen you till today. Just arrived from New Zealand?"

"Britain, actually. And I've been here for six months, though sometimes I still feel as if—"

"Aha. You're English."

"Well, I grew up in Wales. Though I've lived in various parts of England—"

"Wales? Which one is Wales? The island?"

No one ever seemed to know. "The big rectangular peninsular attached to most of the west side of England—sticking out toward Ireland…"

"That's it: Ireland. I knew Wales was *part* of England." Dan shrugged. "Anyway, I could tell you didn't sound English."

Alice opened her mouth to explain that her accent was as generically English as it could be, just one of those things—a bit of a sore point, in fact, since even in Britain no one believed she came from Wales—but Dan plowed on, oblivious: "I've never met someone Welsh before," he said, looking at the door through which two women were retreating.

"Well, I'm not strictly Welsh…"

"Come on," he said, turning his head back. "You just said you were."

Alice supposed she was being pedantic since it was neither here nor there to him. Still, for form's sake, she explained that she was born in Wales, grew up there, but was not Welsh since her parents were not Welsh.

"What are they then?"

"Well…" She thought of listing her forebears' miscellaneous roots. But Sage had come back, and had heard it all before, and she was starting to suspect that Dan cared more about his questions than the answers she gave. "Well, technically they're British," she concluded lamely.

"Isn't that what I said in the first place?" Dan grinned. "Anyhow, I need another beer," he announced and rummaged in the ice. Then he looked up. "Hey, I'll bet you're one of those snooty Oxbridge types that only drinks wine," he said.

"I did my Ph.D. in Cambridge," Alice confessed. Dan raised a frigid bottle top up to his eye again, commandeering her weakening smile.

"Speaking of which," he said, turning to Sage, "when d'you plan to defend?" Sage looked to heaven and changed the subject. One of the men from Dan's earlier entourage crept quietly back and stared studiously at the floor while Dan and Sage sustained a burlesque joke. He looked up, evidently startled, when Alice finally spoke.

"You two know each other?" Dan asked in the pause that followed.

"No. Hi!" Alice held out her hand. The man touched her fingers and muttered a bland hello—distinctly enough to confirm her hunch that he was British.

"I thought you Brits all knew one another, small place like that," Dan said. "And she's from Oxford too, Duncan my boy."

"Cambridge actually," Alice corrected, seeing Duncan flinch as she tried and failed to catch his eye. "And only for my—"

"Close enough," Dan said, looking pleased.

"There you have it," Duncan muttered, frowning at his bottle of beer. "Anyway," he added, looking pained, "Hayley will be wondering where I am." He set the bottle on a shelf. "See you Dan, Sage," he said in a low tone, nodding with businesslike briskness, if not overt suspicion, toward Alice before he left.

Dan burst out laughing when he had gone. "*Anyway, Hayley will be wondering where I am,*" he tried to imitate, his vowels far too short. "But you're not about to hurry off Alice, are you?" He pretended alarm.

"Well, I'm meant to be setting up an experiment." She

looked across at Sage.

"Go on," Sage said. "Another beer won't hurt. I thought it could wait."

"Come on, it's Friday night," Dan said.

Alice had another beer.

THIRTY MINUTES later Sage rose to leave. On his way past, he shot Alice a look and nodded at the door. She shrugged, thinking about following him out, but it seemed unkind to abandon Dan all at once. A couple of postdocs she knew said hello, but they were on their way out. Three other women she knew less well rushed in wearing coats, and one waved vigorously to Dan, and Alice thought her chance had come—until they veered off toward the table and busied themselves scavenging for chips.

"Well, that leaves just you and me," Dan said, eying Alice again. She looked at her watch.

"A pressing engagement?"

"Not really." She shrugged. What did it matter? She felt sorry for him. He seemed to want her to stay. In fact, his eyes were begging her to stay. He must be desperate, she thought. And maybe I am too.

"Personally I'm starved," Dan announced. "Feel like joining me for dinner?"

Alice found herself accepting the invitation though she was not hungry at all. She felt disingenuous; a little guilty, in fact, knowing exactly why she had said yes. After running back to the lab to fetch her bag, she joined him at the elevator, which was still out of service; the staircase beyond it had been cordoned off since Dan came up. So she led him back down to the fire escape exit which, not long before, she had run up in such dismay. Four flights below, she let him hold for her the bright red door. She preceded him through. Beside him she retraced her steps—up that corridor, past the restrooms, through the foyer and out into the cold dark night. And by then she knew she had made the right choice. The lights had been out, the lab on the first floor was empty, he—the two of them—had gone. Well, she could play that game too. Why should she feel ashamed? The shame was that he, whoever he was, had not been there to see.

DAN POURED HIMSELF another glass of wine.

"No thanks," Alice said, covering her glass. He moved her hand away and filled it. "Oh all right, then," she said, starting to get used to him, though it had taken her a while. And he was still talking at her, as if oblivious of to whom he spoke. "So what do you work on?" she had asked as they sat down. "The cutting edge," he had said. "High-tech, high throughput technology." She had smiled and asked him what type. "The details would just bore you," he had said, comically imperious, and before she had a chance to request that he try her out, he had started telling her how hard it was to find good students these days. "You have your own lab?" she had asked, having assumed he was a postdoc just like her. "Not quite yet," he had muttered, looking around with sudden purpose for a waiter. "Man, the service these days…" His arrogance made her laugh. But she hid her contempt, because it was hardly his fault that he had happened to be there when almost anyone would have done. He was only trying to impress her. His effort, at the least, was flattering.

"Well," he said now as Alice sipped from her glass. "Where shall we go next?"

"What, after this?" She looked at her watch.

"Sure, the night is still young. Hey, I'll bet you can dance. I know this great place—near an Irish Pub that'll remind you of home. We could go there first."

Alice said it sounded fun. She was starting to float free, to lose old points of reference. She had never met anyone quite like Dan. His interest in her was explicit, which made it easier to respond.

Every action begets an equal, opposite reaction, a voice chimed in her head. Newton's third law? As if physics were relevant tonight. Besides, she had always liked to dance.

"First, though, I have to take a leak," Dan said, rising from his seat. "What's that thing you say about a dog?"

"Seeing a man about a dog?"

"That's the one. I'm off to see a man about a dog." He snickered and left her alone. She felt exposed as her smile slowly died, though a calm hazy twilight veiled the room. She sipped from her wine; she toyed with the candle on the table, and with the small vase of flowers. Occasional bursts of ironic laughter spiked the hum of indecipherable words.

The youthful waiter who had taken their order reappeared and asked her if she needed anything. She said she was fine. Returning her attention to the food still on her plate, she thought she could have made a worse choice. Flustered, she had chosen a random entrée—still distracted by what 'entrée' meant—after Dan had reeled off his wishes without checking the menu, adding options unasked. She speared a mushroom and chewed. "*Champignon,*" Dan had murmured, catching her eye as the waiter wrote down her request. She had asked if he spoke French. "*Mais bien sur,*" he had said. "Practically bilingual." So it had seemed only natural to show him her new find. "You'll be able to translate this, then," she had said, taking the paper from her bag. He had squinted at the conjoined babies, scanned the text; his focus had waned. "Nah," he had, shaking his head. "That's *old* French. Even I can't read that." Once more she had felt sorry for him.

He had still not come back. In Cambridge, Alice mused, it was not done to visit the bathroom during a meal when people were still eating. The disciplinarians of her college had once sent out a memo when etiquette had lapsed. She decided to tell Dan about this when he came back; he would probably laugh. There had been so many rules like that in Cambridge. But at least you knew what was expected of you, and what to expect. Back then no one would have expected a man like Dan to ask her out—an exhilarating thought, but unsettling too, because it made her feel as if one false move might catch her out.

In fact, she already felt caught out tonight in her casual clothes—her jeans and non-descript grey shirt. The woman at the table beyond Dan's chair was sheathed in a deep red evening dress—satin, sleek and low-cut. Her hair was piled high, a few stray curls coiling toward the tiny pearls clasped around her neck. Alice felt envious and plain. Then again, she had hardly known that morning how the day would unfold. That morning: the punctured tire and missed call seemed a lifetime ago, Diane's engagement belonged to a different world. Alice wondered what was keeping Dan, and looked at her watch—instantly remembering her English teacher, Miss Kernan, trying to tell thirty newly pubescent girls about love. "Time *does* vanish!" the young woman had said, looking up wide-eyed from the Louis Mac-Neice poem they were studying that day. "He's right! Time disappears when you're in love!" As if those twelve-year-old girls might have understood, newly chained as they were to time, month by bloody month. As if Alice understood even now. *Meeting Point*: that was the poem. She touched the vase of flowers again. "The *bell*—the flower on the table in the coffee shop,"

Miss Kernan had gone on to say, "it really does not make a sound!" The flower in front of Alice now was silent enough, but she had no doubt that time was in evidence tonight.

"...There you go again," a man's voice erupted, addressing the woman in red. The woman's back was rigid now, as if carved from stone. "*Just tell me how you want me to be,*" the man mimicked plaintively, his cruel tone making Alice wince. "Always ready to drop everything at the least prompt from me," he said. "God, you're so boring, so predictable. You're driving me insane."

Alice fiddled with her fork. Poor woman, she thought, at the same time guiltily relieved that looks could only go so far.

"I'm back," Dan announced, blocking out the scene as he reclaimed his seat. He patted the table with both hands. "Ran into an old girlfriend," he said, and Alice wondered how many girlfriends he had had.

"And now for a coffee," he said, calling to Alice's mind the poem again. And although she never drank coffee this late, she said she would have one too. Behind Dan, the man with the elegant woman asked for the check. A repulsive specimen, she thought. What did the woman see in him? Soon after, the couple rose in unison as if from a tranquil rendezvous. The man grinned affably at Dan as he squeezed past his chair.

The coffee arrived. Alice knew she would not sleep well. Dan stirred his with a spoon and watched the deep brown vortex flatten.

"Thanks for coming out tonight," he said, looking up suddenly.

"You're welcome—thank you for inviting me."

"Friday nights can be so lonesome," Dan added, and Alice was about to laugh when she realized he was serious. His gaze was focused on her so trustingly, so pitifully, that she turned her latent smirk into a sympathetic smile.

"I know," she said, trying to sound sincere—and feeling so very insincere. As if she were being judged, she thought, but not by Dan or anyone there. *Every action begets an equal, opposite reaction*, that voice inside her chirped.

"To be honest," Dan said, "I'm really kind of beat." His lips curled in a downcast grin. With one finger he drew a circle on the back of one of Alice's hands. "Shall we take a rain check on the dancing?" he asked, his eyes almost moist.

"Sure, I'm tired too," Alice said, though by now she was wide awake even without the caffeine. Well, she thought. That will be that. Dan insisted he take care of the check.

"So," Dan said out on the sidewalk in the cold fresh night air. "Need a ride home?" Alice declined, said her bike was still at work. Probably for the best, she thought with a twinge of regret. Or possibly relief. He was parked there too, he said, and so they walked back together, their arms rubbing accidentally—or maybe not accidentally—now and then as they talked. Alice began to glow inside. Not meaning to at all. She wondered if a metaphorical analgesic, which she knew Dan had been, could go further than assuaging pain.

They reached Dan's brand new SUV. He touched her shoulder and thanked her again. Then he seemed to reconsider, and hooked a finger beneath her chin, raising her face toward his. He smiled into her eyes. Several large and fluffy snowflakes landed on her face and she laughed. Breaking the spell. She breathed a small sigh. Of relief or regret?

"Want to change your mind about that ride?" Dan asked, frowning at the sky, evidently undeterred.

Part II

Incubation Period

Chapter Seven

A SHAFT OF LIGHT from the window high on the wall opposite slashed a trapezium on the rug. Alice closed her eyes again. And then she heard the crisp brisk knocking that had nailed through her dream. Before she thought to ignore it, she had leapt from her bed into her nightdress and sprung into the kitchen where the sound had come from. As her pulse out-beat the ticking of the wall-clock, another rhythmic volley assured her that it was only her elderly landlord on the other side of the door leading up to his quarters in the main house above.

"Come in," she said, knowing she had no choice anyway. She was glad Dan had gone. The key turned in the lock.

"Please forgive me," the old man said as he bowed around the door. "I wondered if you would care to join me for a cup of tea."

His manner, his gentle German accent, his use of the words 'care' made her yearn for lost innocence, and not only hers; it was as if he had opened the door to a crack in time.

"Thank you," she said, her bearings askew as she fought the startling shame his aged presence had evoked. She glanced at the clock: it was almost ten.

"Ah, but you are running late," he said with a nod. "I should have known. You always work on Saturdays."

This was true—though work was hardy on her mind, what with the feel of Dan's flesh on hers still so fresh. She smiled rather than lie to him outright, well aware than she was in no mood for drinking tea with an old man, however quaint and decorous. Besides, his knowledge of her schedule was somewhat unsettling, given that she had barely spoken to him since before she moved in. He had been disquieting even then, and she had only taken the apartment because, as promised in the neatly typed notice she had found in the library, it was fully furnished, right down to the faded counterpane with pleated edges on the bed. Though, if she was honest with herself, it was the lingering smell of mothballs that had swung her in the end, reminding her of grandparents and old woolen coats.

A yellowed sign had caught her eye the day she came to look, still jet-lagged from her recent flight. *Absolutely forbidden: television after 10 o'clock,* it said. *DO NOT VIOLATE.* It was tacked above the door in which he stood now, rust stains circling the pins. The letters curled elaborately, decisively, written with a fountain pen, the thinner strokes almost gone.

"Ah, yes. My wife. She didn't like... The floor is rather thin," he had said that first time, looking up. He was old, very old, his skin yellowed like the sign, seeming almost translucent in the unforgiving kitchen glare. "Just to keep the volume low after, say, 11 o'clock at night," he had confided with a smile. "She is dead now, of course." He had peered at Alice then, his eyes glistening—or so she had thought, though it might have been the light. Feeling that she was intruding, she had mumbled a clumsy condolence, wondering at the stern memento of the woman he had loved.

"Anyway," he had resumed, businesslike, that first day, "this door leads to my place. I keep it locked at all times. I come down once a month to fetch the rent check, you can leave it right here." He had tapped the speckled countertop with one clawed hand. Then, with a solicitous air, he had led her to the front door that opened on the stairwell tucked against the house. "I am so glad you are British," he had said meaningfully as she waved her through, and she had wondered what dubious prejudices he enjoyed. However, he had seemed so sure she would want to move in that she had not wanted to disappoint him. They had parted by the terracotta pots along the side of the house that he had been tending when she arrived—a row of verdant domes splashed through with red, white and pink—and she had felt his eyes on her back as she walked away.

"So, I must let you get on then," he said this sunny Saturday morning. "I'm sorry you can't join me, but please wait one moment while I bring your tea."

Before Alice could process his words, he had retreated up the stairs and soon returned with a gilt-edged china cup balanced on a matching saucer. The rosebud painted on the side of the cup was almost hidden by a wedge of lemon.

"I had an English friend who liked to drink her tea like this," he said, handing her the cup and saucer with a courteous bow.

Humbled and ashamed, Alice pleaded her gratitude. The old man smiled as if he understood, backed behind the door and pulled it closed.

Alice laid the teacup on the table and sat down. The cup and saucer were almost exactly like the ones her father's parents had kept in a glass-paned cabinet that rattled peevishly when you came close. "Your inheritance," Oma used to say, holding a cup toward the light. "A reminder of all we lost." Then she would stare at Alice hard and recount in soft Teutonic tones how they'd had to sell most of their belongings when the markets crashed between the wars. "Less baggage when we left, though," Oma would add and click her tongue and laugh. However, if young Alice moved a hand toward the cup, she would be scolded straight away: "Be careful, very careful. Have a good look. But please, *do not touch*." Inheritance: a heavy word to Alice, a claustrophobic word that made her feel about to disappear beneath its weight and its fragility.

Alice sipped her tea. Slow footsteps cross the floor above. Then it was quiet. A short time later she dressed and went out.

FOR FORM'S SAKE, Alice walked toward work. She knew she ought to restart the assay she had aborted last night, but the lingering sensation of hands sweeping her skin made her feel acutely conspicuous and conscious of her physique, as if the contours of her body had been freshly defined. Her thoughts, however, were disjoined, fickle and amorphous, easily waylaid. As she waited to cross the road a sleek black car rolled past directly in front of her. Like a modern-day version of a black cat, she thought. With portents of bad luck. Or was a black cat crossing your path good luck? The car swept into the driveway of the mock-Gothic apartment building looming beside her, pulling up at the curb beneath its crenelated walls. Two women packed in lime green silk and an older man in a morning coat homed in on the car. A bride emerged in a snowball of tulle and, like the chime of midnight for a displaced Cinderella, brought to Alice's mind the wedding in August.

Always the bridesmaid, never the bride, she though as the bride was whisked off through an archway by her bustling entourage. She felt as incongruous as the man in sweatpants who walked past at that moment, staring at them; she had never even been a bridesmaid before—in fact Diane had said she would be the Maid of Honor. Would she make them wear lime green, truss them in frills and ribbons and bows? Alice pictured herself in a row of identically painted figurines, hair sculpted tidily in place. She shuddered at the thought, checking as she did so the long flat barrette she had found that morning in the bathroom cabinet—left behind by another former tenant, she assumed—and used in a shortcut toward a semblance a French braid; it was holding up so far. Still, she would do what Diane wanted when the time came, she thought. Just as she would do as she was told in the lab—when the time came.

Now, however, was not the time. She had been thinking of fetching her bike, but decided it could wait—decided she was not yet ready to run into Dan, and he might just be there. Turning around, she walked the other way to the far end of the street where a small commercial district spread from the T-junction. Usually she skimmed the near edge on her way home from work when she needed to buy food. Today, though, she entered its heart, moving slowly among the bustling weekend crowds, her fragmented image gliding beside her across storefront displays. Eventually she stopped outside a chic boutique. Gold lettering on the window spelled out *Evening, Bridal & More*, and three smooth serene mannequins displayed one of each. For Diane, Alice thought. Just to rehearse. After a moment's hesitation, she opened the door and stepped inside, trying to look as if she went there all the time.

She felt like a small child as she browsed among the overpriced garments made for women who lived a different life from hers. Most were not to her taste, whatever kind of life she lived. She hoped Diane felt the same way. After a while, though, she came across a low-cut red evening dress that happened to be her size. Why not give it a try? The dead-pan woman at the counter, who had been watching her since she came in, showed her into the dressing room and then left her alone with the full-length four-way mirror.

Alice had not seen herself whole for months—the mirrors in her apartment were all far too small. Even before shedding her coat, she felt an odd disconnect. Maybe Sage was right about the braid, she thought, re-securing a loose strand back into the barrette. It did make her look different. She tried on the dress. It fit astonishingly well—and yet still she barely recognized herself. Had she lost weight, or else changed shape? No: she was still too short and solid to be lithe, too lean to be voluptuous. This mirror, she could tell, did not lie. It was probably the dress; something similar had happened once before, when she and a college friend spent an afternoon trying on ball gowns well beyond their meager means—gowns designed with the utmost care to give an illusion of elegance even where there was none. Afterwards, Alice had bought some imitation silk and used the seamstress skills she had learned from Oma—who had taken in sewing to help make ends meet when she first arrived in Britain after the war—to create a near-perfect copy of her favorite dress. She had been pleased with the result, worn year after year to the Cambridge May Balls, each time cleverly adapted and altered to look new.

She turned to view herself from behind—and might as well have been surveying a stranger's back. Though perhaps, at the same time, the impression was familiar. Shrugging, she pulled the end of her braid over her shoulder, just as Dan had done last night. He had carefully released it, loosened the intertwined strands and spread her liberated tresses on the pillow about her head. Then he had buried his face in her hair, inhaled it and fallen asleep on it. Pinning her to her bed.

Alice liked the dress. It made her look sophisticated. She held the braid atop her head. Still more elegant, she thought—just like the woman in red last night. The image repelled her, though; she let the braid fall. That image repelled her too. This is not me, she thought—or felt, the feeling surreal, she did not understand. But something was wrong. Quickly she slid off the dress as if it bore an evil charm and left it hanging on the rail.

Out on the crowded sidewalk, her heart missed a beat when she thought she saw Dan. Before she could dissect panic from delight, she realized she was wrong. All the same, she dove into a nearby bookstore, where the colorful displays offered the perfect excuse for being too absorbed to notice who else might be there. She found herself looking at a cover illustration that brought Dan to mind again: an aerial view of two almost empty coffee cups. Her skin crawled with pleasure, or perhaps penitence, or both at the same time. Though they might well be tea cups, she thought with a pang of self-reproach and compassion for old age. More likely coffee, she decided, opening up the book. The title story was about a kiss. She blushed and began to read, and continued to read while she waited in line to pay.

"Next, please!" a woman's voice called loudly through tale of unrequited love. Alice looked up, momentarily lost—and looked straight into a pair of unmistakable brown eyes.

"Next, please!" the woman at the checkout called again. Alice leapt to the desk, feeling his presence near the door and those brown eyes on her. She paid for the book with pained attention and spent a long time folding her receipt. When she was sure he had gone, she fled, head down—though she hardly knew why she would react like that toward a man she barely knew. Still, what right did he have to stare at her? She had done nothing wrong. And at least Dan had *wanted* her—and desperately, too.

Out on the sidewalk she continued to feel exposed. Across the road, the billboard of the art house movie theater caught her eye, *Casablanca* spelled out in large black letters as if for her. She crossed the street and bought a ticket to the next showing.

"Twenty minutes in theater A," the ticket clerk said, counting out her change. "What's the book?" he asked.

She took it out from under her arm for him to see.

"English major?"

"Scientist," she said, and the young man grimaced and turned toward the next in line.

Alice made her way inside, marveling at the art deco mythology on the walls. Taking a seat near the front, she returned to her book until the heavy curtain swung—a red velvet curtain like the one in the old Odeon in which she had seen her first feature film and which she had watched being demolished with a ball and chain when she was ten. When the movie began, she closed the book and gave herself up to the romance and drama on the screen, to the conflict between love and doing what you know is right.

The movie ended. The lights came back on. Alice did not move. When the bustle behind her died, she stood up and stretched. Only one other patron was still there. He had already reached the exit, heading out, but Alice froze in mid-stretch. Just in time she stooped, pretending to search for something under her seat—she was sure he had looked back. When she straightened again, the door was swinging to and the startled deer-eyed man had gone.

Gone, that is, until she almost collided with him in the grocery store. All she had wanted was to get some beer in case Dan came back. And maybe some food. She had let down her guard as she swung into an aisle and a second too late turned her attention on a can of soup. Though not before she had noticed the sleek eggplant, the fussy bunch of herbs, the bottle of red wine in the basket in his hand. And yet what did she care what he—they—dined on tonight. She pretended interest in another can, and wondered whether Dan could cook. Probably not. She grabbed the can as if to prove she did not care. Nor did she care how graceful that man's fingers were, or how cartilaginously white the smooth knuckles of his fist.

"Hi," he said.

She looked up as if surprised. "Oh, hi," she said. "Wow. Small world. Excuse me, but I really must dash." Ben had used that line on her more than once—sounding as insincere as she knew she did now. She did not wait for a response, but hurried off to the checkout line as if she had spoken the truth. All she had for her dinner now was one can of soup, but she would have to live with that. Besides, if Dan came back this evening, he would most likely want to eat out.

THE LANDLORD was standing by the terracotta pots when Alice returned. It was on the verge of getting dark. Only a tangle of grey dried-out stems trailed from the pots now, the spent earth dormant beneath discs of ice.

"Hello," Alice said. "Thank you again for the tea earlier."

The old man had been looking at her, but he must have been deep in thought; his focus seemed to change.

"I'll fetch your cup and saucer now if you like," she added as he caught up, wondering as she spoke whether he had come for it already while she was gone.

But evidently he had not: "Ah, yes," he replied, fully present now. "And perhaps, if you are not too busy, you would join me for some sherry? British sherry," he added, one scant eyebrow raised.

Alice was not sure what to think. Was he overstepping the bounds of propriety or just being kind? She did appreciate his old fashioned manners, and the old world charm that was as rare these days as being served tea with lemon in a gilt-edged china cup. She supposed he would be shocked if he knew that Dan was there last night. She was still in shock herself. Though she refused to feel ashamed. Dan had wanted her company. And so, it seemed, did this old man. "That would be lovely," she said, hoping they would find something to talk about. "I'll drop off my bag and get your cup."

"And I will meet you momentarily at your kitchen door."

The old man smiled as he led her up the stairs. The smell of mothballs intensified. He guided her into the living room. Everything in there was pristine, an impression of reflections, some true, some not: large gilt-edged mirrors, glistening glass tabletops, glazed framed sketches and paintings and photographs. A grand piano gleamed at one end of the room, reflecting and reflected, hazy in the polished floor.

"You play the piano," Alice said, glad of a prompt.

"Not any more. My fingers, you know." The landlord held out a hand and she saw the knobby, enlarged joints. With that same hand he took the cup and saucer and set them down on a tray. "I used to give performances," he said brightly. "When I was a boy." He went over to an open cabinet and removed two crystal glasses. "Dry or medium?" he asked.

"Dry, please," she said as if by rote. Someone—Ben, in fact—had told her once that medium sherry, which she far preferred, was unsophisticated. Instantly she felt ashamed of lying, if only to herself. "Actually," she said, "may I change that to medium?"

She examined a photograph propped on a shelf, of two children on a beach. "You have family around here?" she asked.

"Family? No, no. We had no children." He walked over with her glass. "Please," he said, "do sit down."

Alice lowered herself onto the floral sofa. He sat down on a matching chair.

"No," he said, looking at the photograph. "My wife's nieces and nephews and their offspring on the other coast, but no children of our own. It just never happened."

Alice looked at the picture with him, not sure what to say. She sipped from her glass.

"Not that we didn't try," he volunteered. "We tried everything. You would not believe the things we tried. One time they had us sit in mud baths, can you imagine? Covered in mud up to our necks. I thought we would laugh about it afterwards with our children, when they had grown up and heard the lengths we went to for them."

Alice did her best to smile.

"And you," he said. "What about you?"

"Me?" Alice wondered what he meant.

"You have a fiancée? Or a boyfriend?" He grinned at her expectantly. "Or boy*friends*?" He laughed and watched her, cocked an eyebrow, seemed to wink.

Alice felt her cheeks burn. She wondered what he had seen, what conclusions he had drawn.

"Ah well, you're still young," he said with a mischievous grin and Alice sipped her drink again, thoroughly confused. Was he trying to be nice? And was thirty-one young?

"Here, have a look at this," he said, reaching for an album on the glass-topped coffee table. "Pictures from my first summer in America. I was looking at them." He opened the padded floral cover and began to turn the collaged pages. Alice wondered if she would hear if her phone rang downstairs.

"There," he said and turned the album around her way. "This is my favorite view of all time. I was visiting with friends on the coast."

Alice looked at the picture: grey sky, grey sea sliced by the trunk of a tree.

"This was from their house looking down on the beach past this silhouette of a maple." He pressed down on a photo corner that had come unstuck. "The sun was low in the sky," he said. "It was the evening. Then the sun broke through the clouds in the midst of heavy rain making that spot of light far out to sea. Yah, I know it is only black and white but can you feel the radiance? Beautiful, no?"

Moved by his evident emotion, Alice agreed.

"Of course, it was especially beautiful to me." He looked at her as if wondering whether she was ready. From his age and so-familiar accent, she had long guessed he had fled the Holocaust and expected him to talk of freedom and starting afresh. "You see, I don't know if you know it yet," he told her instead, "but there is a layer of beauty that belongs not only to the eyesight, but to a deeper knowledge—perhaps a kind of intuition. This beauty makes you feel more whole and more a part of life, and of love, than you have ever felt before." He was silent for a while and Alice wrestled with her discomfort at such intimate talk from so elderly a man—and the incongruity of this beauty and love and his late wife's forbidding notice in the kitchen. On the other hand, she thought, why ever not? He had been young once and so had his wife. Besides, did age have to change the way you felt?

"Do you know, though?" the landlord broke in. "I always

wondered whether the beauty came of sharing with someone you love, or the other way around." He stared a moment at the photograph. "And the problem is, you do not always see until afterwards the true significance, the true potential."

Alice listened, guiltily aware that she did not understand.

"But in any case," he said, "this feeling stays with you forever, whatever else happens—or doesn't happen."

Doesn't happen? Alice thought again of Dan. Distracted, she commented to the landlord that it must be lonely without his wife. He looked up and smiled—a sad and pitying smile. Then he reached across and tapped her gently on the knee.

"You're still young, my dear," he said. "You still have many things to learn."

ALICE SAT DOWN on her bed. She always said the wrong thing. But surely not to Dan. That had been for the best. She had asked him in knowing she might have to say something— knowing already what he had in mind. Hoping, perhaps, that he was prepared? Hoping he was not—for how could he have known he would end up with her, or anyone, last night?

Alice sat and watched the telephone. In her hand she held the credit card receipt from the restaurant at which they had dined. She had seen it propped up on her stovetop while the landlord fetched her tea. *Ciao*, Dan had written on the back. Had the old man noticed too? Had he known what it signified? Then again, did she? While the phone continued to not ring, she wondered if that small word implied more than an ordinary goodbye, and looked it up in the old dictionary that she thought of as part of the décor in the hallway until now. *Ciao*: dialectical Italian derivation of a word that meant *slave*. Short for *I am your slave*. How flattering, she thought. Especially after just one night.

Besides, who would not have asked him in? He had said, over and over again, that he was powerless in her presence, that he needed her, wanted her—as he pulled her from his car, as she unlocked her door, as he danced her to the bedroom, hands sweeping, Velcro ripping, sticking fast to each other like burrs as they laughed, zippers unzipping, layer by layer peeled away.

And then, inevitably, he had kissed her. A no holds barred kiss. Alice had tried hard to push off the cool grey resignation that descended as his flaccid, moist mouth sealed her lips. She had tried hard to ignore her conviction that he was kissing someone else, that old familiar feeling that she was not really there. He had said that he needed her, wanted her—was that not enough? Deftly he had unbuttoned her shirt and then pulled down her jeans, placing a palm on her warm abdomen, electrifyingly cool. She had lowered herself beneath his weight onto the bed. He had turned to his own jeans.

"Uh…I'm not on the pill or anything," she had said, dismayed by the prim and childlike sound of her voice.

Dan had stopped what he was doing and raised himself, caging her with outstretched arms. "Oh," he had said, looking at the wall, and Alice had wondered at the added implications of the word *anything*.

"Sorry," she had said.

He had laughed. "You really are something else," he had said, shaking his head. His face without glasses had seemed bland, incomplete, as if its key lines of demarcation had been erased; his chin receded into loose folds of skin. Like a lizard, Alice had found herself thinking and tried not to look.

The backs of his fingers had brushed her cheek and he had seemed sad. Then he had laughed again. "Well, never mind," he had said. "It's probably for the best. You are, indeed, my little savior tonight." He had sounded relieved, which took Alice by surprise and ignited a first glow of affection for him.

Rolling onto his back between Alice and the wall he had stared at the ceiling. Then his eyes had swiveled to meet hers and caught her watching him. He had raised himself onto his elbow. "I really don't deserve you," he had said, playing with her hair. She had felt both elevated and unworthy as he untied her braid. Tentatively she had reached out and touched his cheek. With his ungainly fingers he unwoven and combed out her hair. Then he had sighed and she thought he would speak. Instead, he had lowered his face in her hair and soon fallen asleep. Later, she was roused from a half-doze as the lavatory flushed. She had heard the opening and decisive closing of her latch. Moments later, the crisp smack of a car door and the macho roar of its awakened engine. A cloud of cool air had wafted through her room.

Alice lay down on the bed in that same room, still waiting for the phone to ring. *Ciao,* she thought and smiled to herself. *I am your slave.* She did mean at least something to him. She waited, studying the receipt as if it might hold the key. Finally, she reached beneath the bed for a shoebox she had brought with her from home. It was filled with handwritten messages—mostly hastily scrawled notes that had been pinned to her door in college, left in her mailbox or on her desk at work. Some were from men on whom she'd had short crushes, undeclared and unreturned, in which they asked to borrow lecture notes, a textbook or perhaps her bike. Others were more overtly romantic, from men who made it as far as the first kiss that marked the end of what she felt for them but still deserved at least her gratitude—and maybe empathy—for misplaced love. The vast majority, of course, were from Ben, who was clearly getting on with life in

London and not missing her at all. Ben's messages, often in his neatly constrained script, were usually insulting, even when they had been transcribed by other people when he had phoned while she was out. Material evidence of what might have been, of what was not—and maybe also evidence of what was not yet? She placed the credit card receipt on top.

Of course: She had not given Dan her number; that was why he had not called. She had not said the wrong thing. And even if chance did favor the prepared mind, there were penalties for trying to tempt fate.

He could find her name in the directory, directory enquiries. It could not be that hard.

But perhaps—well, perhaps he would not think of it. Besides, he hardly knew her yet. And she would see him at work—on Monday, if not before. There was really no rush.

In any case, the phone did not ring.

Chapter Eight

Peter FOLDED his laundry straight from the drier and stacked it in his bag. Something in the drum beside his thudded out of sync with its cyclical hum. The laundromat door opened and someone came in. He made a point of not looking up, annoyed at the effort this required, and then at his needless caution when a bland young man asked from the far side of the room how to use the machines. Having gone over to explain, Peter stood by at his novice's request as the nervous youth performed a dry run. Then told the kid to have a good evening, grabbed his bags and walked home through the newly fallen darkness, noting how even a stranger's functional gratitude felt good just then.

In the porch he picked up his mail. There was a postcard from his parents. *We've reached New Zealand*, he read in the dim light coming from the window overlooking the porch. *Don't forget to check the house now and then.* When on earth would he have time for the three-hour round trip to the Cape? He turned the postcard over to a view of stunning hills, and realized what had changed: the blinded window had been dark since the former tenant moved out months before, leaving only his name on the corresponding mailbox. That name was covered now, he noticed, by a strip of sky blue painter's tape unevenly handwritten with the name *Joy Adair*. Shouldering his way in, he wondered if the British woman had moved in downstairs. He would hardly be surprised the way his day had gone so far—though she had hardly looked like a Joy that afternoon.

He made his way inside. The door to Joy Adair's unit, leading into the foyer, moved. Peter froze. He had hardly been serious. And in any case she had not wanted, even remotely, to detain him. Quite the opposite in fact. Yet what else could he expect? Twice now she had seen his mood turn dark. Besides, anyone could see that Joy Adair's door, left ajar, had simply moved with the incoming draft. Head down, he crossed the once-grandiose hallway and took the wide wooden stairs two by two to the top.

The rattle of his keys triggered liquid peals from Violet, a small ginger guinea-pig whose previous owners—the family of a former colleague—had moved back to Japan. Peter had taken her on temporarily, but before he had pinned up an advertisement found himself growing attached. He liked her lack of restraint, the way she lived for the moment alone. Pulling a leafy carrot from one of his bags, he made straight for her cage, where she was leaping up and down with unbridled vigor—he had not known before she arrived that guinea-pigs jump. The instant the carrot touched the thin wire mesh, she tugged it inside and gnawed with fearsome relish at its crystalline flesh. As he watched, Peter thought of seizing the moment too, jumping into his car and driving down to the Cape, his sense of obligation to his parents having morphed on his way up the stairs into a means of escape from the mess he had made.

Violet stopped gnawing and gazed up at him with her perpetual smile.

"Don't worry," he said, lifting her out. "Too much to do here. Maybe next weekend…and just for the day." Steadying her on his chest, he stepped over to his flashing answering machine and pressed the button with his free hand, picking stalks of hay from her swirling rosettes while the cassette slowly rewound.

"Dude," his brother's voice said at last. "Does this thing still work? I feel like that time, back when overseas calls cost the earth, when Dad talked to a for fifteen minutes into a microphone, a Christmas message to his UK cousin, and then realized he had forgotten to press down record. Anyhow," Eric added, "I just checked in to say I'm heading for the Cape with Marie and the boys on Friday, so the house is ours for the whole of next weekend."

"Damn," Peter said, and pressed reset. The cassettes whirred and clicked and then fell still. And then the phone rang, intrusive and shrill. Violet scrambled on his chest.

"Peter. You're there."

"Tom." Peter held his breath. The last time Tom called him at home, the main lab freezer had failed.

"I know who got the California job," Tom said.

Peter exhaled. "Who then?"

"Your arch-nemesis."

"My what?" Peter answered himself: "Ah, Sarah. I see." He stared at the wall, at another of his salvaged wild-flower prints, this one of *Rubus*—brambles. Sarah was chief author of the modeling paper that had stolen his thunder.

"On the bright side, that's one less to compete with from here on, eh?"

"True." Sarah also happened to be Peter's former girlfriend, though he had never mentioned that to Tom—Sarah with her sweet dimpled smile behind which she hid a caustic wit and ferocious ambition and the opportunistic streak with which she had ground him into dust. "I should have guessed, though," he said, gritting his teeth. "Some prig of a grad student started on about her model in the middle of my talk, as if her word were lore. It's all about who gets there first, isn't it? All about who makes that goddamn first impression, imprints their screwed up version of the truth on naïve unsuspecting minds—"

"Ease up there, kiddo. The way you speak about her anyone would think you two had—no, don't tell me, not my concern…"

Tom was unbelievable. "Her model's wrong," Peter said. "Any fool can see that." He knew he was no more of an immunologist than Sarah, but at least he had studied how lymphocytes behave, and taken into account the critical fact that the same signal can trigger opposing responses, depending on whether or not the lymphocyte has met that signal before.

"People see what they want to see," Tom said, and Peter thought about the British woman and how her response to him had altered after that first time. "Forget about her," Tom advised. "*We* know her model's crap. Besides, all she did was get a job you didn't even want."

"I guess." He could have told Tom there was more to it, that Sarah had stolen his idea—even if she had then adulterated it—during their farce of a relationship. A relationship that had begun all too fittingly during an evacuation of the building in which they both worked, the claxon ululating an alarm that turned out to be false. Only she had not really stolen his idea; he had shared it willingly. Hard as it was to believe now, he had been smitten by her, blindly infatuated once upon a time.

"Well, I'll let you get on now," Tom said. "And we all know the pain of a job search, so anytime you need to rant just give me a shout."

Peter thanked him and set down the phone. It was true: He had not wanted that job any more than he had wanted Sarah by the time she left. But he was not going to discuss Sarah with Tom. What had he seen in her anyway? As Tom had just said, we see what we want to see.

Goddamn Sarah, he thought. She had called him her knight in armor when they first met—mocking his impenetrable up-tightness, however, and not his chivalry. At the time she had not known about his actual armor, the full-size chainmail vest he had made in his late teens, spending days on end obsessively coiling wire and clipping rings that he linked one by one into a huge fluid garment—a creation he had not known what to do with beyond trying it on now and then to marvel at its encompassing weight and breath-taking compression. By the time she seen the real thing in his parents' garage—on what turned out to be their last trip together to the Cape—she had forgotten about him being a knight of any kind and called him an anachronism; and not long after that, when everything turned truly sour, she had called him a chronological error, one whose shelf-life has expired.

In retrospect, he knew what had gone wrong. What Sarah wanted, what she needed, was rivalry: clear evidence of competition by which to validate herself and the choices she made. She had even said so to his face, more or less, that last time on the Cape.

"So," she had whispered, rolling on top of him one night on the beach. "How many times have you…had passionate *intercourse*, you prude, on the sand beneath this bright summer moon?"

It was fair enough to call him a prude: he had told her himself that he did not use profane language to describe to making love. And her question had been fair enough too: she knew he had been a lifeguard in his teens, and most of the others had, indeed, spent their days looking out for willing prospects when they weren't bragging about the night before. However, Peter had not been like that then or now—had she not realized that yet?—and he had told her as much.

At which she had twisted without mercy from his crotch. "Oh what a good boy you are," she had said. "And you know what? You've never said a word about the previous women in your life."

Peter had never thought it relevant. Sure there had been women, or at least girls. Not many, it was true, and none for long. But why should that matter? It had mattered to Sarah because soon after that she and Peter's roommate Dave had found their own place together—Matt, Peter's onetime good friend and a mathematician extraordinaire, to whom he had introduced her without a second thought after telling her more than once that Dave never went anywhere without a woman at his side and never the same one twice. So no wonder she had risen to the challenge—entered the competition, and won—and in plain sight of Peter, too. Though of course he had not seen it coming, trusting in the decency of friends. Friends? They had added salt to the wound by collaborating professionally on their stupid contrived model based on complex mathematics, so much cooler than the ordinary math and sound biology of his according to the scant few that cared.

"Don't you care?" Sarah had asked when she had told him about Matt and herself. "Don't you have anything to say?" But what could he have said? That it wasn't fair? Who was he to argue about two people falling in love? He had introduced them to each other of his own accord, and if she liked Dave more than him, then so be it; he was not going to compete. He had seen it for the end it was. His feelings were his business, and he had kept them to himself—though no doubt they had shown in every muscle of his face.

"Ow!" Violet had moved and dug her claws through his shirt. He pried them free again. "I'll give you the benefit of the doubt," he said, setting her back down. "You didn't know what you were doing." She circled a few times as if chasing a non-existent tail and then curled up to sleep.

Peter retrieved his laundry from near the front door. As he lifted the bag, the phrase *mass times height times the force of gravity* came to mind, complete with an image of his high school physics teacher vigorously chalking the words *Potential Energy* in white across the board. "*That* is what you guys need," Old Cross had told an especially languid class one day. "Stored energy to convert into…"—Cross had added an arrow as he spoke—"*Kinetic Energy*, a.k.a. action." In his gabled bedroom Peter unpacked clothes and linens already pressed to his satisfaction in the bag on his way home. Even the pile of paisley bandanas evoked Old Cross tonight: Cross had always insisted that a gentleman never left home in the morning without a clean handkerchief. Peter had never been prone colds or allergies, but he had worshipped Old John Cross and still habitually followed his advice—as well as using the multicolored squares for many other things besides.

Cross's life lessons had often resonated with Peter far more than the physics he had been hired to teach, though he had also taught science with flair. He had introduced his freshman physics class with an elaborate set of cranks and cams which he turned while humming old show tunes to demonstrate the many facets of rotary motion—rotary motion preserved or transferred between his intercalated cogs and levers of many different shapes. Peter had especially liked the square ones, and the ovals and ellipses, and the cam with an off-center axis—known as an eccentric according to Cross. These ones, with their awkward traits and irregularities, caused the most momentous transformation, turning rotary to linear motion as its axel revolved beneath a pivoted lever that rose and fell as the radius changed. *Linear motion: motion up and down or back and forth,* he could still quote by rote. *A.k.a. reciprocating motion.*

Reciprocating: the word touched a nerve tonight. It made him feel…not alone—he had never minded being alone—but unusually lonely. Old Cross had lived alone, and told them he transcended loneliness by adhering to small rituals, such as eating three square meals a day, laying the table before he ate, and reading a few pages of a good book every night. Sound advice, Peter thought, moving into the kitchen and realizing in retrospect that Cross had not even been old, simply prematurely white. Maybe not much older than he was now.

Peter sliced, diced, sautéed and simmered, intercalating his culinary tasks with the same well-planned efficiency he used in the lab. Tonight his timing was off. The rice was cold before the eggplant was done, and the tofu was a mess. He decided against the wine. Dividing the meal between his plate and three lidded containers, he washed out the old pans he had inherited from Mike Burns. "You'll be next," Mike had said, tossing one across the lab like a bridal bouquet shortly before he moved in with his wife. Hardly likely, Peter thought, laying his place setting at the table he had salvaged from the curb outside. Peter's current good book was by Elizabeth Gaskell, contemporary of Dickens but far less well known—an injustice that had resonated with Peter even before he read a word. He empathized acutely with her protagonists: reserved misunderstood men who tried to do the right thing, and modest women of limited means who refreshed last year's dresses by trimming them with lace and learned to see through life's hypocrisies. As he ate, however, he read a recently published article on emerging viral pathogens.

Now and then muffled gunfire rumbled in the room below. Peter's concentration failed. He tossed down the article and meditated on his framed print of brambles—on the intricacies of different varieties: prickles that ranged from absent to dense, the leaves of some subtypes under-laid with felt. He was meant to have disposed of the field guide when they rearranged the store, but its water-stained illustrations, painted in the early nineteen hundreds by a British clergyman, had reminded him acutely of his naïve childhood notion of becoming a naturalist. Back then he had thought a biologist could look forward to a lifetime of taking notes on plants, classifying, sketching, writing lengthy monographs—he still loved that word, monograph—at an old roll-topped desk in a cottage near the sea. For a few years in his youth he had filled an entire journal with careful sketches of leaves, flowers and buds of native plants. He wondered where that journal was. "Very nice," his father had said when Peter showed it to him, "but it's hardly going to earn you a living." Which, let's face it, was true. "Besides, it's all been done before," his father couldn't help but add and ask what era he thought he was living in.

Been done before: the story of his life. He squeezed his temples till they hurt. That's what they had said about his model, as if Sarah's were identical, as if his different assumptions and conclusions were beside the point. As if he cared about Sarah. What he cared about was that a girl he barely knew already hated him.

Loud gunfire rattled in the room below; someone shouted an obscenity. Peter turned on the radio to drown out the din, but the jazz was too insipid and the rock too soft. He thumped the floor to no avail. So, late thought it was, he went into the bedroom and pulled on his running gear. A piano played close by, the notes so distinct they seemed to be coming from inside his room. Impossible, he thought, for a moment wondering if the laws of nature were being defied. Then he realized that the tune was spilling from the heating duct and spreading across the dull parquet—until it unraveled into furious chords. Bizarre. He flipped the lever, sealing the vent. After knotting a red bandana around his head, he made his way downstairs. Suddenly the melody resumed Behind Ms Adair's closed door and the mystery was solved.

For a long time Peter ran through the night-frost and the dark urban streets, while warm blood laced with endorphins worked its magic on his mood.

Chapter Nine

EVEN FROM the far end of the corridor Alice noticed that Dan hesitated when he caught sight of her. Perhaps she had startled him; it was Sunday afternoon and the fourth floor was especially quiet.

"Hi," she said, perhaps a little too soon, as she approached.

Dan had backed into the alcove by the darkroom door.

"I happened to be passing on my way up the stairs," she added, feeling as if she were pulling herself toward him hand by hand along a taut rope. "So I thought I'd stop by and..." She reined in her words, in actuality having stopped by to face her doubts and try to prove to herself that she had no regrets.

"Hi," Dan said, and glanced back the way he had come, as if afraid of being watched. "Listen. Umm—I have to get this done right now. I'll catch you later, OK? In your lab. You'll be there for a while?"

"Sure," Alice said as he slipped through a concealed gap in the folds of lush black drapery. She wondered if he had heard. Then she went upstairs to work and to wait.

DAN FOUND HER later. Much later. Long after she had done what she came in to do—except for going to the library to dig up more on Sharden's, which she had struck from her list after telling Dan she would be in the lab. Instead, she had resumed the assay she had aborted on Friday, which she should have been working on anyway.

Gloved hands moving like puppets beyond the Perspex of the hood, she pressed the nozzles of her multichannel pipette firmly into a corresponding row of plastic tips in a newly opened rack. With practiced care, she withdrew the tips and dipped their tapered ends into a trough of clear red fluid, and had just drawn a synchronized blush up each cloudy white tip when a voice behind her said, "Hi."

Forearms frozen mid-task, she turned around to smile. However, Dan had stopped in Sage's bay and stood half-hidden by the open shelving, so she could not see his face even craning her neck. Besides, the sudden constrained movement had caused the tips of the pipette to rip the glove on the hand steadying the trough, and when she turned back a string of bright crimson pearls was welling neatly from the revealed skin.

"She wondered why I didn't pick up on Friday night," Dan said, oblivious of the wound.

"She?" Alice wished she had misheard.

"Near enough jammed up my voicemail," Dan said, moving into view. "She was"—he cleared his throat—"out of town for a few days, you see." He held an unused tube up to the light. "I told her nothing happened," he added, squinting at the tube. "That I spent the night with friends."

"Oh." Alice ejected the row of spoiled tips. So that was that, she thought. Even an idiot might have guessed.

"Yeah," Dan said, leaning forward on Sage's bench and doodling on its surface with the pointed base of his tube. "She doesn't understand, you see," he said to the tube. "She doesn't understand that I'm just a man, that all men have needs. And like, well…. Like, this would be a truly bad—I mean *truly* bad—time for her to suspect. Know what I mean?"

Life is not a fairy tale, Alice told herself. He's just a man. "I understand," she said, wishing that she did.

Dan looked up, apparently surprised. "So we're agreed that nothing happened," he said, meeting her eye at last—and Alice did understand: he was scared.

"Sure," she said with her most guileless smile. "Nothing happened."

"Good—I knew I could count on you," he said, straightening up. He aimed and jettisoned the unused tube into the trash. Then he grinned, turned and sauntered from the room. Somewhat callously, she thought. What if it was a bad time for her too? But at least he knew now that he could count on her—that she would not betray their secret.

At the sink, she doused her hand with cold water and tended to the graze. Back at the hood, she picked up the micropipette and resumed her rhythmic task, drawing fluid in and squirting it out again one row at a time into tiny plastic wells, each iteration seeming to emphasize the incontrovertibility of what she had just learned. Why on earth had she not guessed? Someone always got there first. She should be used to it by now. It happened every time.

Tolerance and understanding, she reminded herself. It takes tolerance and understanding to love and be loved. That was what her mother had said when pre-teen Alice, having finally understood that Grandma was divorced, had asked about her parents' marriage and what made it last. After that, whenever Alice expressed irritation or impatience with siblings or friends, she had been told she would end up a spinster, a dried up old maid, if she did not learn to be more tolerant. Well then, here was her chance to show that she had learned. She would demonstrate her tolerance and understanding; she would tolerate second place and make the best of what she had.

As the rosy-pink solution filled a new row of tips, Alice wondered what the other woman looked like and how she compared—and why she had never before noticed that the multi-channel pipette looked like a poison-laced comb. Then again, she observed, this sterile fluid that nourished cells was hardly toxic, and—for better or for worse—she was hardly a match for Snow White's wicked queen. Besides, she thought, the queen's evil ploys had failed even in the fairy tale.

Stacking up her plates, she took them to the incubator. On her way back, her mirror image overlaying the nightscape outside converged toward her desk. For a moment the bright red beacons of the incinerator tower bloomed around her virtual head. Like a garish tiara, she thought. Like a princess. And once more she had the feeling, not unsatisfactory this time, that she barely knew the person looking back. Stepping close, she noticed that her image was made up of two not quite overlapping duplicates in the double-glazed pane. Yet that was not what struck her the most; it was her hair. For years she had worn it in a bob around her chin because she had been told it looked flattering and framed her roundish face. Grown out now by default rather than design, and thanks to Helen's momentary whim and her own incompetence in trying to copy Helen, it was now styled, she realized, in a way she had idealized ever since that rain-soaked day on the cliff-top when she had seen the girl with the turquoise umbrella and the long thick braid down her back: the kind of girl a boy would want.

Maybe I'm now the kind of woman a man would want, she

allowed herself to think. *Looking-glass, Looking-glass, on the wall,* she recited as she packed her bag, and dared to wonder if her pale reflection—not the wicked queen at all—did still stand a chance. It was worth considering, at least. Provided there were no poisoned apples or deep comas that went along with it, of course.

*

"I HEAR YOU'VE BEEN landed with the *pièce de résistance,*" Ken said, coming over to Alice's desk. It was Tuesday afternoon. "If you have time right now, I'll fill you in."

"Sure," Alice said, looking up from the paper she had been trying to read. The previous day, Helen had rushed in and told her Ken was leaving. "Defecting to biotech," she had hissed. "Trading intellectual freedom for the well-paid constraints of a corporate job—fool that he is." But what really bothered Helen, it turned out, was that Ken had walked out on his high-stakes project just as it was reaching fruition. "And that leaves me in dire need of someone to take over," she had said. "Immediately. And you're the obvious choice. Besides," she had tossed off, "it's time you stopped wasting effort on that artifact." As if she had thought so all along.

However, Alice could not complain. The entire lab knew that this project was a gold mine, and not only because it promised to link function to molecular mechanism and a top notch paper was guaranteed, but because it made use of a reagent engineered by Helen to which no other lab had access yet. This reagent's possible uses extended far beyond Ken's project—in fact, its future application to Sage's experiments had been one of the key incentives when Alice first chose to work with Helen, although

Sage was nowhere near that stage as yet. Alice also knew that Richard, among a great many others, was eager to gain access to it, which now made her wonder whether he had been negotiating behind-the-scenes again. In any case, by chance—and these things did boil down to chance—this reagent triggered the very interaction it had been designed to block, at least in cultured cells, and so acted as metaphorical key to the pathway-in-question's lock. All Helen needed—and fast, she had said—was for someone to start churning out data in live mice instead of interviewing for jobs.

Ken pulled up a chair and sat down beside Alice. "What d'you do to your hand?" he asked, peeling off a sweatshirt with frayed cuffs. "Looks like some kind of animal clawed you."

"Oh, nothing serious," Alice said and touched the parallel scrapes. She thought of the blustery Sunday in the fall, when Ken had told her what a hazardous place a laboratory was. He had brought in his three-year-old daughter that day, depositing her at his desk where she sat quietly drawing while he disappeared to pulse some cells. "Don't you know it's yucky, Maya?" Alice had heard him say several times before that, holding her up to wash her hands. Later he had explained to Alice that having a child had made him realize that you never knew what nasty things people spilled and didn't bother to clean up, "—and don't even get me started on germs and pesticides in the real world," he had said.

Alice noticed a white crust on the sleeve of Ken's shirt. She was glad to be distracted from Dee's incessant singsong about love—about being in love, how she'd seen it coming, known the signs—on the far side of the shelves where she was nominally helping Sage.

"Yeah, kids," Ken said, following her gaze. Then he leafed

through a notebook he had brought over. "Not that there's much to show that you haven't seen at lab meetings—mostly proof that it works in culture, and doesn't cause artifacts in disease-free mice."

"So we inject it during active disease, comparing different administration protocols?"

"Got it in one. Although not *we*, I hasten to add. I'm washing my hands of all this, bequeathing it to you. This project is yours from here on, first-authorship and all."

"Wow," Alice said. "Thanks. Thank you very much." Few people would be so generous with what they had begun.

"You're welcome," Ken said. "Though I doubt you'll be waiting with baited breath for your results."

Alice deferred to his cynical smile despite her eagerness. His lack of enthusiasm surprised her. She had thought he was at least blandly content, though she hardly knew him well; he never took time out to chat. "Too few hours in the day," he often said in his mild way, with a blend of detachment and tangential focus that Alice associated by now with the phrase *married with kids*.

"Anyhow," Ken said, "let's go downstairs and see the mice."

In the subterranean dressing room, they gowned up like surgeons and entered the maze-like domain. Ken led the way to one of Helen's germ-free rooms. As in every windowless cell down there, the sound of gentle rock music—found by trial and error to best calm the mice—helped to soften the glare and the austere implications of the rows of standard issue cages filling the floor-to-ceiling racks. A water bottle rose out of each cage top beside a depression filled with smooth pellets of chow. Alice stepped up to examine a huddle of soft pink neonates in the corner of a cage. They looked startlingly exposed.

"More like human babies than you'd guess," Ken said.

"Yeah," Alice said, though the thought had not remotely crossed her mind. She sensed the qualitative difference between herself and Ken—or anyone raising a family. "How old is your younger one?" she asked, hearing herself sound like her mother.

"Seven months," Ken said, "and what, ten days? Man, they're so much fun at this age, but our life's in disarray—man, you just can't imagine."

Alice laughed, well aware that she could not.

"But that's one of the reasons I'm quitting," Ken said more soberly. "Two lots of daycare doesn't leave much on our current income. My wife's a postdoc too, as you may know—but she's a darn sight more successful than I am, so I'm the one that has to go." He shrugged. "You're still single, aren't you? Make the most of it while you can."

Alice smiled, not meeting his eye.

"It's not exactly what I had in mind when I joined this lab," Ken said with sudden vitriol. He began, somewhat violently, to open and close the drawers in the cabinets along the wall. "Syringes," he said to one drawer, "vials and tubes," to another. "Sterile hood, of course." He waved at the hood. "Basically the same as any other room down here. And you already known how to inject and harvest and the like—intravenous, intraperitoneal, the usual stuff; the finer details, of course, are in the protocol."

"Not exactly rocket science, I guess."

"You can say that again. So tell me," he said, looking straight at Alice. "Can you think of anyone who has gone on to greater things after passing through Helen's lab?"

Alice had not considered this before. "I don't suppose so," she said.

"Interesting, isn't it? You see, I thought I was coming here to complete my training, become one of Helen's prodigies. But all I've really done is use what I already know and pick up this and that from other postdocs who got their expertise from who-knows-where. Helen hasn't taught me a thing."

Alice had never heard Ken speak this way. His manner was as startling as what he was saying. Surely this was not how science was meant to work. "When I was a student," she said, "my advisor was always telling us—students and postdocs alike—that we were his apprentices. In fact," she added, even as she remembered how much fun they had made of Richard at the time, "he believed our purpose in life was to be instilled with everything he knew."

"Oh, he had a point," Ken said. "I'd like to meet the guy."

"But surely Helen wants us to take away something from our time in her lab?"

"What, like this precious reagent that she's 'still refining' and that, rumor has it, would never have been noticed among all the other duds if not for her first technician, a super-smart kid from Vietnam who *on her own initiative* developed a double-function screening system, did all the work, presented her findings to Helen and then went off to do a PhD in some other field and never looked back. Alice, you're opening a can of worms here. Ask Sage; he'll tell you a thing or two. I would say more, only I have a ton to do upstairs and have to be out of here by five forty-five. Daycare closing time, you know—keeps you on your toes!"

"THIS IS HOPELESS," Sage said, brushing past Alice on his way in. She was standing just outside the lab finishing a tuna sandwich. After washing down the final crumbs with the dregs of her cold tea, she followed him in, by which time he had flung himself into his chair with his head on his desk.

"What's wrong?" she asked.

"Everything," he said, sitting up. "To cap it all, Dee didn't set up the infections last week, so my plans for the whole of this week are shot. Got distracted, she said. In too much of a rush. And don't we all wonder why? Man, I've had to listen to her drivel all afternoon—my boyfriend this, my boyfriend that...you might have stepped in to help."

"Sorry," Alice said. She knew she could have helped—and not only when it came to Dee. Even before she met Helen, she had known more about the Sage's project than he did now. That was why Helen had hired her, or so Helen had said: someone with the relevant experience to take charge of a microbe in a lab that had, until now, never worked with live stimuli. Helen had been attracted by this particular virus—LCMV as it was known—because of its versatility: Depending on how it was administered to mice, it either caused an anti-viral immune response that attacked virus-infected cells—an analogy for the response against one's own cells in the case of autoimmune disease—or, conversely, shut off the anti-virus response, allowing the virus to persist both harmless and unharmed in the infected host. "Just like self-tolerance," Helen had said in that conference restroom. "Imagine the implications for autoimmunity if we could work out how the virus does this, and mimic that 'don't attack' signal with some kind of drug."

Alice had indeed imagined the implications; and not only for autoimmunity, but for her career. Besides, the opportunity to work on LCMV was rare. At the same fateful conference, she had overheard a fresh-faced delegate saying he would die for the chance, only it needed one more level of containment than his lab could afford. "And that's just because it's fatal to a *tiny* fraction of the already small minority of infected people that even show symptoms," he had said with a sneer, "and even those few symptomatics usually just figure they have mild 'flu." Unlike that bitter young investigator, Helen had already negotiated access to the stringent safety facilities dictated by protocol. While Alice was waiting in London for her visa to come through, she had read every paper she could find on LCMV.

"Well at least it's quiet now," Alice said, referring to Dee. Stupid female, she thought. Distracted indeed. With a tug, she broke open the seal of the incubator door, and carried her warm plates to the microscope. There they were, she observed, adjusting the stage: nice healthy clusters of proliferating T-cells that looked like bunches of luminous grapes—she could almost see them multiplying as she watched. And, as she had known all along, only multiplying in the positive control wells given a tried and tested stimulus. The ones treated with the supposedly disease-initiating protocol that had once—and only once—seemed to break down self-tolerance looked as calm and inert as the negative controls. As inert as my career, she thought and gave in to another surge of pent up covetousness for the LCMV project that was languishing with Sage. She could have done so much with it by now. What chance did Sage stand, even without Dee in the way, when he did not have the touch?

She slid the plate from the stage and her cells almost spilled. Not that it would have mattered if they did. It wouldn't matter if she tossed them out, but she never abandoned experiments mid-way—sometimes not even afterwards, she thought, glancing at the tubes she had given a reprieve on Friday though it had already been too late to analyze them over, and they would not have shown anything different even if she had. Besides, she was already purifying cells for the next step of this one, so she might as well keep going. Lifting off the lid, she peered into the water bath in which those cells were being treated in an orange capped tube. Warm stale vapor bathed her face and she dropped back the lid with a harsh metallic clash.

"Sorry," she said, looking over at Sage, who seemed unusually inert and was staring at a book lying open on his desk.

"What's that?" she asked, more loudly this time.

Sage pushed the book away. "Nothing."

Alice persisted, worried about his mood: "Did you hear I'm taking over Ken's project?"

"So I've heard."

"Isn't it a shame he's leaving?"

"Yeah."

"The money, he said."

"The what?" Sage perked up. "Is that what he told you? Really? That's not the half of it." He looked toward the door. "Hey, come down to the coffee room; I'll tell you some more."

"I only have…oh, twenty minutes—that's fine." Clipping the timer to her belt, she washed her hands and followed him out.

Sage told her about the fight mild mannered Ken had had with Helen the year before. He had been looking at academic jobs, Sage said, and every department he visited—and there had been quite a few—had been excited by the project he proposed. This project was, as it should have been, a direct tangent from the work he had been doing with Helen. But although Ken swore he had talked it over with her many times, all of a sudden she claimed he had never said a word.

"Too close," she told him one day. "It touches too closely on what we're doing in my lab. It would be pointless for you to compete when I only have to lift a finger and I'll be way ahead of you. Let's face it: I have the balance of resources and manpower. Surely you see that." Needless to say, Ken had argued—

110

politely, at first. This was his idea, he said, his unique slant; surely some kind of amicable agreement could be reached. "Anyone could have thought of it," Helen had said. "How do you know I haven't thought of it already? It's your word against mine." And clearly she had put her word about fast, because soon after that every department had dropped him like hot coal.

"Poor guy," Sage said. "He tried coming up with other ideas, but what with the baby and all that he didn't have much time, and never got around to talking it over with Helen again, let alone pursuing any other ideas. Oh believe me, he's turning to industry in despair—though in the end, I have to say, he's landed quite a job.

"But at least you don't have to worry about any of that," Sage finished with a sigh. "Footloose and fancy free, with your future all mapped out."

"Well, only as long as I—"

But before Alice could finish pointing out that her future was still conditional, Dan stalked into the room.

"Hi Sage, what's up?" he said, waving a large plastic jug and making a beeline for the water dispenser. "We're out of this pure stuff downstairs. Knew you'd have a ton of it up here." While he held down the tap, he and Sage exchanged comments about last night's game. Alice waited her turn. And waited. Not even the tiniest briefest glance. Dan stopped the water with a flourish. Amoeboid bubbles struggled to fill the void left in the tank. Dan leaned over the table to examine a copy of *Nature* on the far side of Sage. "Huh. Last week's," he scoffed with the down-turned smile she had recently thought quaint. "So, don't work too hard," he said, slapping Sage's arm before sauntering off.

"Jerk," Sage mouthed toward Dan's fading steps. "Oh, and sorry for abandoning you on Friday but I really had to go—"

Alice opened her mouth to speak, not sure what she would say, but at that moment Duncan, the dour Englishman—likewise from Friday night—poked his head around the door.

"Happened to see you on my way past," he said, beaming at Alice. She stared dumbfounded at his genial grin. Since when had she and he been friends? Sage mumbled that he had to go and quietly fled.

"So, I hear you know Ben Chamberlain," Duncan said, stepping in to the room to make way for Sage.

"Yes," she said, not sure whether to laugh or cry. "We were…post-grads together in Cambridge," she said, awkwardly settling on the British term. "How about you?"

"Old friends since primary school."

"Wow!" Alice said, caught off guard by nostalgia as she pictured Duncan and Ben as small boys during a childhood that must have been, relatively speaking, quite like to hers.

"Good old boy is Ben. Did he get through to you in the end? You know he's coming over next week…"

Alice whimpered her surprise.

"Mostly for some high-powered symposium, but he's staying with us first. Said he planned to look you up, so I told him we'd already met. Thought we could all go out to dinner one night—Sunday week perhaps?"

"Sunday—I don't know." Alice tried to give the appearance of scanning an imaginary diary as if she might conceivably have plans. "Yes, I think so," she said.

"Good. Sunday week it is, then." Duncan raised a hand and was suddenly gone like a fairy godmother whose task is done.

SAGE WAS LISTENING to the radio when Alice returned, though all she could hear was an irritating staccato of indistinct words. Stopping the timer with two seconds to go, she fetched her tube from the water bath. The cell suspension within had turned a dull cloudy pink. Behind the part-raised window of the sterile hood, she opened the cap and drowned out the reaction with an excess of fresh medium, transparent and bright red.

Jerk, she thought, echoing Sage. It was obvious now that Dan had meant what he said. Nothing had happened; she was nothing to him. He had purged all memory of her—of that night—from his mind. She had been nothing but a fool.

Filling a second tube at the tap to balance the first, she dropped them into opposing buckets of the centrifuge. Pressing closed its lid, she turned the timer dial to ten and felt the rotor start to turn—and the casing start to shake with escalating violence. Alarmed, she turned the dial to *off*. The casing juddered and was still. She opened the lid and found a forgotten balance tube in one of the other buckets. And now here came Ben, she thought, removing the erroneous tube. She would see Ben next week. It was a way to pass the time. Besides, it was probably not such a bad thing. *Better the devil you know…* Once more she pressed down on the lid and turned the timer dial to ten. Beneath her hand the casing barely vibrated as the rotor sped up smoothly as it should have all along.

Part III

Initial Non-Specific Symptoms

Chapter Ten

PETER WAS FURIOUS. He had just come up from the animal room and his dead and dying mice, and knew who to blame. "Do you have a warm water bath?" she had said from the door. "I have to thaw a couple of tubes, and my own lab's way upstairs and—" So much devastation from a couple of small tubes. He forced an arm into his coat sleeve, exited his office and, struggling with the other sleeve, locked the lab on his way out. All those days of wasted hope when it had already been too late. He felt like showing her the mice, dumping them out in a gruesome pile in front of her. Though even if she was likely to be there on a Sunday evening, and even if he knew which upstairs lab, he was not sure he would recognize her; all he had noticed was the way she talked—and boy, could she talk.

Outside, the wind had picked up and he had not grabbed his hat. By the time he reached the library, his head ached—though that could have been from his foul mood as much as from the cold. Either way he had come to the right place, he thought, heading for the deepest stacks. It was peaceful down there, silent but for the soft air conditioning roar. Rather too warm, as it turned out. Too much like the climate-controlled animal floor. The mere thought of all those expiring bodies still turned his stomach. Long before he had taken on Violet, he had disliked working on mice. One of the great hopes for his model was its possible use—at least eventually—as an animal-free way to investigate disease; because although the term 'multivariable calculus' often aroused terror in non-mathematicians, its descriptive equations would allow for harmless exploration of far more interlinked dimensions and levels of complexity than could ever be achieved with hands-on experiments. However, in order to justify his theoretical approach and save future generations of unwitting mice, he had to show that his predictions mirrored real life. The irony was not lost on him that his very first attempt had caused especially needless suffering and death.

He had always liked the odor of old books, but tonight their sweet acrid mustiness was making him feel ill. Or was it just the sickening memory of those mice lying limp on their sides? It crossed his mind that, if not for his brother, he might have been down on the Cape now in a state of blissful ignorance—or at least stuck in end-of-weekend traffic in the middle of nowhere the dark. Though it was dark in the stacks too. A naked light bulb dangled grey above each aisle—which was not such a bad thing, he supposed, given his headache. His muscles were as stiff as if he had, indeed, spent all day in the car. He regretted going for a run earlier; far from focusing his mind, it had worsened the tightness in his lower back and thighs. Now his metabolism seemed to be failing, and his brain was expanding as if frozen and then thawed too fast—like those goddamn samples in the water bath, he thought, closing his eyes.

"Just use a separate rack from mine," he had told her, trying to keep his place as he squirted tiny volumes into miniature tubes. He had remained civil, if not especially friendly, when he had to tell her to replace the lid—but evidently friendly enough to keep her leaning against the bench beside him, delivering her stream of chatter about broken water baths and floors being waxed while she played with his pen at the edge of his vision. He had even hidden his irritation when she dropped the pen and tapped with her nails on the black Formica surface, because he had known that if the woman from the library was there instead, he would not have minded at all.

But he had minded when, just as he had set down his pipette and was peeling off his gloves, she had reached over to touch the untouchable: a flask of ultra-pure RNA-free medium. Sure, it was a curiously shaped flask, but no one—not even he— touched his RNA-free medium without wearing gloves.

"Don't," he had said, catching at her hand.

"Don't," she had echoed in his face, coming startlingly close as she reared up. In one swift motion she had freed her hand and grabbed his wrist.

"Look, I'm sorry," he had said, backing away, his raised hand still gripped by hers. "But seriously, please don't touch that."

"Seriously. Please don't touch me, either," she had rejoined, leaning in too close and dropping his hand. And turning away from her fierce disdain he had sent the force of his shock and embarrassment directly into the eyes of the woman he had been wishing was there instead. He remembered that part with exacting clarity. Somehow she had appeared outside his lab like in the worst kind of dream. And there was no question that she had seen him and recognized him, and no question that she had flinched. When his eyes met hers she had flinched and run away.

"Besides, can it really matter so much?" the girl beside him had said.

"Of course it can," he had told the void outside his door. "Look, feel free to use the water bath, but please leave me alone." Which she had done quite literally in a flounce of long hair, slamming door behind her and masking his vain reminder not to leave without her tubes—just before he heard the tell-tale pop as their frozen contents thawed too fast, the pressure building up inside and forcing off their snap-on caps.

He should have warned her not to heat up snap-cap tubes; she was only a kid. Maybe no one had told her about microfuge tubes with screw-on caps designed to stay on securely under just these conditions. Still, there was no point in wondering what she had or had not known. By the time he had opened up the water bath, salvaged her rack and run after her, it had been too late to see where she had gone—and evidently also too late to stop whatever was in her tubes from contaminating his.

However, that did not make sense. She had used a separate rack. Or had the aerosol sprayed far and wide? What else? He had fished her rack out fast in the hope of catching her, but when the corridor was empty, he had come back in, placed the rack high on a shelf and sat, head in his hands, neither thinking nor moving until his beeping timer nagged. All he had done after that was scoop up his own tubes from the still-open water bath and take them downstairs. That must have been was when the damage was done. He had re-closed her tubes before following her out and maybe gotten whatever was in them on his fingers— though he knew he would have put on a fresh pair of gloves before getting back to work.

Well, he could change nothing now. He rubbed his temples and his eyes. His head still ached; the muscles of his body too. He had been thinking about going back after this and sampling the few mice that had survived, but all he wanted right now was to curl up and sleep. Holding his coat against his chest like a pillow, he followed the aisle toward the desks along the wall.

Toward one desk in particular. He felt like a ghost drawn to its favorite haunt. An adolescent ghost.

Around the final corner he stopped short. It was one thing to think about her, but it had not entered his head that she might be there. And yet she was: in the very same place, trapped in a dome of radiant light. With her head propped on one forearm, eyes cast down, the faint trace of a smile on her lips, she looked like a woman in a pre-Raphaelite painting—only far better looking and without the red hair. She must have sensed his presence, because her arm abruptly fell. She sat up straight and closed the volume she had been looking at. Somewhat defensively, he thought. Her soft cheeks glowed pink as dimensions disappeared again, and from the vacuum that remained Peter spoke.

"I'm…I'm sorry," he said, his voice far too loud. "About the other day."

The woman looked away. Extreme tension filled the air.

"It wasn't you," he continued. "I wasn't mad at you." And then he saw the ambiguity of what he might be saying and started again. "That paper, the one you weren't reading," he said. "It was an old one of mine. It's complicated, but…it's…well, it's sensitive. I—" I sound pathetic, he thought.

"It doesn't matter," the woman said, staring at the fine ellipse that spilled from the lamp onto the desk and up the wall.

It was obvious that she did not want to talk to him. Regardless, he wanted to talk to her. If only he knew what to say. He searched her desk for a prompt, and saw the handwritten lines on the pad beneath her hand—a far cry from the childlike penmanship of Joy Adair, and strangely reassuring with it not quite regular yet balanced flow that constantly adjusted to each off-kilter slant. Quite unlike Sarah's too-perfect script, he thought, his gaze moving on to the row of photocopied articles bordering the desk and settling on the book weighing down the closest pile.

"May I look?" he asked.

She shrugged.

He picked it up and examined the cover, an aerial view of two cups on saucers. It was the title that had caught his eye, though: *Kiss in the Hotel Joseph Conrad. Kiss in the Hotel* was written on one line, *Joseph Conrad* just below. "Do you like Conrad?" he asked.

"It's not *by* Conrad. That's the name of the hotel." She spoke to the desk.

"I can see that. I just wondered if you liked Conrad."

"I wouldn't know."

He wondered if this was the book she had been buying that day. "Is *this* one good?"

"Very," she said. Still she would not look at him. He knew he should go. She sounded so defensive—and so British.

"You're British," he said, tracing the edge of a saucer with his fingertip.

"Yes I am." She sounded fed up.

But Peter could not stop himself. "Which part of Britain?"

"South Wales," she said with overt hostility. "If you know where that is."

"Of course I do," he said. "But you don't sound Welsh."

"I'm not. I always have to explain—as if anyone cares or knows the difference. I was born there and grew up there, but don't have Welsh blood."

"I do."

"Oh." At last she had looked at him.

"I'm part Welsh."

She studied him. With mild suspicion, he thought.

"My grandfather," he said. "On my father's side."

She seemed to think about that. "Have you ever been there?" she asked tentatively.

"A long time ago." He frowned. "It was…" He searched for a word.

"I suppose you're going to tell me it rained the whole time," she said with a sharp edge. "People always say that and it's not remotely true. It's very pretty if you bother to look."

"I know it is. I'm sorry, I didn't mean to— I did think it was pretty." Pretty, a word he never used but he was clutching at straws. She was pretty, too. He wanted to kiss her. The thought must have shown, because when her eyes met his again, she shot him a look of such condescending disgust that he almost did give up. "I thought it was magnificent," he said instead. "The cliffs, the rocky shore, the miles and miles of meadows grazed by cows and sheep—"

"Fields," the woman cut in.

"OK, *fields* grazed by cows and sheep…" He looked up at the ceiling, wished she would see that he was actually on her side—and looked down just as rapidly as his headache bloomed again.

"Well, I'll have to read this," he said, wincing in defeat, laying back the book—on top of a familiar illustration. Of conjoined triplets. His copy? Impossible. And yet what was the chance of her finding too? Miniscule enough for more dimensions than he knew of to collapse. He took a step back—and bumped into the nearest bookcase with a jolt that pierced his brain. He buried his face in his bundled up coat.

"Are you all right?"

He lowered the coat. She must think he was unhinged. "Just a splitting headache," he said with a forced smile. "I'll be fine."

But the woman looked concerned. Hauling her backpack onto her knees, she rummaged inside. "I have some Advil in here somewhere," she muttered.

"Really. I'm OK," he said, catching at the book she had knocked aside. He felt feverish and sick. "Anyhow, I have some back in my lab," he added, straightening out the book.

She stopped rummaging, her eyes instantly cold.

"Thanks all the same," he said, wondering what was wrong.

She glared at her bag.

"Well, I guess I should be getting back," he said.

She did not respond.

"Good-bye, then," he offered as a last resort, and she shrugged a vague farewell. So at least he had tried. Though he might have been more eloquent if his head had not ached, if he had not been subject to what felt like magnified gravity. There was nothing he could do beyond leaving her alone.

WHEN SHE WAS SURE he had gone, Alice stared at the bookcase against which he had leaned. She wondered why he had stared at her like that, as if waiting for something, wanting to say more. Though why should she care? So what if he had some Advil in his lab? The same lab in which she had seen him with Dee, who would, no doubt, see to his woes.

Yet why had she been so harsh? Fields, meadows, what difference did it make? Why had she blamed him? It was hardly his fault. She had longed to call them meadows once upon a time— all those stretches of grass filled with buttercups, grazed by cows, bordered by streams. *The sheep's in the meadow, the cow's in the corn*, she had chanted as a child. *The cows are in the meadow, eating buttercups...*; *It happened one day, as Bo-peep did stray into a meadow hard by...*. Except that no one back home had ever called them

124

meadows, they had only ever called them fields. She had no idea why—it was just one of those things. As a result, she had thought that meadows, like milkmaids, were confined to fairy tales and rhymes, and she had imagined coming upon a real meadow in the same enchanted light as she had imagined waking up to find she had turned into a princess overnight.

Perhaps they had been fields all along. Even the butter-cups had usually turned out to be celandines, lesser celandines at that. Although she did remember sitting astride the old stone style near the end of the wall that had once stopped several yards further on where there was no cliff-top any more, her legs bathed by the straggling stems of real buttercups. She had sat there looking down at the rock-strewn beach—at the giant steps of limestone pavement that up close were pocked with rock-pools shimmering with life, at the hammered iron grey swell, at the ebb and flow of molten waves that bubbled like lava around the tide-line stones. How magnificent, how magical it had been back then—before she realized that other people used the word beach to describe endless yellow sands lapped by waters of a post-card blue. And what was wrong with rain? It was the rain that made the grass so lush, so thick, so green—so much greener—over there.

Alice wished she could go home, or back in time, or both.

But it was hardly his fault that she could not. She reached for the book she had been using as a paperweight, and traced a saucer's edge—until she realized what she was doing and pulled her hand back as if she had been burned. And in a way she had. She wanted to scream, to yell, to lay the blame on someone else, and maybe it was his fault after all. His fault because that first time he had made her feel so—

She took a deep breath. She felt nothing now. She laid her

head on her arms, now folded on the volume she had slammed shut when he appeared. All she had wanted to know was what he had noticed that first time—and now that mystery was solved. Faced the end of Rollins' article was the start of a paper by Peter Young and Mansfield Hall. Mansfield Hall had been famous for years, and so even before he appeared in front of her like a summoned genie, with his depthless amber eyes, she had guessed that he was Peter Young—as if she cared about his eyes. He had cared about his paper, though. Peter: a name she had once thought fictional, like milkmaids and meadows, because she had never met a real-life Peter. Peter: a rabbit in a little blue coat with brass buttons down the front; a boy who never grew up; a man who ate pumpkins, kept his wife in a pumpkin shell. His wife.

What did she care? Rows of differential equations had run like intricate lace between the compact blocks of type. Mathematical models. Not her kind of thing at all. Pretty enough to look at, but not her kind of thing.

Chapter Eleven

"GOOD MORNING, Peter. What's up? New data?"

"No." Peter dropped his modeling paper back in its slot and closed the filing cabinet drawer. "And don't expect much anytime soon. Most of the goddamn mice are dead."

Tom balked. "They can't be. The virus isn't virulent."

Peter sank into his chair. "They can be," he said. "Because they are. Some kind of lousy contaminant."

"You're sure?"

"I even know how—and when, right down to the hour."

"Shit."

"I know." Peter was too tired to think.

"On the bright side," Tom said, "the tropical parasite guys over in Public Health—remember, they spliced a possible vaccine protein into the original construct and saw marginally decreased infection rates in immunized mice? Well, they're keen to try now with each of variants, which could really take this to the next level!"

"Cool."

"Show a little enthusiasm. It should be cool—very cool!"

"So should this. Only I've just lost more than two weeks' work. Besides which I feel like death." He clamped his head with his splayed hands.

"That's too bad. But I've seen it happen before—all that stress over jobs preys on the body as well as the mind. Get on home, then. You should have taken that work-study student who stopped by last week—he'd be an extra pair of hands if nothing else."

"The last thing I need is more hands getting in my way."

"So you always say. Anything urgent need attention while you're gone?"

"Not really now that this round is screwed."

"And the second batch of mice?"

"Too early to process yet—but infected from separate stocks if that's what you're asking, and they look fine so far."

"You checked the viral titers of any survivors of that first lot? Just for the record—or at least to figure out what went wrong?"

"I already know what went wrong: goddamned contamination from someone's samples in my water bath. And I would have checked last night, only this headache hit me."

"Man, I always loved setting up those titrations. Used to run them the time—could do them with my eyes closed even now."

Peter closed his own eyes. "I'll run them later if you like. I'll be fine in a couple of hours." He pressed his palms against his eyelids.

"Kiddo, you look beat. This is simple. I know what to do. I'll find my way around. Still, you should train up an assistant. You'd get twice as much done. Besides, once you have a lab of your own and teaching duties, you'll find—"

"Not much to worry about on that count."

"No more job news then?"

Peter shook his head. He stood up, feeling queasy as he did.

"Something'll come up eventually."

"My breakfast if I don't get home soon." Not that he had eaten much that day.

"When you have a moment though, we should talk."

"Sure—this afternoon, I guess." Gently, Peter pulled on his coat, flinching as he picked up his bag. "On second thought," he said, "maybe tomorrow."

"Tomorrow it is, then. Off you go, and try not to breathe on anyone else. Take your time—and relax, I know exactly what I'm doing here."

ALICE WAS in a good mood. It was the start of a new week and a new phase at work. Not only was she starting on Ken's project—she still thought of it as his—but the evening before, as an antidote to the latest incident with Peter Young, she had been forcing her way through the last few Sharden's papers lingering on her list when she had the epiphany for which she had hardly dared hope.

It had begun with a small-print footnote mentioning three enteric bacterial strains found in the muscle biopsies of two Sharden's patients—something promising at last. Alice had long associated the word enteric with infection, knowing that enteric parasites lived in the gut. Moreover, she knew that even typically benign bacterial strains could pick up virulence factors from other bacteria by a process rather like infection, effectively turning them into pathogens. So she was disappointed to learn that the authors had checked and detected none of the virulence factors associated with enteric bacterial pathogens, and concluded that their muscle biopsies had likely been contaminated during collection or analysis.

Benign enteric bacteria were by definition harmless. In fact, Alice recalled a long-gone Friday seminar—not because of its relevance to her work, but because of its different slant on how microbes can be viewed—given by a nervous young man who had spoken too fast in his eagerness to propose that the significance of commensals was often overlooked because people typically think of microbes exclusively as pests. Commensal, he had explained defensively, meant *eating in the same house*, and he had revealed several newly discovered ways in which this diverse flora of meal-sharing commensals was not only harmless, but often beneficial, helping furnish that house by biochemically assisting with the gut's healthy development.

It was only after she had begun to tackle the next article that a new implication dawned. As her eyes had travelled over words explaining that symptoms of Sharden's were proportionately more common in adults who claimed to have been neglected during infancy, she realized—even with her mind elsewhere, or perhaps because it was elsewhere—that this was the critical catalyst. Far from being yet another baseless attempt to correlate disease with anecdotal patient history, few of which held up for long or hinted at a mechanism, these stories of maternal neglect seemed to do both.

Intestinal health and maternal neglect had been inextricably linked in Alice's memory ever since she was told so by the elderly professor affiliated with her Cambridge lab. Professor Chapman had been given the bench next to Alice's after he retired—an act of charity to a faded has-been, people said. As he pottered about with his make-shift apparatus and obsolete technology, Alice's colleagues had ridiculed him—in his absence, of course. However, his archaic enthusiasms and evident pleasure in small discoveries had reminded Alice of her Grandma, and she had tried to be kind. Besides, he had always been kind to her. One day, after rigging up an odd contraption on his bench and then stringing it with what looked like worms—like giant versions of the parasites she had worked on back then—he had pulled her aside and whispered that he was studying the influence of mind over matter. He had just discovered, he said, that intestines of mice separated from their mother for a few hours a day since birth were more permeable—at least to large molecules—than those of mice left with their dam.

At the time Alice had indulged him with her interest to divert him from her colleagues, who would likely just have laughed. And in all honesty, her awe had been for the most part an easy echo of his. Now, in retrospect, it was genuine. Enteric bacteria outside the gut, intestinal permeability and neglect, neglect and an increased likelihood of Sharden's: there simply had to be a link! She only wished she had listened harder to what Chapman had said, instead of working so hard to look as if she was listening. And apparently no one else had listened either: neither of those two Sharden's papers referenced his work, or even the concept of gut permeability. Either he had not published his findings, or no one had made the connection yet. Because if Chapman's increased permeability applied to bacteria as well as whatever large molecule he had used, didn't all of this suggest that location alone—in versus outside of the gut—might determine whether the immune system perceived a microbe to be harmless versus harmful?

Just before the library closed for the night, Alice had run a quick search on the main frame and found the abstract of a paper written by Chapman at around that time. This morning, after leaving a barrage of reagents thawing on her desk, she was off to the library again to find the obscure journal and photocopy the full text.

Alice knew, even before she set foot on the stairs, that it was

Dan's voice she heard. He sounded irate. She stopped mid-step—and heard a woman's voice. Dan's again, facetious and caustic. They were arguing. Alice had half a mind to leap down the stairs and pretend he was not there. He needed to know she did not care, that this was what he deserved—she would not have nagged like that if he had picked her. Then again, what if he caught her eye and glanced longingly at her, filled with remorse? Tough luck, she thought. Or could this be her chance? Just then the elevator doors opened behind her and Sage called out.

"Hey, Alice! Wanna help?" He was dragging one end of a large old fashioned wooden-ribbed trunk. "Couldn't resist," he said. "It's the kind they used back in the day—and it really *was* used. Check this out!" Lifting up the 'Free—Please Take" sign taped to its side, he revealed an ancient label bearing an address in Sioux Falls. "Pre-Edith Wharton, I swear. Back when the frontier was new." He had found it in among a pile of worn-out furniture outside a fancy apartment block on his way in.

Alice grabbed the dried out leather handle at the other end and they took it to the lab. By the time she returned, the stairwell was quiet. She set off, one hand sliding down the banister, and swung around onto the fourth floor landing. And realized her mistake. She should have taken the elevator. Dan and the woman were still there. Mercifully though, his back was to her, tightly locked in the woman's arms.

"I do love you," Alice heard him say at the same moment she noticed the ring.

"I know."

The ring on the woman's left hand.

"See you downstairs at five, then," he said.

The simple golden band.

Alice bounded down the next two flights of stairs. Slow footsteps circled above. She continued her descent, feeling shamefully exposed although one full spiral of the staircase hid her from the woman she had wronged. Her skin felt transparent and seemed to burn, as if branded—albeit in her ignorance—by Dan's illicit touch. She reached the first floor and fled from the echoing stairwell, but had to stop for some students crossing her path. By which time the footsteps of the other woman changed as they too left the stairs. Curiosity got the better of Alice and she looked back. She looked back for the briefest instant only, but saw more than enough. The woman was pregnant. Alice felt ill. In her horror she failed to look where she was going and collided with someone coming from the left. Recoiling, she stepped back and away from Peter Young, who was walking with a hand over his eyes. Alice muttered an apology, and he grunted and moved on without dropping his hand, but that hardly mattered; her regret was not for him. He had disappeared from Alice's mind even before he left her line of sight as she watched the mother of Dan's unborn child follow in his wake.

MUSIC DRIFTED past the mailboxes as Peter crossed the deck. It was sweet and dreamlike, lapping against the halo of pain into which his perception of the world had now shriveled and shrunk. When he opened the door into the foyer the music swelled, seeming to press him back against the paneled door. By now his body was aching as much as his head. He wanted only to lie down, and had half a mind to curl up on the old Turkish rug lying between him and the stairs.

"Hi!" Joy Adair's door had flown open; the music had stopped. She was noticeably tall; her large feet were bare.

"Hi," he said, looking away. There was no way he could

navigate the facts and platitudes required of first time introductions.

"Do you have some cash?"

"Not on me, no."

"Just ten dollars? Give me ten, I'll give you twenty back."

"Sorry." His nerves felt damaged and raw as he stepped across the rug, though at the bottom of the stairs he broke out in a cold sweat and for a moment that soon passed he felt a little less unwell.

"Quarters, then," she said right behind him. "I have to do laundry."

"I don't have any," he said, studying the carved post at the end of the banister.

"What's the matter with you?" she asked.

"I have a headache."

"That's not what I goddamn mean. What's the matter with you all? Why does no one ever want to damn well help?"

"Sorry," he said. "But I can't even help myself." He started on the stairs.

"You're all the goddamn same," he heard her yell out before rapidly played chords began to follow him up the stairs. The chords transitioned into a wistful waltz as he reached the second floor, but time was running out. There was no prospect of redemption now; wave after wave of peripheral sensation rolled away. With one last burst of effort, he hurried to the top. In one swift movement he unlocked his front door, Violet's squeals clashing with Chopin on the stairs. In urgent and despairing haste, he slammed it closed behind him in a brittle shattering of glass as its central pane gave way, and felt a measure of release as he scrambled, lurching, into the bathroom where he leaned over cold white porcelain. Moments later he vomited.

Chapter Twelve

ALICE SAT DOWN at her desk in the stacks. She hugged the
backpack on her lap, reminding herself that she was trying to
move forward. Dan meant nothing to her. Only she had made
the mistake of looking back. She had looked back and seen the
woman, seen that missing piece of information that changed
everything. Though it really changed nothing, since the woman
had been oblivious of her; and besides, no harm had actually
been done. All the same, how could she have even begun to be
part of something so sordid? As for that sense of being exposed:
now she felt more as if an opaque membrane had been peeled
back from her surroundings, from where it should have stayed,
revealing not only the burden of what she wished she did not
know, but also showing her the range of possibilities that might
lie ahead. Clearly there was no safety net, no predictable limit
within which her future would unfold. She had been lucky this
time, but there was simply no knowing where her next error of
judgment might lead.

And there was no denying that her judgment was at fault.
What had she seen in Dan anyway, with his reptilian sneer and
condescending fake sincerity? He was shallow and patronizing,
and she had known that all along. Was she really such a fool?

Ciao, he'd written on the credit card receipt. *I am your slave.* She had even read meaning in that.

Then, on top of everything else, there sat the guilt-ridden fact that in her smallness, even after she knew there was someone else, she had—if only for a moment—imagined coming between Dan and his other woman. The woman soon to bear his child.

It had not even crossed her mind that he was married—she had noticed straight away that he did not wear a ring. She examined her own ringless hands. The wound from the pipette tips had very nearly healed. A purulent sore would have been more apt, she thought. Or at least a lasting scar, a perpetual reminder that she had not even liked Dan and had only looked twice at him because she liked someone else, someone at whom she had looked twice and been glaringly forewarned. Seeing that man in his lab with Dee was exactly what had sent her flying into the arms of whoever came along. Even so, Dan must have cast some kind of spell on her to make her want him. Who on earth had she thought she was? Some kind of charismatic *femme fatale*? It was almost as if he had turned her into someone else.

"Hi there!" The greeting rang out behind Alice and wiped clean her thoughts. She spun around with a smile. The voice belonged to a stranger, not looking Alice's way, one of those huge new cordless phone devices pressed to one ear. Alice wished she could dissolve.

"Yeah, it's just me." Hard heels hammered on the vinyl floor. "I'm over in the library," the woman said in her clear shrill voice. "Thought I'd get some work done…"

Alice thought she would, too. She unzipped her bag.

"No don't worry," the woman's voice went on, "no one else is around, I'm down where they keep the obsolete stuff."

No one, Alice thought. Obsolete.

The footsteps lost their sharp intensity, the words dissolved to nebulous noise. Alice started to unpack, laying her notepad and pen beside the pristine periodical that sheltered Chapman's work. The words came back into focus, syncopated by the clack of heels.

"I don't know. It's just that he's so...well, so possessive. I mean, what's wrong with needing space? I don't have to spend every minute of my existence with him. Besides which...uh, I don't know if I should tell you..."

Then don't, Alice almost said out loud. She stood up, letting her chair legs scrape the floor to show that she was there.

"...Oh, you don't want to know that, believe me!"

No I don't, Alice cried out inside. Hastily she repacked her bag and slung it on her back.

"...Just don't tell anyone," she heard within a giggle. "...I know, but he said—"

Alice grabbed the periodical and pushed in her chair. She was beginning to feel she was destined to have other peoples' private lives thrust upon her, like it or not. Crossing the stacks toward the stairs, she inadvertently stepped into the ambling woman's path. Blank eyes met hers very briefly, but the low-voiced narrative flowed on. Alice stood aside and let the woman pass. So I'm no one, she thought. Evidently she was nothing, no one, of no consequence to anyone. She knew intimate facts about other people's lives that she had no business to know, and did not want to know either, but they were forced on her anyway—which she supposed was what happened when you were ready to respond to anything and everything that came your way.

Slapping the pages on the glass, she copied the Chapman paper, stuffing it into her bag as she walked past the guard. To her relief he did not wish her a good day. Head down, she pushed through the door and was blinded by the sun as she met the chill outside. Then again she was always blind, she observed. So blindly adaptable and eager to please. That was why she had been so perfect for Dan: she was so placidly adaptable, conditioned to please and meet anyone's needs.

Where had she gone wrong? "You have to be adaptable if you want to be liked, if you want to be loved," her mother had added to those well-meant warnings about tolerance and old maids. And yet here she was now, for better or for worse, a bitter old maid precisely because of that—so adaptable, so malleable and ready to be shaped into whatever was required.

Malleable: that was the word Ben had used one night at a party when he had drunk far too much. Alice had seen him watch with sad bloodshot eyes as the object of his unrequited love lucidly seduced another man. Then he had wound an arm around Alice, found her breast and begun to knead it. "Malleable," he had whispered in her ear. "You're so malleable." Said with venom rather than lust. And she had not flinched, knowing already that he did not want her and knowing also his pain, thus prepared to be a salve for him when he coaxed her to his bed. Afterwards he had kicked her aside and turned his back on her, which might have been the end of it if Alice had not already suspected that love was just the stuff of poetry and sentimental dreams; too many first kisses had spoiled the illusion and also been the last. It might also have been the end of it if Ben had not continued to come looking for her on other bleak nights. Besides, Ben had never kissed her—not that or any other night—and had gone straight to the point of his substitute relief using a condom meant for someone else. Ben had never spoken of those shared nights by day, never validated their existence by giving them a name.

Alice stopped on the steps into her building. Only three more days to go. What had possessed her to say yes? The again, Ben was different. He was not like Dan. She had always known exactly where she stood with Ben. Like it or not, she had no illusions about him. Besides, years had passed since those unmentioned nights. She and Ben had found their ideal distance, settled into a mutual understanding that went beyond insult or guilt. It was all going to be fine.

As if on cue, Duncan burst from the entrance, hand raised in crisp salute. Alice returned the gesture, feeling happier as she did. She walked on. Yes, it would be nice to see Ben. After all, he had been right. "Come on, you're not the type to like the States," he had said when she phoned him back in August to say that she was going. "You won't be any happier there." She had thought he was just being his usual vindictive self. But he was right: she was no happier here. He had suggested that they meet at a Fulham pub three or four evenings after that, only she had had to cancel on the day. She had left a remorseful message with his colleague saying she was overwhelmed at work and would have to stay late—which had, in fact, been true. Ben had never called her back.

Still, he understood her so well. It was a lost cause to think of staying over here—as if the thought had ever even crossed her mind. Of course she would be going back. She reached the fifth floor and moved with purpose down the corridor. She had things to do. She knew it was a cliché to drown your sorrows in work, but she also knew that clichés arise from excessive use. And if this one worked for so many other people, why should it not work for her?

ON HER WAY through the lab, Alice glanced over at Sage, who

was sitting at his desk, seemingly examining his palm.

"What happened?" she asked, taking off her coat.

Sage did not respond.

"Is something wrong?" She moved into the bay, at least as far as she could with the trunk in the way.

"This line here," he said, touching his palm. "My lack of flare for science."

"Your flare for arts, you mean." Alice wished she were the kind of person who would grab his hand and trace the other line.

He continued to regard his palm.

"You can't take that stuff too seriously," she said.

"The facts speak for themselves."

He did have a point. Then she noticed the scattering of printouts spread over his desk. "What, another disaster?"

Sage leaned back and closed his eyes. "I just don't know what I'm doing wrong. Absolutely no signal. Don't know if the infection got screwed up, the cell prep, the stimuli. All I know is that there's not the slightest hint of anything there."

"But I thought you'd seen some kind of effect lately."

"Really?" He squinted at her and then frowned. "Oh, that. False alarm. Negligible in the context of the whole once I'd plotted it with the controls."

Like my love life, Alice thought, sitting down on the trunk.

"You know, everything was going so well for a while," Sage said, lifting up a sheet of data and dropping it back. "Just not the way Helen wanted. It would have upset too many of her friends—and she also didn't trust me enough to be sure of my results. Good easy experiments, too. But that's why she moved me to this LCMV stuff. The irony is that I always wanted to work on pathogens, design vaccines and all that. Part of my 'grand plan' in life."

"LCMV can be pretty nasty, can't it? Wasn't someone in the news lately—got really sick from cleaning out their attic?"

"All those old mouse nests—yeah. But that's the thing. Alice, these mice aren't even meant to get sick when they're injected our way—though of course I excel at screwing up, which is why Dee's supposedly helping out. And we're not even remotely trying to make vaccines here, it's just a great model for faking self-tolerance."

"Not a bad one though—nice clean read-outs, chronic exposure without pathology and all that. Wow, if you could figure out a mechanism that would switch off autoimmunity—"

"You sound just like Helen"

"Sorry. I didn't mean—"

"But like you said, it's a great tool for looking at clean responses—only my responses are so damn clean there's no sign of them."

"Look, I'm sure..." This was going to be hard.

Sage touched his forehead. "My intellect's fine, you know. I'm just no good with my hands. I only need to look at an experiment and it turns to trash." He swept the sheets of data to one side. Suddenly he laughed. "This guy I met once in a bar—it was late, and I guess we were both drunk—but he said he'd been a scientist for a while, only he gave out some kind of weird electromagnetic force that skewed his results. And he was dead serious when he told me all this. I believed him, anyway. But I mean, don't you think, maybe I could be the same?"

"Don't be silly!" Alice did, in fact, wonder.

"You used to work on microbes, though" he said. "Any thoughts on what might help?"

He had put her on the spot. "Every pathogen is different," she began. "And I've never worked with viruses as such." She

141

thought for a moment, weighed the facts and costs and benefits. "But as it happens," she resumed, "I've at least *read* a little about LCMV. Maybe we could look through your notes and see if anything obvious stands out."

He shrugged and pulled over a notebook and a folder filled with histograms. Alice scooted to the other side of the old trunk, catching her jeans on a splintered rib. Together they looked through his notes and found no glaring mistakes except that the records from half of each experiment were not there.

"Yeah, those are the parts that Dee did," Sage said. "Helen thinks it's more efficient if we split up the work."

"That's how she taught you? That's like—well, it's like trying to paint a picture with someone else without being able to see what they're doing."

"Come on, it's not as if she actually *taught* us. You know how it is: 'Run over to *x*'s lab and have them show you the protocol, then come back and set it up here.' Anyhow, this can hardly be compared to a work of art."

Some science can, Alice thought. Science at its best felt very much like art. She wondered what to do, having vowed to steer clear of interfering, having tried to forget how much she had invested in this project that belonged, and always would belong, to Sage. Then again, it also seemed wrong not to share knowledge that might help—donate it for the greater good.

"OK," she said eventually. "It's a long way off, but I'm not busy next Monday. Find the original protocol. I'm not up on the practicalities, but sometimes an impartial eye sees past the obvious. Let's set the whole thing up together, every step, and figure out what's going wrong."

"You're an angel." Sage smiled with melancholic gratitude. "Let's only hope that you can save my doomed skin."

Chapter Thirteen

ALICE HAD SEEN no need to ease herself into Ken's project—she still thought of it as his—since it rested on techniques she already used. After reassuring Sage the day before, she had channeled her attention into setting up several long term assays that would run in parallel, meticulously mapping out their overlapping steps. She biked into work early that Tuesday with her mind focused on the day ahead—focused to the point that she almost failed to stop at a red light, and had no patience for her lingering disquiet as she climbed the stairs past the fourth floor. The morning passed in quiet efficiency as she moved between workbench and hood, between one assay and another. However, by early afternoon her carefully optimized staggering of incubation periods in some assays with bursts of action in others had fallen out of synch. She had counted on small subtle differences between Ken's protocols and hers, but had not anticipated the cumulative effect of each brief delay caused by her stopping to check Ken's notes, or waiting for Sage to leave the hood or Dee to finish centrifuging cells. Deadlines converged.

Helen came in and ranted to Sage about safety and irrelevance and snagged hosiery. "Just get rid of that damned piece of junk," she said and kicked at the trunk.

Sage apologized, but after she had gone muttered, "Yes Ma'am. Right away, Ma'am," and likewise kicked the trunk. Then he called up Bill and mumbled into the phone for a long time. Bill stopped by while Sage was downstairs and, much as she liked Bill, Alice was glad when Sage rushed in again and she could turn her attention back to her assays and the clock—all the while trying not to listen to them bickering about the trunk and whether it would fit in Bill's small car. At last they carried it away, leaving Alice in a welcome silence tainted only by the realization that she had no one like that to bicker with.

Wednesday morning brought her first real coup: only when she reached the fifth floor did she think about Dan, and even then it was only to wish she could yell at him. What did he matter to her anyway? With every small step she was moving closer to worthwhile results, and even the stress of frantic busyness was outweighed by a sense of purpose, a feeling of responsibility, the prospect of new data by the following afternoon. The day passed with satisfying efficiency, and by the evening all her assays were in sync again and very much on track. With the bulk of that day's manual labor done, she was sitting at the hood aspirating fluid from her last set of centrifuged cells—and wishing Sage would tire of the constant crackle of staccato voices from his radio— when Sage suddenly called out 'Warning!" across the lab.

Alice froze, her glass pipette sucking air.

"Storm watch upgraded to a warning," Sage said, laughing at her alarm—and Alice realized she had not heard him laugh like that for a while. "Starting around midnight tonight through the best part of tomorrow, fourteen to eighteen inches by four, the first major storm of the year."

Alice was awed. "They can really predict that level of detail?" As a child she had never known when it would snow, and in fact it very rarely did. All the same, she had hoped every morning that it would, rising to stand beside the blue squared curtains of her bedroom closed against the dawn. *Please God,* she would whisper, *let it have snowed, let the snow be thick and drifted and let there be no school.* And then she would wait, because until she looked, there was still a chance that it had snowed; she could still at least hope, even though she already knew that if she did see white it would most likely be hoar frost and not real snow at all.

But there it was when she woke up on Thursday: deep accumulating snow, rising softly on the rim at the top of her window well. On the radio they said to stay off the roads, stay home if possible to let the plows through; only essential personnel were advised to go to work. As she ate her toast, she heard those plows drive by, one after another careening out of nowhere in a harsh metallic rumble that made the fixtures in her basement shake. She wondered what they meant about staying off the roads. She hardly counted as essential—and yet she had work to do, protocols to follow, assays to complete at precise times. The talk of snow emergencies called to mind curfews and check points and who knew what else. Was walking still allowed? Surely it was; this was just snow. After wrapping herself up, she stepped out to face the blizzard and get on with her day.

The strength of the wind came as a surprise, but Alice forged her solitary way along the untrodden sidewalks. Once in a long while a car inched past, muffled and hazy through the matrix of unstill flakes, though few pedestrians crossed her path. Snow clung to her jeans, and soon packed itself into the tread of her boots, hindering her grip, weighing down each step. She felt noble and brave as she kept going, and almost cathartic when she realized that she cared about science enough that for all her childhood prayers that it snow, that the snow prevent school, she was going to work despite the warnings to stay home.

No one else seemed to be around. The department was officially closed and the building eerily quiet. Ultra-violet spilled into the dim-lit corridors through the windows of closed laboratory doors, the silence buffered by a hum of compressors and fans. In her own lab, she turned on the lights and created a microcosm of startling clarity—an island of sharply focused brightness. For once she also turned on Sage's radio and listened to updates on the storm, looking forward to results by the end of the day.

The hours passed. There was something pleasingly self-sacrificial about working through a storm. And something curiously restful about this particular storm, the heavy density of each wet flake, the density at which flakes fell, the soft and silent way they merged with the ground. The snow had fallen all morning, an incessant, wind-worried curtain between Alice and the world. Undisturbed, her assays ran according to plan.

Toward late afternoon there were voices in the corridor, and laughter and footsteps. The lashing winds of the morning had died down, the snow falling more slowly, a diffuse veil over the slow crimson rhythm of the chimney tower beacons and the bright rows of hospital wards spreading out below.

"Hey, that looks good!" Sage said, springing up beside Alice. "What does it mean?"

"It means," Alice said, squinting at the monitor, "that I have my first results."

"Great! Helen'll be pleased—or aren't they what she wants?"

"Don't worry, they're exactly what she wants." There was no question about that—or about Alice's antipathy.

"Excellent!" Sage said. "Listen, if you're nearly done, we're off sledding. Want to come along?"

"I don't think so."

"Come on, why don't you celebrate?"

"No, I—I have to print it out, get it ready for Helen."

"I can wait."

"No, really. I need to take my time."

Sage shrugged and left her alone, his voice receding down the corridor among shouts and squeals. Alice should have wanted to join in. For the first time in months she had a reason to be excited. Instead she felt cheated, or maybe even like a cheat though she knew the data were real. She was starting to wonder if Ken's disenchantment had been passed along with his project; maybe the project itself was cursed. Without enthusiasm, she busied herself living up to her excuse to Sage and, having transformed her numbers into lines on graphs, took them down to the office and laid them on Helen's desk—where she happened to see a draft of the paper Helen had obviously written preempting these results.

Furtively, she turned a few pages—though of course she had a right to, her own name headed the list of authors, penciled in instead of Ken's. Midway down the third page, within a space left in the text, she saw a hand-sketched replica of one of the graphs she had just brought in. As if Helen had had a premonition, Alice thought. Unaccountably annoyed by what she had just seen, she tried to console herself with the fact that at least she had managed to correctly fill in the blanks.

Part IV

Remission

Chapter Fourteen

PETER WOKE UP feeling fine. For a while he lay listening to the wind work its way through the eaves. He had not forgotten that it was Thursday and his big interview was the next day—along with his seminar, the key to selling himself. It was just as well, he supposed, that nothing had changed since the California trip and he could give them the same talk—and lie there wrapped up and warm for a couple more hours.

Now and then small projectiles tapped the windowpane. He grew restless. Eventually he decided to go in and start processing that second batch of mice. One hot off the press piece of data, however partial and preliminary, could make all the difference—*would* make all the difference, he was sure. Rising, ready to face the day, he pulled up the blind and discovered that the world outside was monochrome. Shapes were muted, edges blunted by the smooth white mantle absorbing with placid indifference the steady plunge of earthbound flakes. As he watched the gently simplifying scene, the sheer unpleasantness of the past few days seemed to fade. Perhaps it had not been so bad. Moreover, even in the depths of his misery they had been looking out for him. Slipping on his unlaced boots, he stepped out into the hallway to inspect his newly repaired door.

He had not had to call. Sometime later that same day he had become aware of people in his room. "Jeez," a man's voice was saying. "Maybe we *should* have called the cops."

"At least he's still breathing," another voice replied. "No more blood?"

Beneath the forearm covering his face, he had opened his eyes from a particularly bad dream in which the girl who left her tubes came back and breathed into his lungs while the woman from the library watched. He had seen his landlord and a man he did not know at the foot of his bed. They both seemed distressed. Out of a vague sense of decorum mixed with fright, he had scrambled to sit up. He felt sick; his head still ached horribly, his throat was parched and it was far too warm.

The two men peered at him. His landlord looked pale. Peter knew him—Mister Coe—only from the annual meetings during which he told his tenants he regretted he would have to raise the rent. Coe's impeccable attire as usual failed to hide the impression of having long since gone to seed.

"What happened?" Coe asked tenuously. "Are you hurt?"

Feeling unsteady, Peter raised a knee on which to lean his head, registering the skin of his thigh—yes, he remembered he had undressed before dropping onto his bed. "I don't think so," he said, unable to think.

"The door," Coe prompted. "The glass?"

"Yeah, I'm sorry," Peter said. "But right now I'm not feeling all that great." He rolled back down onto the bed.

"I think he might just be sick," the other man whispered. He sounded relieved. "Are you sick?" he asked Peter loudly, as if talking to a child.

"I guess so." He wished they would go. And then he understood: he had been sprawled there half-naked, a pitiful mess, quite the innocent victim. He almost wanted to laugh, wondered if he should feel embarrassed or see the whole thing as a joke.

Coe had pulled the silken square from his breast pocket and covered his lower face. "So you weren't hurt, then," he said into the fabric, a statement rather than a question.

"No." He did not feel at all well. With some effort he pulled himself to his feet. "I'll see you out," he said, ushering them into the hallway.

"My friend here will come back to fix this later on," Coe said, stopping at the broken door. He worried the frame and a loose shard fell.

"Excuse me," Peter said and left them standing there. He slid across the bathroom floor.

"So it's all good then," Coe called from the landing. "Take it easy now," he added as Peter retched.

At least all that was over, Peter thought, picking up the debris the repairmen had left and checking the floor for splintered glass. He wondered what kind of idiot would install a door like this. Then he lowered the blind they had raised while they worked, and released a fresh sprinkling of shards. By the time he had scoured the floor again, showered, dressed, and broken his fast of the past few days, it was mid-afternoon and he was eager to be off.

On the landing he saw drops of dried blood. No more blood, they had said. He checked his hands and rubbed down his arms; he still seemed fine. However, someone else was not. He saw more scattered drops on his way down, like a trail of bread-crumbs leading the way. Coe's visit, he realized, had not been about him, but in response to something else. He thought of Joy Adair's bare feet and bit his lip.

At the bottom of the stairs he met a damp frigid breeze, the vestibule doors propped open with a pair of flip-flops. As he stepped onto the rug, one side slid slowly closed and sent it flimsy doorstop skittering and in almost perfect synchrony, Joy Adair's door swung wide and someone staggered out behind a large cardboard box.

"Jeez, that eff-ing door again," a woman said behind the box. "Can you get it then?"

Peter leapt across to help, not failing to see on his way past the stack of boxes piled up inside the room, or the piano draped with a discolored dustsheet.

"You're moving out," he said, ashamed of his relief. "I'm sorry about—"

"What's to be sorry about?" She squeezed past with her box, seeming smaller than before.

Maybe it was not her blood after all. Besides, why would she have gone upstairs?

"And it's my sister that's moving out, not me," the woman called back breathlessly. "Besides, I'll bet you're the guy whose door she smashed in."

So it was indeed Joy Adair's blood. "But wait," he said, following her out and now thoroughly confused. "She didn't smash it in. I broke the glass myself." He saw the sticky patch left on the mailbox where the tape had been peeled off.

The woman stopped in the porch and turned to look him up and down. "Well she might as well have," she said. "You're lucky that she sliced her foot and came back down. She's a sucker for a pretty face," she added with disdain, "but piss her off and...well, you're not the first. What d'you say to her, anyhow?"

"Nothing...I don't know. Hardly anything."

"Ha! That's what they all say. Don't look so scared, though, she won't be bothering you again. And blame your friggin' self-appointed social worker of a landlord—always wants to let 'em sink or swim, but she won't take her goddam meds so what can you do? Anyhow, here's my help," she said, peering into the road, and then winced as a white van crunched against the snowbank between the sidewalk and the road. She made for the van's rear. "All I can say," she said over her shoulder, "is that she's lucky I was here."

Peter stayed where he was, lost in the ambiguities of cause and effect, blame and actual guilt. Besides, something far too similar had been said about him once. *He was lucky that the girls were there*, the local paper had claimed, long ago and far away. Lucky? If it had not been for those girls, he would not have needed that luck.

A large man had jumped out of the van and begun to argue with the woman.

"And what the frick are you looking at?" he yelled across at Peter, who pulled himself together and set off, feeling like a pawn caught in other people's crossfire, far preferring not to know who lived behind closed doors, or why. These days every interaction seemed rigged with tripwires, missed cues, misunderstandings and inadvertent consequences.

A frenzied swarm of kids hurried by dragging sleds, and he backed up against a leafless shrub until they had gone. He walked on, waiting at each junction as crisscrossing plows took turns to neaten the streets with no thought for sidewalk access to the road. At the final intersection, a verbal fight broke out between a man in front of him—rushing to scale the bank and cross the road before the light changed—and an older woman trying to escape from the road she had just crossed. By the time Peter made it to his building, he was glad to be alone.

Unlocking his lab, he turned on the lights. They flickered

briefly as if dragging out the suspense—and revealed a wasteland of abrupt abandonment. So Tom had come in to help. And evidently been called away or lost interest, and left. Typical. Peter gathered up the lidless tubes and culture dishes and the half-used boxes of pipette tips Tom had strewn about. Then he found his lab book, still lying on his desk in the office exactly as he had left it except that Tom's wide open script now followed his own last dismal entry. All Tom had written down the date and time—Monday 12:40 pm—and two words, VIRAL and TITERS, underlined. And that was it—no numbers, calculations, nothing more. Which was neither here nor there since he had told Tom not to bother, he reminded himself. Only now he found himself agreeing with Tom that he should have run those assays in the first place. Maybe he still could. He was going down there anyway to start on the second batch, and a few more samples would hardly break his back.

Pulling on some gloves, he gathered his supplies, in the process noticing the rack of microfuge tubes left by the girl. The source of all his woes, he thought, pushing aside his tray—taking no risks this time—and inspecting her tubes. Nothing but a finely drawn V in the center of each lid. What was that supposed to mean? Well, whatever it meant, it had not helped his mice. Holding the rack at arm's length, he tipped the tubes into a bio-hazard bag destined for the autoclave, and sealed the bag. Then, after washing his hands thoroughly, even obsessively, he picked up his tray and made his way down to the mice.

The moment Peter opened the door he smelled death. One quick look into the urine-soaked sawdust confirmed his fears. Another look—his heart beating fast, breath held behind his mask—reinforced his suspicion that this was no arbitrary apocalypse. The pattern had reproduced absolutely and completely.

The attrition was confined to the groups given his variants. And not only that: it was worst among the variants that should have been cleared. This had nothing to do with contamination, or co-incidence, or chance. The only explanation was that his model was wrong.

He leaned his head against the rack, mortified by his baseless over-confidence—and his distasteful instinct to blame someone else. Though in all honesty he felt no bursting wrath, no tempestuous sense of devastation, just a strange and benumbed willingness to take each step as it came. Only which step did come next? He had no idea. His imagination appeared to have failed—his one key asset, critics of his paper had said, though they had meant it as an insult to his hypothetical science. For a while he stared at the bodies, at the languishing survivors wandering around their deceased kin. Then he lifted out the corpses and lined them up in a zip-lock bag that he laid in the deep-freezer morgue. Let the others live another day, he thought, setting back the final cage. It seemed wrong to take more innocent lives for the sake of a lie.

Back in his office he stood at the window, looking out at the lamp-lit parking lot. The lingering storm had already laundered the sidewalk that had been clear when he came in. All that trouble for nothing, he thought. His predictions were wrong, so his assumptions must also be wrong. His mathematical methods were sound, but that was all. There was no meaning any more to his equations, to his mutually dependent variables—host defenses versus pathogens—and their intertwined trajectories moving with satisfying predictability across the screen. There was no truth to his calculus-bound phase planes swaying like ghost-sheets in a breeze of advanced math. Their points of intersect—possible endpoints slipping and shifting, appearing and disappearing as parameters changed—had been obliterated once and for all. With the outcome of this last experiment, his hypothesis had become ballast in an oversized volume reproduced too many times. This latest result, likewise reproduced too many times, would go no further than his handwritten lab book that would gather dust on a shelf, or be buried in deep storage, never to be opened or thought of again—

Peter caught his breath. The girl from Wales had just come out of the building and walked down the steps. So near and yet so far, he thought and moved back from the glass to watch her walk past the bike rack and turn into the road, leaving a thin trail of dark even footprints. He had half a mind to grab his coat and run after her—and then what? She would be horrified. Besides, he had things to do—such as prepare for tomorrow's interview. One step at a time, he reminded himself, shuttering himself in with a cascade of blinds. Then he turned on the desktop computer and found the folder that contained the figures from his California talk.

He had been pleased with that talk—as far as it went. It told a logical story from his past work through the present to a speculative future that promised great things—speculation that depended on exactly what he had just failed to show. He thought of Tom's friend Joe and his false assumption that spoiled everything. But this was not the same. For one thing Peter was not tenured—far from it—and had no captive audience who could at least learn from his cautionary tale. Besides, he did not even know which assumption was wrong, only that the narrative had shriveled, instantly transforming those painstakingly prepared figures into meaningless shapes slashed with arbitrary lines. His elegant story of mutual dependence and definitive—if not always happy—endings had become nothing more than a work of fiction. Though not even that. A work of fiction could at least be enjoyed, still reveal essential truths. Whereas this? With a few quick clicks of the cursor he corralled all the figures illustrating his cursed model and dragged them into the trash. With one more click they were gone.

Now what? He took a deep breath. There was no cause for alarm. He had plenty more to say, other sound and ongoing projects with which he could sell himself—Tom had made sure of that. All he had to do tomorrow was show them he was out there on the cutting edge. Or at least make them believe he was. He began to dig through his old files, trying to remember catch-phrases and punch lines from half-forgotten lab meetings and departmental talks. Only there was a tightness in his chest, sapping his drive. He felt ragged, torn apart. Maybe that was what happened, he thought, when you touched the cutting edge and it was blunt.

He closed his laptop and, elbows on the desk, buried his face in his hands. Had he really cared so much? It was only a model, an idea. And she was only a woman who did not care for him. The suffocating feeling tightened, hurting his throat. He tried to ignore it. He had work to do. But he kept on picturing the murdered rodents that should have been just fine—and that bleak black string of footprints: an ellipsis beyond which there was no more.

Chapter Fifteen

BY THE TIME Alice left for home, snow had covered up the footprints of Sage and his friends. Not far off, a snow blower ground against a curb, its engine jarring and shrill. Car tires hissed along the slush blown road beyond the gaping heads of parking meters, fleshless chrome handlebars and sinewy brake cables emerging from impacted snow-banks like sand-swept skeletal remains. Even the trees had changed shape, boughs hanging low toward the ground instead of reaching for the sky. Alice thought of the picture drawn by Ken's daughter Maya that one Sunday in the lab. "Look," Maya had said, showing it to Alice. "It's a sad girl. I drawed it for you." And indeed the girl she had drawn looked sad. "Eyebrows going down like this," the girl had explained, industriously mimicking her art as she looked with clear brown eyes at Alice.

The bushes bordering the landlord's yard had buckled and splayed, closing off the path. Alice pushed through anyway, the gap opening at her touch as the shrubbery's burden fell, and tried to step where she thought the paving stones would be. The snow was un-disclosing and knee-deep—almost as deep as it had been during the fluke storm that had spawned her childhood prayer. When that blizzard had died down, she recalled, she had scrambled up a giant yielding drift, sinking each time she climbed, until at last she had seen the quilt of black-trimmed fields through which two parallel dark hedgerows snaked. They had been cut off for a week then, while the excavators inched their way closer along the impenetrable lane to town, moving one drift at a time to connect the village back. Then again, the village had always seemed separate, disconnected from real life. She had always felt safe there, she realized, far away from urban ills like pollution and crime—and from adulthood in general, with all its bitterness and cynicism and failure to take pleasure in the simplest things.

Snow was clinging to her jeans like a fine white mold. She stopped to brush it off her thighs, and then looked up to see a shadow in the overlooking window. The curtain twitched and then was still. Frowning, she turned the other way. So he really was spying on her. There was no escape. Stomping with intent around the corner, she almost slid down her partially-submerged steps. Snow tumbled in across the hallway when she opened the door, and she kicked it out before sealing herself in. As she set the kettle to boil, the floor creaked above. She listened for the sound of footsteps on the stairs and anticipated his curt knock. She tried to think of an excuse. She listened. The footsteps had stopped.

Alice listened to the kettle warming up. She stared at her empty mug, picturing the curtain's discrete twitch, the pristine snowbound yard. He was just a lonely old widower trapped indoors on his own all day. What was the matter with her? Splashing cold water on her face, she turned the burner off. A minute later she had traipsed back around to the front of the house, pressed the landlord's decorative doorbell and heard its glad chime within.

"Hello," she called through the narrow slot while he fumbled with the chain. "I wondered if you had a shovel—I'll help clear the path."

FOR A GOOD HOUR Alice labored outside. She dug a trench from the front door to the garage and exposed the driveway from garage to street. Now and then the old man stood in his doorway quietly watching her; now and then she waved and resumed her shoveling, drawn hypnotically into her task. Blisters formed on her ungloved hands, but it was easier without gloves. And it was fun; pleasing to see cause and effect, instant evidence of her hard work: the sheer sides of the trenches, the compressed vegetation and wet tarmac that showed where she had been. She understood now the old custodian who, in the cold light of a Cambridge dawn, had swept his way through the labs guiding his wide dust mop like a plow. "Drive me nuts if I had to do a job like yours," he would say as he passed by on those mornings when she was already—or still—at her bench. "Days to wait for a result you can't even see."

The evening sky had almost cleared and only the occasional flake floated down. Alice tapped the shovel on the black-top one last time and scraped aside the dislodged clumps, only wishing that her satisfaction with a job well done extended to her work in the lab. Because as she exerted herself outside, she had begun to acknowledge that her recent apathy arose from something more complex than seeing or not seeing a result. It was one thing to churn out data of no consequence, but today's outcome had been positive and meaningful; it should have rekindled her old wonder in science—wonder that was meant to grow with each new discovery and not wane to colorless indifference, or turn into this bland suspicion that that she was merely an impartial instrument of someone else's truth.

A tiny snowflake alighted on her sleeve: a minute six-pronged asterisk. Like the asterisks she drew in her lab notebook to highlight experiments that worked: her symbol of excitement. The snowflake vaporized before her eyes. She let her arm fall and looked back at the path—at the thin layer of slush that absorbed and annihilated every asterisk that fell on it.

"HOW ABOUT A CUP of cocoa?" the landlord asked when Alice handed back his shovel. He had been watching television, but had switched it off by the time she joined him after showering. The cocoa smelled good.

"Come and sit down," he said and left her in the living room.

"Sit, sit," he insisted when he returned, setting down a tray laden with two brimming gilt-edged cups on matching saucers, one of which he handed to her.

"Yes," he said. "My friend and I drank cocoa the night that photograph was taken. The night of the summer storm. You remember the photograph?"

"Of course." Alice wondered how long he had been waiting for this chance.

"I'm so glad you are British," he said, watching her intently.

Her feeling of unease increased. She shifted position and her cocoa almost spilled. The day she first came to look, he had said he liked to rent to British girls and despite her misgivings she had accepted it as a mere sales pitch in which he switched details as need be. Now she was not so sure. "You're German?" she asked, realizing as she spoke that her attempt to deflect his partiality was opening a minefield of potential common ground.

He frowned, but then waved off his expression with a cupped arthritic hand. "Many years ago," he said. "But yes." He shook his head and then smiled. "When the world was a different place."

"I can imagine."

"I doubt that you can, my child. We had a wonderful house in town beside a lake, a summer estate on the Baltic. And then…then it was all gone. Just like that." He snapped his fingers soundlessly.

Alice wondered whether to insist that she did have some idea, and tell him about her grandparents: how Opa's family fortune had snowballed in three brief generations from traveling peddler forefather to his socialite parents who had entertained artists, politicians and scientists in fine apartments in pre-war Berlin; how Opa had seen that lifestyle and much of that company vanish before his eyes. Opa had written a lengthy memoir in his later years—"Here I am, practicing my shaky English," he would joke with Alice when she found him at his desk, though among the grown-ups she had heard him say he was trying to record the process of starting again in middle age without a penny to your name.

"I'm sorry," she said to her landlord instead.

"It is hardly your fault."

She knew that too, and tried to keep her frustration at bay. It was also not her fault that her father had left the memoir in the garage and the pages, soaking up the damp, had inseparably fused, and all that now remained legible was a page of discourse on the weather and the soaring cost of tea. At the bottom of the page Opa had written, "On such matters I must dwell—how sad." Which, according to her father was par for the course; apparently Opa had never revealed much about himself. By contrast, Alice had always wondered how much had been lost, not only to material atrophy and the limitations of a foreign tongue, but also through the opaque filter of an unreceptive mind.

"But even for me it was hard to believe," the landlord was saying. "I wanted to be optimistic. It was my wife's family that made me face the facts—though she was not yet my wife. They made all the arrangements. They were not wealthy, but they had influence, friends overseas. They helped arrange the visas, affidavits, generous hosts to put me up along the way. They did it because we could not have married if I stayed. Jew to Gentile was not allowed by then, you know."

Alice did know: an old family friend had helped her grandparents leave—her baptized Jewish Opa and his Gentile wife. She wanted to tell him, but it did not seem right to compare loaded facts like these, even if only to commiserate. Besides, her knowledge was second-hand and perhaps not hers to share. And the old man was not listening anyway.

"We were happy before the war," he declared, eyes fixed on sights unseen. "We lived next door to one another in two large houses by the lake. There was an island, a romantic place where you could row among the willows dangling near the shore. There were peacocks on the island; we would hear them cry." He paused and Alice saw him glance at a Chinese vase that held a single shabby peacock feather with a bent shaft. "My brother was in love with her too," he said mildly. Then he was quiet for a while.

Alice stared at the floor, wondering why he was telling her.

"She remained in Germany, my fiancée," he resumed. "She was studying—something not allowed to me. There seemed no urgency for her to leave." He laughed, a single mirthless bark. "They burned down the houses at the end of the war. She watched. Our house and hers. She saved these." He held up his cup. "She buried them in the garden with a few other things. They had belonged to my mother. The rest—" He imitated conflagration with his hands.

Alice looked at her cup that was now emptied of cocoa and rested on her knees.

"My wife joined me a year after the war ended and, as planned, we were wed. She would have come before but those were not predictable times." He hesitated again as if pacing himself. "They were glad when they heard the Russians would come," he said. "Despite the rumors they had heard of looting, pillage, worse. Occupation meant liberation; freedom was in sight. My wife and her family and neighbors sheltered in their basement while the fighting raged above—fifteen of them cramped down there for three whole days. They listened to gunfire overhead, but they were safe. The Russians posted a guard, a pleasant, understanding man. He joked with them, played with the boys. Then the fighting stopped and the Russians left. But soon they came back. The SS had counterattacked. When the Russians came back they were different. My wife—" He sighed. "Well, at least she was not destined to bear a child."

Alice knew she would never look at the note in her kitchen in the same way again. *DO NOT VIOLATE*, she thought. "I'm sorry," she said again and set down her cup.

"But I have kept you far too long!" the landlord exclaimed. He stood up and started fussing with the crockery like a genial hen. "Off at work all day, and then all that shoveling for me…"

"Oh, it was nothing, really." Trivial pleasantries sounded odd, light and fluffy after the weight of what he had said. She handed him her cup. *Don't touch*, she had always been told.

"Well, we must talk again soon," the old man chirped and waved her away as she reached for the tray.

"Yes we must. And thank you so much for the cocoa."

His face brightened. He looked happier than he had all day. "Exactly the same," he said, his eyes wide with delight. "Just like old times."

Alice smiled, not following at all.

"Just like old times," he repeated, chuckling quietly as he showed her to the stairs that joined his quarters to hers.

Chapter Sixteen

ALICE SPENT most of Friday in the small computer room opposite the lab. She barely remembered having wallowed in the discontent of the over-privileged, and felt like hugging her old landlord tight. Not only had his silent suffering driven home for her how lucky she was to have been born when she was—let alone to have a job and a project that worked—but his elderly wise presence had reminded her again of Professor Chapman and the copy of his paper waiting untouched in her bag. Having read through and around it last night, and having slept on what she had read, she had now consolidated the evidence and outlined her aims, and was absolutely sure she had a powerful case.

After sending an introductory e-mail to a professor across town, whose collaboration would be sure to enhance the project's goals, Alice was ready to go home. Not since writing up her doctorate had she felt so immersed, and took a moment to reorient herself as she surfaced from the physical torpor of prolonged cerebral focus. The corridor was quiet, as it often was so late, though the lights were still on in the lab and Sage's fringed leather jacket was draped on his chair. Out of caution, Alice locked the lab anyway, then grabbed her mug of stone-cold tea from the shelf by the door to drop it off in the coffee room.

The lights were likewise still on in the coffee room. As Alice drew near, the frosted door swung open—pushing her aside—and Helen emerged.

"Perfect timing!" Alice said, recovering herself. "I was just hoping—"

"No it is not," Helen countered and walked on.

I was just hoping you might be around, Alice finished in her mind with a virtual sneer. Hoping I could share some good news that you'd relish if you knew. Well, too bad for you, she thought and slipped through the door.

At first the coffee room seemed empty. There had been no Friday gathering and a bright green apology had been scrawled across the whiteboard. Then she saw Sage standing by the window with his back to her, facing the buildings of downtown. From that angle, the broad expanse of clustered high-rises overlapped in the darkness as a single glittering pyramid.

"Isn't it spectacular?" she said.

Sage grunted, but did not turn around.

"Is something wrong?" Alice noticed that the table was covered with a slew of papers laid out in a checkerboard of columns of raw numbers and graphs.

"Only Helen." Sage's voice sounded strange.

"What's she done now?"

"Nothing much." Sage paused, then added levelly, "She thinks I should quit."

"Seriously?"

"Come on, it's hardly surprising. She happened to see the latest data on my desk. Kind of blew up when I summarized my progress—or lack thereof. Then she dragged me down here so I could lay it all out bare." He glanced at the tabletop. "Just one look and she says there comes a time when you have to take stock and cut your losses."

"I'm sure she didn't mean—" Alice was embarrassed by her recent good luck.

"Yes she did mean it. Alice, you know damn well that nothing ever works for me." He turned to face her, his eyes hard and dull. Then he leaned against the windowsill as if suddenly tired. "I'm not stupid," he said. "I just can't do experiments. Only you don't find that out until you try. And it was her idea that I start to work on this, not mine—I hope you realize that."

"I do." Alice felt troubled, as if she were to blame. "Listen," she said, "we'll figure it out on Monday, I'm sure we will."

"I've thought of quitting a million times," Sage told the floor. "I've dreamed of walking out of here, packing my bags and heading west—like they did way back when. But it's not like that anymore, is it?" He sighed long and hard. "Apart from which, there's Bill."

"Yes, of course—"

"Besides which, it always seemed more…more worthy, I guess, to keep on trying. At least I wasn't doing any harm. Or so I thought. Jeez, you could have said something, Alice," he said, glaring at her.

"What do you mean?"

"Oh nothing… Anyway, you're on your way home." He glanced at the watch on the underside of his wrist.

"I'm not in a hurry," Alice said. "In fact I'm all fired up by my proposal—it's taking off at last!" Her mind was still racing around her new conjectures and she had hoped Sage might want to be the first to hear.

"Good for you," he said, not meeting her eye. "But go on home. It's getting late. You're looking pretty wrecked if you don't mind my saying."

"I'm really not that tired—"

"Don't worry about me. I'm going home myself."

"Shall I wait?"

Sage shook his head. "I'm not in the mood."

"I'm sure it's not as bad as you think." Alice backed through the door. "She's probably just had a bad day. We'll figure out what's going wrong and you'll be fine. And I'll be here all weekend if you want to talk."

"Go on home. I'll be fine." Sage smiled into the distance.

"OK. See you Monday, then—if not before."

"I guess."

"Are you sure you don't want—"

"Go."

Alice went.

Chapter Seventeen

ALICE RETURNED to work first thing the next morning—though she had woken with a stiff back and could barely move her arms. Overnight she had thought up several improvements to her ongoing draft, and also realized that some of the methodology of her first fruitless project could be reapplied to this one; she could at last make use of her cleanly controlled—if uninformative—data to show that the technique worked in her hands.

She stopped off first in the computer room to update her draft, and to discover that the professor she had e-mailed late the night before had already replied with cautious enthusiasm; he had even attached a confidential pre-print of a relevant paper that had just gone to press. Having sent her new draft to the printer, she crossed the corridor to the lab. The door was open and the lights were on, though it was barely seven thirty and a Saturday at that. The lights had been off, and the door closed when Alice arrived, which had reassured her at the time that Sage had gone home last night. Perhaps he had come in early this morning to turn over a new leaf, she thought and looked with hope into his bay as she walked past—and was startled to see Helen jump out of his chair.

"Alice! I didn't know you were here," Helen said, backing against the desk like a cornered rat.

"Do you need help finding something?" Alice asked, fearing for Sage.

"I'm looking for some data to peruse on my flight. Ideally something that'll justify the long trail of garbage Sage has left in his wake." She touched the picture book and grimaced.

"You're going somewhere?" Stupid question, Alice thought.

"San Francisco." Helen pulled over a notebook. "Jesus," she said, opening it up. "I don't even want to think how many dollars have been drained on experiments that don't even begin to work—and I don't mean uninteresting, I mean downright disastrous." She turned a page audibly. "Look at this," she said. "Readout unclear, controls not doing what they should. How the hell does he make such a mess? By the way," she added in a brighter tone, "I'll be seeing Richard while I'm there."

Alice was taken by surprise. "Great!" she said. "Say Hi from me. Tell I'll be in touch soon—maybe let him know," she added, sensing an opening, "that things are really starting to pan out."

"But of course," Helen said, and then she cursed. "Honestly, I thought it would speed things up, giving this to Sage. If your visa hadn't been delayed, he wouldn't have a clue what LCMV stands for—if he knows that even now. And you, of course, wouldn't have gone off on that waste of a wild goose chase."

Alice remained calm. "Talking of projects," she said as sweetly as she could, "would you like to see what I've come up with for the Sharden's? I've made some real progress. I can show you right now if you're not in too much of a rush."

"Sure—I still have a good hour. Especially if it's something worthwhile." And as Alice had hoped, Helen abandoned Sage's desk and came around into her bay.

"I'd been hoping to start on this when I returned," Helen said, pulling up a chair, "but the earlier the better." She sat down beside Alice in a scented haze.

"Well," Alice said, her hand on a royal blue folder. "The papers I found hinting at autoimmunity are all pretty weak—especially when you check the supporting evidence."

Helen's features stiffened.

"They're all in here, though, if you still want to look," she added. "But in the meantime, I've found several independent observations that, taken together, look far more interesting. They suggest that normal commensal bacteria might actually be leaking through the intestinal mucosa into other parts of the body."

Helen's expression had not changed.

Alice persisted: "One of the papers was even by someone I knew in Cambridge!" The mention of Cambridge, she had noticed, often worked with Helen.

One of Helen's eyebrows did indeed twitch. "Who?" she asked.

"Albert Chapman. He—"

"Never heard of him."

"Well, he was already retired by then but—"

"Alice," Helen said, features aslant, "I have to say that this is really not my thing—bacteria, mucosa…"

"It's all right, I've typed up what I've found, including a list of preliminary experiments we'd be wise to do—and there's at least one local group who'd be happy to show us the ropes, I've already asked. You know, once you start reading, it's a really interesting field. I've just sent a draft to the printer so you can take it with you—I'll just go and fetch it." Alice rose as she spoke.

Helen caught her arm. "I think one microbe is enough

around here," she said. "Besides," she added, reaching for the royal blue folder, "you found several papers on self-reactivity—what more could we ask?"

"Yes, but the data's so weak." Slowly Alice sat back down, retracting her arm.

"Don't worry. It's all about wording. As long as there's something in here that I can make a semblance of a case with, we're all set."

Alice stared in bewilderment. "But…isn't it a waste of time to work on something we don't believe in?" She tried to sound lighthearted.

"Oh, don't go thinking we'll actually *work* on this. I just need to convince them of its feasibility to get hold of the funds. The fact is,"—Helen grinned superciliously—"the committee chair is an old friend of mine. It shouldn't be that hard."

Alice was speechless.

"I must get back to my desk," Helen said and glanced at the clock. "This will be great." She stalked off down the corridor, hugging the folder to her chest like a newborn child.

Fuming, Alice stormed back to the printer and retrieved her draft. This was her labor of love. She slapped it on her desk and dropped into her chair. Her breath came in short outraged bursts. What had happened to decency and objectivity? It was not only the wasted effort that hurt, and Helen's complete lack of regard, but the unquestioning trust Alice had put in her boss. The woman was insane! Alice had to say something. Now. Abruptly she stood up, sending her chair spinning across the bay. She marched from the lab, along the empty corridor and into the outer office where she stopped at Helen's door.

"I—uh—You realize I won't be around for long once the money comes through," she stuttered, words tumbling forth, not at all what she had meant to say.

Helen tapped a little longer at the keyboard and then turned, one serene eyebrow raised. "Yes," she said, apparently unconcerned.

"I mean I just don't think my name should be associated with the grant."

"Don't worry, it's not. It never was. Oh, and thanks again for the papers, I do appreciate the help." Helen smiled. "And now I suggest you focus on our magnum opus and make up for all that lost time. I have to say, the data looks great so far."

"Thanks," Alice had said before she could help herself. Flattered into submission, she found herself withdrawing. For a moment she even basked in the compliment. By the time she had returned to her desk, she could not have said which she hated more: Helen's devious ways and rigid preconceived ideas, or her own compulsive and irrational inability to speak her true mind.

*

ALICE STARED at the clothes in her closet. It was the long awaited Sunday on which she was seeing Ben, and she needed to look good. In fact, the prospect of having dinner with him was the only reason she had gotten out of bed. The day before, after watching from on high as a liveried driver ushered Helen into a sleek black limo and whisked her away, Alice had packed up and gone home and lain inert on the faded counterpane on her small bed until she tired of her own thoughts; then she had turned on the ancient television and crawled between the flimsy sheets while action and adventure, heartache and romance filled the static-snowed screen. At some point she had fallen asleep, and had awoken this morning just as she was sitting down to a big exam for which she had completely forgotten to prepare.

Maybe life was rigged with safety nets after all, she thought, knowing that even one kind word from Ben tonight would cheer her up. It was almost as if the timing of his visit were governed by some great cosmic scheme. She picked out a dark blue dress she not yet worn over here, which Ben had told her once looked nice. The main snag now was that she was not mentally in tune. With Ben she needed a sharp mind. Sorting through the tangle of tights she had likewise brought from home and not touched since, she tried to think of them as pantyhose while keeping a straight face. The word still sounded silly to her British ear, and the tights themselves made her feel just as silly when she pulled them on. The fine knit was perversely constraining, both mentally and physically, coating her skin with a smooth dull sheen that seemed to gloss over the mental chaos of the past twenty-four hours. And she had to try to get a grip, she affirmed, because with Ben she had to be able to think.

The good news was that she still had several hours. Her best bet, she decided, was to go into work and stay busy and engaged—to go through the motions until the right frame of mind came. At least she knew that Helen would not be there. And if she rode her bike in to avoid the single file trudge along narrow snow-bound sidewalks with no means of escape, she would have a good excuse not to wear tights—and like the dynamo-powered lights on her first bicycle, she stood more chance of glowing for Ben if she revved herself up. Compromising with her favorite jeans and a nearly new plaid shirt Sage had given her a while back after it shrank, she clipped back and braided her hair, pressed her helmet snugly over it and zippered up her coat. Though she had to carry her bike high so as not to damage the neat walls of her carefully dug trenches, the roads themselves were salt-bleached, clear and bone dry, and she felt ready to face the day by the time she reached the lab.

An air of diligence filled the fifth floor. One or other student or postdoc from the neighboring labs came in, did what he or she had to and left. Alice kept herself busy, mostly by trying to look as if she was busy, because nothing else seemed worth the effort. She could have set up another assay for Ken's project, but the urgency had gone now that she was merely reproducing what they already knew—and she was also taking a perverse pleasure in her power to delay Helen's gratification. There was always the library, of course, always more to explore for her new proposal—if only Helen cared about it, and if only Alice felt less like bursting into tears at the thought that she did not. Besides, a glowering band of grey had appeared in the west and she did not want to get wet. One of Vivaldi's Four Seasons—Spring—trickled over from a nearby lab. For want of anything else, Alice sorted through the pile of papers that had been mounting on her desk for weeks and filed them away.

By the time she was done, it was starting to get dark. Clouds hung heavy overhead. If she went straight home she might beat the rain, but in less than an hour she was meeting Ben down-stairs. An early dinner, Duncan had said, and then they would see. Alice supposed she would indeed see—not least whether even Ben could help her now. Ben used to joke that he got his highs from research, that for him learning and discovery were like mind-blowing drugs. Alice had known what he meant, had felt the same way this past week with her Sharden's epiphany, until it all turned sour. Really, Ben could not have picked a worse time to come. She imagined his smirk when he asked—as she knew he would—if she was happy over here. She did not want to lie. She wanted to pour out her frustrations, her disappointment and disgust, and even possibly admit her defeat. But she wanted Ben's sympathy, not to see him to gloat.

She also wanted to talk about commensals and neonatal stress. Ben had never been interested in her science, nor in any kind of science not relevant to him or his life. When it came down to relevance, Richard was her last hope. He, at least, would understand the broad significance, and might even be impressed—surely more impressed than he would be with the discovery that Helen did not share that coveted reagent. As long as Helen did not taint his viewpoint first. If Alice e-mailed now, she might yet catch him in time…or maybe not, she thought a moment after she logged in: a brand new message from Richard had appeared since she last checked. Then again, the subject was *Good News,* almost definitely referring to the job he had promised her back home. Alice clicked on the message and read: *Here I am in sunny California. Jill and the boys have gone to look at Stanford, and I'm finally catching up on a little business before Helen's talk. Helen's already told me how productive you are, and I'm looking forward to hearing more over lunch. Meanwhile, I thought you'd be glad to know that the higher echelons have just approved your lectureship, and we'll be advertising the post later this month.*

Alice tempered a moment's knee-jerk panic: Richard had already explained that they were bound by law to advertise, but that in cases like this, where they had someone specific in mind, there were ways of tailoring the wording so that only she would fit the bill.

As I suspected, Richard continued, *we were wise to move you into autoimmunity. The dominant forces here are adamant that they don't want another microbe buff. And also—I know you'll be glad to hear this—we'll now need you back by the end of the year. Eighteen months with Helen*

*should be more than enough, what with your paper almost out of the door.
If you could just add the finer details to the paragraph I've attached and
send it back—making profuse and specific mention of Helen's reagent—
I'll forward it on to the powers that be.*

Surely this was, indeed, good news. Why, then, did her viscera constrict? All the more so when she read the attached
paragraph. Richard described her as *a much-needed addition to the
department, bringing with her a fresh focus on autoimmunity, employing
cutting-edge techniques for measuring gene expression as developed by Jonas
et al. Moreover,* he claimed, *Dr. Gaines will provide a local source for
Jonas's unique and especially versatile reagent, helping other interested parties adapt it to their needs. She will also continue to develop her already
active independent research program focusing on....*

Alice sat back. What on earth was Richard thinking? Autoimmune disease? Already active independent—*independent*—
research program? She imagined the person she should have become going back to London, getting on with the life that was
meant to be hers. That person did not exist. No doubt he would
learn soon enough that she had no program—at least not one
devoid of microbes—and most certainly not one employing
Helen's reagent. Helen would never in a million years let her take
it from the lab, let alone share it far and wide. Had he not asked
Helen himself? Helen was ruthless; Alice had seen what happened to Ken. And when Richard found out that Alice could
not bring back his holy grail, he would not want her any more.
There was nothing she could do. She would not be able meet
her obligation, and that would be that.

Unless, Alice realized with a deadening heart, he had been
scheming again with Helen behind her back. Maybe he had
asked her for that grail, after all; and maybe she had said yes. All
the more reason, Alice thought, not to want Helen's projects or

reagent. Alice had her own ideas. Ideas that evidently no one else wanted. Not even Richard. No more microbes, he had said.

The chimney beacons bled into the runnels of raindrops now smearing the windowpane, and then withdrew again. Alice felt abandoned by fate. Or was this feeling rather one of abandon—an absence of restraint? What would happen, she thought, if she simply let go? Just then the beam of a headlight sliced through the parking lot below. She cupped her hands against the glass. A small sedan drew up at the curb and a front and rear door opened in unison. There was Duncan—and yes, that must be Ben. They hurried toward the building entrance and out of her line of sight. Sighing, she put her thoughts on hold. After shutting down the computer and locking the lab, she made her way down, taking advantage of the empty stairwell to practice smiling and expressing interest and delight in her visage.

BEN AND DUNCAN were standing in the lobby with their heads bowed. They were looking at Ben's shoes—probably at the white wavy tidemark rising up from each sole. Through the opening of Ben's ski jacket, Alice recognized the Aran sweater she had borrowed from him one cold spring night. He looked all wrong without the shapeless navy anorak that had always been a part of her mental image of him—although so had the white plastic shopping bag dangling now from his left hand, so at least something was the same. The lift pass cinched to his zipper tab looked especially out of place.

Ben looked up as she drew close. "Damned snowmelt," he said, eyes narrowing as he scrutinized her. "Long time no see." His gaze was intense. "Fancy you and Dunc being here under the same roof." Suddenly he grinned and took her hand. She squeezed his palm back as if to check that he was real—glad for once that it was not his habit to embrace—and then realized in the awkward grapple that followed that he had been trying to raise her fingers to his lips. He dropped her hand and shrugged. Just like the good old Ben, she thought.

"You've changed," he said, steering her around to examining her back.

Spinning around again, evading his almost flatteringly proprietary grip, she awaited the inevitable derogatory verdict, having just remembered that he had once declared long hair was frivolous and girls with braids always uptight.

"Looks good," he said instead, apparently meaning it. Perhaps he had just been goading her before, testing her out.

"Thanks," she said, and looked at him quizzically. She could have told him that he looked good, too; and by all measures he did, with his overgrown bronze curls and congenitally mascara'd eyes. Only that was not how conversations went with Ben. He smiled his tantalizing smile that used to make her day despite its overtones of mockery—though she noticed that the overtones of mockery had paled. She felt a heightened sense of vigilance, as if at risk of exposing herself, or perhaps exposing herself in an unflattering light. A door slammed in a distant corridor, causing her to jump and glance over her shoulder. She was glad when Duncan clapped his hands and declared they should be off.

After spilling out onto the portico, they ran for the car, dodging large drops of sleet. Alice slipped into the back seat with Ben, and noticed as she buckled up that he was bathed in cologne. This was unprecedented. Meanwhile, Duncan introduced her to Hayley—bubbly, pretty and American—and Alice realized she had expected Duncan's girlfriend to be British and humorless and plain. As Hayley drove them into town, she talked about the people she and Duncan had met at Christmas when they visited

Ben, and Alice felt left out, never having been introduced to any of these supposedly great friends. She had spent a quiet—though actually quite pleasant—Christmas over here on her own. Not that any of them asked. And so she stared out of the window, waiting for a chance to mention Diane's wedding and start rounding out her summer plans—until Ben steered the talk toward Cambridge and began to reminisce with her instead. But whereas he was jauntily recalling dinners, dances and May balls, her thoughts settled on the moonlit pavements of King's Parade, on the gothic grey facades, on her echoing footsteps on the flag-stones of deserted streets as she walked home in the early hours after staying late in the lab. And as the car jerked through dense and halting traffic, it occurred to her that what she missed most was the moonlight, and being alone, and escaping to the top of the tower in the corner of the quad where she had hidden to write her thesis for those last three summer months. She had stopped wearing her watch then and lived outside of time—or would have done if the clock towers had not chimed the hours and quarter-hours across the rooftops day in and day out.

The car stopped. Sharing two large black umbrellas, they backtracked to the restaurant. On the door, a large white sign warned them: *SORRY, RESERVATIONS ONLY TONIGHT.*

"For goodness' sake, we've never booked before," Duncan said, opening again the umbrella he had just closed. "What on earth do we do now?"

Hayley looked up and down the street. "The place we went that time with Hugh?"

"Jolly good idea. Off we go again!"

Alice trotted with them back to the car, thinking how much she could have done meanwhile in the lab. She caught Ben's eye, wondering if he felt the same way; he had always had a strong aversion to inefficiency and wasting time. He smiled placidly back, as if sharing a different joke.

A short while later they pulled up at the restaurant at which she had dined with Dan. The place was busy, crammed with murmuring pairs, but they were not turned away and squeezed as directed into the overcrowded bar to listen out for Duncan's name.

"But don't you miss the fundamental *Britishness* of things?" Ben asked as Alice wedged herself against the wall. "It's all the fake good cheer over here that gets to me. *How are you today*, they say when you know perfectly well that they don't give a damn."

Alice laughed, falling back on faked good cheer. Because amidst the listless crisp accents, the dry British wit—all of which had been familiar to the point of invisibility not so long ago—she was feeling disoriented, buffeted in turn by keen waves of longing for and aversion to home.

"But you'll be back before you know it," Ben assured her. "Two years really isn't long."

"Perhaps not," Alice said, noticing as she spoke the ambiguity of her reply. Ben craned his neck and scanned the room. And in the lull that grew from the side-stepped opportunity to talk about August, she examined more critically the one-time object of her dreams.

She had met him one evening on the train back from London to Cambridge. He had taken a seat opposite her just before they left King's Cross, but had not said a word until they were racing through night-shrouded fields.

"Are you happy?" he had asked, penetrating an empty reverie spun by the rhythm of the train.

"Are you talking to me?"

"There's no one else here. I've seen you around college—

you're always smiling, so I wondered if you're happy."

"Of course. Well, not especially. Does it matter?"

"Does it matter to you?" Ben had grinned and stared out at the obscure fields.

Later that week their paths had crossed again—on King's Parade at a quarter to eleven at night.

"You've been in the lab, haven't you?" he had mocked, falling into step. In his hand he held the soon-to-be-familiar shopping bag in which she later learned he carried his thesis-to-date. He was about to join some people for a cappuccino, he said. She could come too. If she wished. If she had time. She told him she did.

In the coffee shop, he introduced her as Jean, his longtime childhood friend. In her astonishment—to her astonishment—she played along.

The next day, he had placed his tray opposite hers in the college cafeteria. "May I join you?" he had said after he sat down.

"Why did you introduce me as Jean?"

"I just wondered what you'd do. So what did you think?"

"You have some interesting friends." Conversation had, in fact, been stilted—not least when Ben made an inflammatory comment about women that Alice tried to downplay.

"Friends?" Ben said. "Mere acquaintances." He paused to chew a forkful of peas. "I'd hoped for more from them, in fact. *La crème de la crème* indeed, what with their bland responses to my insightful comments on life. The fact is," he confided, "few people say what they think. Too busy worrying what *other* people think, trying to say the right thing." An experiment: that was all it had been. "And your placating comments hardly helped," he had added, one arched eyebrow raised.

But after that, it seemed she had earned her way into his life.

On his dark nights of the soul, when no one else was around, he would seek her out in her lab or in her room. On the whole he would discuss the meaning of love—in the abstract, of course, strictly impersonal; his dissertation, he said, dealt with love in literature. "But you're not capable of love," he would sometimes insist. "Says who?" Alice would reply. "Why don't you love *x*— then?" he would ask and name a mutual friend—even as he unbuttoned her blouse. "He's good looking and intelligent," Ben would add. "What more do you need?" And Alice would also wonder what more, and wonder why she listened, why she let him unclasp her bra, let him cup her small breast in his always-warm hand. Except that deep down, she still half-believed that he understood, that he really did see beneath the vacant smile he had pulled her up on that first time. And sometimes, on those never-mentioned nights, she would wonder if Ben was unhappy too.

He seemed happy enough now. Alice looked beyond him at the dining room. She saw the same studied twilight, heard the same toneless chatter as on that other night with Dan. Duncan and Hayley stood a short way off now, separated from them in the crush. Ben was talking with an air of modest understatement about developments at work. He had gained some recognition, he said. A book was in the offing.

"That's great," Alice said, remembering the well-thumbed paperback on pop-psychology she had found in his bathroom, in which she recognized the mind games he had often played on her. In seeing through him, she had felt sorry for him. She understood that he needed her; he always came to her when all else failed. So she had maintained for him her sham of innocent ignorance. Besides, he had kept her mind sharp, provided traction for her labile thoughts. And she still remembered the way his presence had sparked in her a vibrant charge, as if he brought her a little closer to some bright amorphous truth.

She felt no vibrant charge or proximity to truth tonight. Trying not envy his success, she listened to him say he'd bought a small house in Cambridge, commuted back and forth to London three days a week. A small house by the river, he said, and told her exactly where. She followed his directions in her mind, saw the river and Jesus Green, and was soon wandering on her own: along the towpath, through Granchester Meadows and back into town, across Midsummer Common—the names alone were like a dream. She had often walked along the river that last summer, during those final days of writing up. She had wished those days could last forever more.

"And," Ben was saying as another name was called, "there are still three decisions pending on college fellowships—and I have inside information that...well..." He grinned. "I'm on my way back."

Two stools were vacated and they sat down at last.

"That's great!" Alice said, genuinely pleased for him. He had always been enthralled by college life. As she had too, she acknowledged—she had loved those formal dinners when they had robed up in academic gowns, and the all-night May Balls when she had worn flowing velvet or stiff taffeta, when she had danced in the moonlight until the sun rose on a flat grey dawn.

"You must come and stay with me next time you're home."

The directness of his statement pulled her up. Really, he was far more attentive than he had ever been before—distinctly personal, in fact. It had never been him with whom she dined or danced or watched the sun come up. She looked for the snag, the twist that would trap her. Such was his way.

"You'll like it," Ben said eagerly. "Four bedrooms, a big back garden, perfect for…" He cleared his throat. "And when you're back, it's really not a bad commute. An hour either way if you time it right, not counting the Tube ride—but you can work on the train. Look, Alice, I'm not much into all that sentimental stuff but what I'm trying to say…"

With chilling clarity it dawned on her what he was trying to say. She tried to imagine herself living with him—married to him. *Marry the boy next door*, Alice's Grandma had once said and then confessed she had learned too late, and later Alice's mother had explained about the social mismatch Grandma made, the father she had barely known because he left when she was three. There was no question that Ben was the perfect boy-next-door, born to the same rung of social hierarchy that was so difficult to escape because even if you did escape, you knew exactly where everyone else still expected you to be.

Alice supposed she could, indeed, commute—prepare lectures, grade papers on the swift London train. Except that there was no prospect of that job anymore. She had the brief sensation of being on a train rushing past her destination without letting her get off. Then she remembered Ken's project and her latest results, the line of minimal resistance she had been ready to dismiss. With a paper in *Nature* or *Science* she might even find a job in Cambridge; and one day she might want to stop working, mind the children instead, take them to play on the towpath as she had watched other mothers do during that summer without time. It was all falling into place.

"By the way," Ben said, interrupting the gravid pause. He reached into the carrier bag. "I found this in my car and thought it might be yours." He held up Alice's black velvet jacket, the one she had worn so many times to Cambridge functions.

She laughed. "Yes, it's mine!" She had not realized it was lost.

"Don't tell me—I left it in your car after that last dinner dance…" With a small struggle, she put the jacket on. Its tailored formality looked ridiculously over her thick flannel shirt. Smiling, she slid it off again, half-wishing that she had dressed up after all. She placed the jacket on her lap. It would be so easy to go back. There had been so many opportunities to dress up in Cambridge—to be just like her mother on those nights her parents kissed them goodnight in a hurried haze of aftershave and perfume and left a neighbor in charge. Sometimes Alice and her siblings had played in their mother's closet then, amidst the out-of-bounds cellophane-clad splendor, though making do when they dressed themselves up with plain cotton scarves and bright polyester blouses, feet pressed into the toes of too-big high heeled shoes. How grown-up they had felt, heels tapping compactly on the bare linoleum tiles…

"Thanks," Alice said and stroked the velvet like a much-loved pet. Her nostalgia was acute—for Cambridge, for home, for dressing up, for dress codes, etiquette and form.

"Reminds me of May Balls and the like," Ben said. "It'll be nice to be part of all that again."

Part of all that? Now she thought about it, Alice had never really been part of all that—no more than the Little Mermaid in the court of her rescued prince, trying so hard to play along but never really understood.

"It sounds as if you've got your whole life falling into place," she said. Falling into place like puzzle pieces. Solved.

"Yours, too—it'll be just like old times." Ben stepped, confident, into the future. But Alice could not accompany him. He had indeed shown her the truth. She was thinking of the paper that might have been Ken's: follow the protocol, fill in the blanks correctly and it's yours—yours, whoever you are. This was not the timelessness for which she had yearned; this was time standing still, not the same thing at all. She would be trapped within his expectations, the puzzle solved around her, around someone she was not—around a Mrs. Chamberlain, three thousand miles away. She would end up playing make-believe for the rest of her life. Poor Ben. Here he was, trying to seduce her, offering her the kind of future of which she had dreamed, and she was no longer the person that had dreamed those dreams. Perhaps she never had been. The person who had dreamed them was just someone she had created by following the protocols—whether Ben's assertions or institutional rules or quaint traditions—and filling in the blanks that were not really blank.

"And I think I should apologize," Ben said uncomfortably. "Sorry I was such a…well, such a jerk. Thanks for sticking by me through it all." He looked at her expectantly.

"It's all in the past now."

"I knew you'd understand."

This was not going to be easy. Alice looked at the jacket. It belonged to her past. Ben belonged there too. She, however, did not—and, unlike the Little Mermaid, she was not mute. *One of the heads was already deprived of life*, she thought, and folded the jacket into her bag. *This one was amputated.* "Thank you," she said, and looked into Ben's eyes. "Thank you for everything, but I'm afraid… I'm sorry…"

Ben's expression changed. He had understood.

Alice looked at her watch. "Oh dear, I didn't realize it was so late," she lied to set him free. "I must get back to the lab."

Ever the gentleman, Ben saw her out. They stopped beneath the canopy outside the door. The sleet had turned back to rain, and bounced merrily on the sidewalk. Just beyond Ben, Alice saw a red heart in the restaurant window. *Reservations recommended tonight* was written above the heart, and a large *Valentine's Day* below. I am heartless, she thought. But the pretense had to end. And no one was going to tell her when, or for whom, she should feel love. Ben was standing in front of her, apparently not sure what to say. Then he pulled her toward him and planted a kiss on her lips. Especially the kisses, she found herself thinking. All part of the game and yet spoiling the game; kisses always spoiled the game because they made her feel as if the man who kissed her was really kissing someone else. And this time she knew why: because they were.

Ben drew away. He held the end of her braid in one hand. "A good thick braid," he said as if to the braid. He squeezed it and then let it fall.

"Goodbye," Alice said. "And thank you again." She meant it wholeheartedly, and felt unusually buoyant as she turned to face the rain. The restaurant door sighed closed as Ben went back inside. She walked away fast, her heart aching as if she had just been given news of the death of someone she once vaguely knew.

Part V

Acute Resurgence of Symptoms as the Virus Enters the Central Nervous System

Chapter Eighteen

WATER POOLED straight away beneath the chair on which Alice draped her coat. Peeling off the yellow Post-it note that still clung to the glass, she let down the blind, covering the image she had been so pleased to think of as the type of woman a man would want. She had been right, though: she had indeed been a type—a generic someone; anyone; no one in particular.

Poor Ben, she thought. All these years she had known that he, of all people, could reveal to her great truths. Her mistake had been in guessing what those great truths might be. The greatest truth—the one that he had now revealed—was that he was just a small drop in the ocean of currents she had let carry her along, just one source of directives she had allowed to shape her life. She could see now that to Helen and Richard, too, she was no more than a vehicle for carrying out their plans. That is, until she started on her Sharden's work. Her eyes fell on the printout fanned across her desk. True, that proposal had germinated from Helen's request, but it had changed since then, been thoroughly reborn, taken on a life of its own. She could not let it die. That document was hers, and not only by default because no one else wanted it; it had taken shape from *her* perception, *her* experience, the merging of *her* divergent thoughts.

Skimming the front-page summary at which Helen had not even glanced, she felt slighted and wronged. Even Richard had closed off his mind. Was she really meant to resign herself now to being at the mercy of other people's blinkered needs? *One resigned, one sorrowful, one at peace*, she thought, picturing the three fused babes. Picturing them, she realized, not by way of confirmation, but because there was more to the story than mere resignation or sorrow or peace. *Not without further mutilation*, the doctors had said. Maybe that was true here, too. Her options began to separate, her preferences to take shape in unambiguous relief. A clear solution emerged—one that would circumvent both Richard's constraints and the roadblock to independence from Helen already met by Ken. Mutilation, yes; but Alice had already made the first cut with Ben. She knew exactly what she had to do next—because she was damned if she was going to spend the rest of her life in a state of resignation!

Dear Richard, she typed on the bright computer screen. *Thank you so much for the news about the job.* The job you say you are tailoring to fit me, she thought, when the opposite is true. *I do appreciate the effort you've made on my behalf*, she added, *but as my perspective has broadened, my focus has changed. I've found a new niche, one I care about, centered on microbes, which is clearly not what you are looking for. So I plan to stay on here for now and pursue this idea. I sincerely hope you find your ideal candidate soon. With best wishes, Alice.*

Perfect. The message was dispatched with a click of the mouse. There was no turning back. Alice felt light as a feather as she prepared to go home.

*

IF PETER HAD KNOWN the sidewalks were clear around the

medical school, he would have headed down there earlier to run off the stiffness that had started that morning, aftermath no doubt of his trip to the Cape. On Friday he had come home cold and exhilarated to another flashing phone message from Eric, who had seen footage of downed trees on the national news and was worried about their parents' house—adding humbly that they might also have left an open carton of milk on the table by the door. So, although Peter would have liked to think of it himself, he was glad of the reminder that he had meant to head down anyway, and had set off on Saturday morning, spent an hour in standstill traffic leaving town, and arrived before lunch to a breath-arresting stench of inevitably sour milk. After a bracing afternoon clearing the driveway, he had warmed a can of soup, and then—as an antidote to the sensation that his present was upside down and his future anyone's guess—spent the evening excavating the sediments of his past in the cold and cluttered garage. He had driven back that same night with a large cardboard box filled with sketchpads and old artwork piled on top of his long-neglected and beloved chainmail vest.

That vest weighed a ton; no wonder his back ached. His neck was stiff, too, though that was probably because, after being trapped between two elderly pedestrians in the high-walled furrow of a sidewalk for the first block of his run, he had given up on it and gone swimming instead. He rarely visited the pool, with its limited lap times and mildewed locker rooms, but in no time at all had been lulled by the rhythm of his still-powerful stroke and could have kept going all day. Even then, his neck would have been fine if he had been left to cool down, if the lifeguard had not blown her shrill whistle at the end of his lane. When he surfaced, finally realizing that she meant him, she had yelled at him for wasting her time, for looking as if he was drowning, when all he had been doing down there was trying to relax.

He neared the crosswalk to his building, feeling like a ghost moving through its bygone life. Tiny pellets of ice burned the skin of his face, and each arduous step drove a nail through his brain. He stood at the curb without crossing the road, and considered going home. Then, up ahead, he saw the woman who was not Welsh. She was standing at the bike rack in the parking lot, facing his way. He froze. And then he realized she was crying. Moments later, without even knowing he had moved, he was standing beside her—by which time she had turned away from him, one hand shielding her face.

"Are you okay?" he asked, touching her sleeve. Through the padding of her coat and his thermal glove, he felt her tense. "I'm sorry," he said, dropping his hand. His forehead hurt.

"I'm fine," she said, still hidden behind her fingers and quite obviously still crying.

"I don't think you are." He massaging his brow. And neither was he—he felt more desolate than she looked. "Why don't you come inside?" he asked. "Out of this…this rain, or whatever it is." He squinted at the sky and the pain flared again. "I could make you some tea," he added. "It might warm you up."

"I'm fine," she said again without conviction, brushing her wet saddle with a mottled gloveless hand. "Really, I'm fine."

"Okay, then." Pulling off his glove, he reached under his jacket into the pocket of his jeans. "Well, at least take this," he said, holding out a paisley kerchief, faded deep green today.

She stared at it.

"It's clean," he said.

At last she looked up. "Thank you," she said with a blinding smile that just as suddenly disappeared as she dropped her inflamed gaze. But she did take the handkerchief—with a hand that felt astonishingly cold against his.

"Thank you," she repeated, drying her eyes. "I'll wash it and give it back."

"Really—no need," he said and a lump came to his throat at the finality of what he had said; he had left no room for more. "And I should go," he added, backing away, feeling her eyes on his hand again as he forced his glove back on. His left foot slipped from the curb, and to save himself he turned around, catching his balance as he started to walked off, spasms of pain gripping his skull to the beat of his heart.

"Thank you," she called one more time, as he reached the building's steps. He raised a hand to one side in acknowledgement and then to his head again, unable to look back, though when he had wound his way robotically through the doorways and corridors that led to his lab, he went straight to the window without turning on the lights. She was still standing at the bike rack, now grappling with her lock. And from the way she was moving, he suspected she was crying again.

"Hey Peter. Long time no see!" The lights flickered on. "What's with the gloom?"

"Hi Tom." Peter moved in closer to the glass so that he could still see out. She had freed her bike—and then a car drove past, temporarily hiding her, and pulled up at the steps. Elaine, Tom's loyal long-time secretary, stooped to pick up her bag in the light of the glass-clad foyer. Peter hoped she had not been there when he walked in.

"What's so fascinating?" Tom said, coming over and following his gaze. "Yep, she's a gem. Came in to help with the grant renewal, we're running way behind. Meanwhile," he said, turning to face Peter, "how'd it go on Friday?"

"Friday?" Peter had almost forgotten. He looked at Tom and

then outside again. "Friday," he repeated as the car's passenger door opened, illuminating Elaine's portly husband leaning across the empty seat. Elaine hurried down the steps and plumped herself inside, her husband's bearded face touching hers before the closing door wiped out the light. The car rolled from the lot, past the woman with grey eyes that had looked lilac tonight, who was wheeling her bicycle out toward the road. Then she, too, disappeared.

"Yeah, Friday," Tom said expectantly. "The interview—how did it go?"

Peter hugged his chest. "It didn't."

"What, they cancelled?"

"No."

"So what happened?"

"Nothing."

"Well then, who's to say how it went?"

Peter shook his head.

"Come now. You're over-reacting."

Peter massaged his neck.

"Look, how about we discuss this over food?" Tom said. "Now that Marion's away, I could use an excuse to eat out. How about Chinese?"

"Sure," Peter said doubtfully, sensing a shadow of last week's queasiness. His skull was tightening on his brain like a vice. Perhaps it was a vice of withheld truth. It might help to come clean. Still, before following Tom out, he detoured to his office and swallowed down some ibuprofen from the bottle in his drawer.

The rain had turned into true sleet, already coating Tom's car with a limp pock-marked shroud. The car was parked, Peter noticed, opposite the spot where the woman had stood and cried.

"Can't abide getting cold and wet," Tom said, slamming his

door with uncalled-for vigor. Peter concurred, a new sensation in his spine. The indicator clicked as they drove from the lot, the wipers laboring to a different beat.

"So Marion tells me she's *still* enjoying it," Tom said, diverting Peter from the bi-rhythmic lure.

"Enjoying it?" Peter's neck felt tender.

"Looking after the kid. My theory is that she's making up for the third child we never had—though I tell you, she was the one who put her foot down, said two was enough." Tom chuckled, and Peter turned his head too fast as they drove past a pedestrian wheeling a bike—an older man. He wished he taken one more ibuprofen tablet.

"Sound like South Wales is a treat," Tom continued. "Nice house, right on the coast, great view of the Bristol Channel—" The car lurched, Tom's foot on the brake. "You OK there?"

"Sure." Peter leaned back again. He still held the dashboard with both hands as split realities re-fused. hey were waiting at a stoplight. "I almost drowned in the Bristol Channel once," he said. "When I was kid."

"Jeez. How did that happen?" The light turned green and the car stalled.

Good question, Peter thought. "I capsized," he said. "During a storm."

Tom shifted into gear and moved on. "What the hell were you doing out in a storm?"

"Good question," Peter said.

Every car that came toward them seemed to have its headlights on full beam. Peter closed his eyes. The way the traffic was, she would be home by now even if she had walked—though of course he had no idea where she lived.

"So, here we are," Tom said, swerving and pulling to a halt.

He ratcheted the handbrake, leapt out and slammed the door again. Sleet spattered on the windshield, sullying the view.

Peter eased himself up from the car. The cold moist air revived him somewhat, but not quite enough. As he caught up with Tom, three couples spilled out of the restaurant in a cloud of spicy aromatic heat. "To be honest," Peter said, taking a step back, "I don't have much appetite."

"No sweat—you can just watch. Then again," he said, "why don't I get a takeout? Your place is close by and I haven't been there for months." He held open the restaurant door. "What, not even coming in?"

Peter leaned against the outside wall. "I'll wait here."

"You OK?"

"I'm fine. Just in need of some fresh air."

Tom frowned. "It's goddamned raining—or whatever this shit is." He fumbled for his keys. "Here, take these," he said, tossing them across. "Go wait in the car."

ALICE STEADIED her bike as it rattled down the stairway. She let herself in and leaned her bike against the wall—and saw her bike lights on the shelf. She had thought they were lost! Really it would hardly have mattered if they were, but when she realized they were neither in her bag nor on her bike, she had burst into tears right there in the dismal parking lot. As if the end of the world had come. And in a sense it had. She had known even then that it was not about the lights—though she had used them for years, day in and day out, part of a mundane existence that had morphed in the parking lot into a treasure trove of sacrosanct memories entwined with those lights. As she sorted through her keys, trying to tell herself they were just battery-driven bulbs, they had felt like a symbol of her rapidly retreating past. Somehow the weightlessness that had made her float as she clicked on the mouse—burning bridges and setting herself free—had solidified and turned into doubt, maybe even into fear, by the time she had left the building for the second time that night.

Irrevocable, she thought, her eyes by now quite dry. The past was irrevocable, and always had been. It always would be, too. She should feel cleansed and cathartic, but felt empty and dissatisfied. Without taking off her coat, she moved aimlessly around the Spartan kitchen, opening cabinets and drawers without intent, until she registered the undeniable craving for peanut butter from the jar, and dark chocolate in large chunks, and honey spread on soft thick slices of freshly baked bread—none of which she would find on her poorly stocked shelves. As she reached up for an open pack of whole-wheat crackers, her suspicion was confirmed: a peevish cramp spread its way across her pelvis—a dull, familiar and telling cramp. Why on earth had she not guessed? That, of course, explained the tears.

However, it did not explain the way she felt whenever she saw Peter Young. Or the way she felt now as her fingers touched the folded handkerchief, the electrifying jolt like the one that had stunned her when she saw him staring at her from across the road; or the way he had paralyzed her mind when his hand—his beautiful lean hand—had touched her arm and, despite his glove and her thick sleeve, sent a deluge of uncalled-for longing flooding through her soul. And yet how could his presence made her feel more alone than she ever had felt before? She had tried so hard to retain common sense, to pull herself together and pretend she was fine. But too much had been happening too fast and she had been unable to pretend. Closing her eyes now, she held the paisley to her lips. He, of all men, with his tender brown eyes and articulate eyebrows, had come to her aid like a hero and offered her tea. He had been candid and matter-of-fact; and it would have been so nice, so very comforting and civilized, to go inside and drink tea with him—and so very easy to forget about Dee. But Alice had not forgotten. And it still made her flinch with frustration and shame when she pictured the two of them side by side in his lab that night.

She sat down on a hard wooden chair, glad she had held firm. She was not going to get involved again in something that could only end in more tears. Yet this man Peter Young had been so kind even about her tears. Not like Ben, who had blithely made fun of her the few times he had seen her cry. She laid the faded fabric on her thigh. He had offered with it his warmth—she had seen it in his eyes, in his expression, even felt it quite literally when his bare hand touched hers. She stroked the patterned layers, wishing life were an old fashioned movie in which this would have been the start of something beautiful—as beautiful as his hands and his brown eyes, and that look of sharp regret as he had backed away from her. It had been so very sad. And when he reached the concrete steps, he had raised one hand up to his forehead as if in abject despair, and as he disappeared inside, she had thought how pale and wan he had looked in the sparkling rain, and been gripped by an impulse to run after him, find him and embrace him and sooth his woes, as if he were the one in need. It had all been upside down.

Besides, why had he been nice? She had not been beautiful at all: she had been crying like a child, which always turned her eyes bright red. Maybe he had not even recognized her, had just seen someone in seeming distress. Why should he recognize her anyway? Especially when her hood had been up, covering her hair and more specifically the braid which was all anyone saw of her these days. She pulled the braid forward over her shoulder, wondering why it made her so desirable—or rather why it made someone who was not her so desirable. No one ever wanted the real her, she was well aware of that—not Dan, not Ben, not anyone. No one knew the real her. She had only to think of her carefully preserved notes: all those sweet cascades of feelings she could not return, those mundane comments and requests from men who barely knew her name, those glib declarations of fake sincerity from men who knew her name but were in love with someone else.

Then again, she could hardly blame them when she barely knew herself. Even this evening, out there in the rain, if only for a moment, she had considered accepting that cup of tea, throwing caution to the wind—forgetting about Dee, seeing how far she could go, how far he would go. Even after what had happened with Dan. So it really served her right that the car had pulled up soon after that and illuminated a cozy caring kiss as if to remind her how these things *should* be. It served her right that she had been be landed with that image of straightforward happiness, stuck with the knowledge of what was not hers as she wheeled her bike home—wheeling it because it was dark and she had lost her bike lights, and she had always been a good girl and played by the rules.

A good girl. What was happening to her? What had happened to the sweet naïve girl who, in her budding pubescence had been determined to wait? Yes—it was all coming back now—she had wanted to wait, had even wanted to save her first kiss for true love when it finally came.

What an ignorant romantic. What had she thought she was saving? She remembered it well, that non-event of a day. The first lush growth of summer had been overflowing along the trail, flowers pink, white and yellow among the rain-varnished leaves as she dreamt of saving her handsome stranger from peril on the cliff top trail—until she had seen him come to life down below, and turned her back on him and on the danger he was in, and on her pleasure in the wind and the rain. One kiss—one accidental brush with an eager young man's lips—and there she had been on the mud-slick path lashed by driving rain, wet weeds clinging to her calves as she made way for the girl with the turquoise umbrella and the long thick braid down her back.

I am your slave, Alice thought and wrapped a hand around her braid. With her other hand, she reached for the kitchen scissors that were lying on a shelf. She made the first decisive cut. She sheared as close as she could to the nape of her neck.

NO SOONER HAD ALICE swept up the last trimmings than she heard the landlord's knock. He timed it so well—she was in her nightdress again, fresh from the shower. She asked him to come in, which he did with considerable difficulty carrying a large ceramic bowl like an offering in both hands. Mangoes, grapefruits and oranges were heaped up within.

"Ah," he said, stopping short. "You have changed. It looks very…very modern."

"Thank you," Alice said cautiously, touching the damp layers that felt curiously like fur.

"Modern but nice," he added, stepping over to place the bowl on the table at her side. "For you," he declared.

"Oh no, I couldn't possibly—"

"Please. My friends in Florida, they like to send me fruit but I can never eat it all. So much ends up going to waste. Do take it, please."

"Oh…well, that's very kind—"

He looked at her again for a moment and then sat down. Alice stood behind the other chair.

"You do so remind me of her," he said as if taking up from where he had left off. "Even with—without, I should say—the hair."

Alice looked over at his wife's severe note.

"Ah, no," he said, following her gaze. "My wife was a fine woman, but it was not a good marriage. Not good at all."

And this is none of my business, Alice thought.

The old man turned back to her. "Perhaps the lack of children did not help," he pressed on. "We never did know why not. However, the trouble....it started long before that. And it was not the fault of either my poor wife or my dear English friend. Young lady, you remind me so much of my dear English friend."

"I see." Alice was struggling to keep up.

"May I tell you something, please?" he asked—somewhat belatedly, she thought. His suddenly anxious tone made her feel he had just tossed her a gilt-edged cup and shouted *Catch*!

"Of course," she answered, pulling out the chair and sitting down.

"I have been thinking, you see—how many things we leave unsaid."

Alice had no idea how to respond, but he seemed not to mind.

"We met that first summer," he said. "Just before the war. On the beach beyond the tree—the tree in the photograph. And this young woman, like you, was here just for a while, staying with the eminent biologists in the house next door—Doctors Earnest and Maria Wilson," he enunciated slowly as if remembering as he spoke. "My first day down on the beach at dusk, I came upon her walking alone, the low sun haloing her hair. We talked of many things—such as how she helped the Wilsons catalogue their samples—but even that first evening, many things were left unsaid.

"She had silver-laced hair," he continued. "Premature white strands that made me tell her, to sound less naïve, that my fiancée would be joining me soon. She replied by picking up a shell, a small translucent yellow disc, that she dropped into my palm. She picked it up with her left hand." He held out his own, turned it this way and that so that his wedding band glinted in the artificial light.

"These things we knew," he declared, "and took as fact. We assumed out time together was incontrovertibly separate from real life. But afterwards—even long afterwards—she remained here." He placed a hand on his heart. "Ah, I do not mean to embarrass you—"

"Really, it's OK." Alice meant it this time, knowing this was not about her.

The old man shook his head. "The problem was that I had assumed too much—about her and about myself. Most of all, I was grateful to my fiancée, glad to have escaped the uncertainties ahead." He stared at the fruit and Alice thought he was done.

"And my gratitude turned out to be our curse," he said, making Alice start. "If not for that, if I had known what would happen, I could have said something, tried to change fate. There might still have been time—for all of us. But I said nothing. And when I saw my wife again, it was too late. My brother...they had come for him long since. And my wife...my wife-to-be, as you know, had suffered too much. So I did my best for her. I owed it to her—and to him."

Alice thought of the brother who had been in love with the same girl.

"He might have been here in my place."

Alice pictured weeping willows, peacocks crying across the lake, and games of romance so easy to mistake for love.

"Who could have known how unhappy she would be married to me?" the old man said quietly. "I heard many years later that my English friend and her husband had divorced. She raised her only child alone. She gave birth not long after the war began. Oh, I don't know exactly when," he said as if Alice had asked, and waved a dismissive hand. "You could calculate back but you could never know for sure, perhaps even she did not know. I do not want to know in any case," he muttered to the countertop. "Why know what I have missed or what delusions I have dreamed?

"So. I can change nothing now." He shrugged and turned back to the faded sign. "I simply felt the need to speak, I hope you do not mind. Do forgive the intrusion." He leaned forward to rise with effort from his chair. Alice leapt up to help him but he brushed her aside. "It was good of you to listen," he said almost severely. "And you do so remind me of her." He placed an arm around Alice's shoulders and squeezed her close. For a moment she thought he would kiss her but he let his arm fall.

"In fact," he said, "I came down here to tell you that my nephew's daughter—my late wife's nephew's daughter—is coming to Boston. Not until mid-September, but he wants her to live with me, down here. I feel I cannot say no. I thought I should warn you. I am sorry."

"Thank you," Alice murmured, barely registering. September seemed a long way off.

He nodded and took his leave, locking the door behind him with one swift click.

Alice stood at the table, stunned. Never before had she been so irrelevantly and yet so precisely chosen, let alone chosen to hear to such private and intimate thoughts. As the floorboards creaked above, she picked through the fruit. It was ripe, some was starting to rot, especially the mangos that gave beneath her touch. Yet the scent of those mangos was sublime. She closed her eyes and inhaled, thinking of all that he had not said, and had never said even back then. His silence seemed to confirm nascent truths about freedom and the future, obligation and the past; about looking at one thing and seeing something else. She thought of her own past, of moonlit meadows and May Balls, and of a long procession of fading might-have-been selves. A little later, in her bedroom redolent of mothballs, she opened up her shoebox full of notes, emptied it out on the counterpane and, starting with the credit card receipt, ripped that carefully preserved evidence of nothing to shreds.

Chapter Nineteen

PETER UNLOCKED the door to the peal of Violet's squeals.

"How's my girl?" Tom yelled and disappeared inside. He was crouched by Violet's cage by the time Peter had followed him in and turned on the light.

"I always enjoyed ours more than my girls did," he said—as he had said the last time he stopped by. "But man, this place is a tip."

"I guess so." Peter tilted the lampshade to lessen the glare. He had forgotten about the mess.

"Having a turnout?" Tom stood up and peered into the cardboard box Peter had not yet unpacked. "We should do this ourselves, only the last time Marion took a car-load to Goodwill she came home with twice as much…. Hey, what's all this?" Tom unfurled a roll of high school artwork.

"Nothing," Peter said, but too late.

"Signed and all! Never knew you were an artist," he said, raising his eyebrows at the partial sketch of a girl. "Nice…" he added, leafing through some more.

"Thanks." Peter pulled over two chairs from the table and dropped into one as Tom examined the sketch of violets Peter had taped to the wall earlier that day.

"This one's new, too." Tom observed. "Yours as well?"

"Yep, from way back."

"Pretty goddamn good. You'd have made a great old fashioned naturalist, you know—like your Reverend Whatsit and his book of wildflowers, eh?"

"I wish." Peter massaged his neck again. What he really wished was that Tom would sit down and be quiet. Despite the medication, his headache was worse. If not for the urgency of the matter at hand, he would have told Tom he was tired and gone straight off to bed.

"And this," Tom said, lifting out the chainmail vest.

Peter watched as entropy reversed, the jumble of wire rings spreading upward and aligning in neat and tidy rows.

"Don't tell me—you made it yourself. Jeez, it weighs a goddamned ton." Tom shifted his weight and poured it onto Peter's knees. "Who knew what treasures you have hidden in your lair," he exclaimed and leaned over to inspect a bookshelf as the chainmail clattered to the floor in a liquefying heap. He pulled out a paperback. "Conrad," he said, shaking his head. "Great Short Works indeed. Pretty long if you ask me. Great works, but long—long stories about long storms at sea." He pushed the book back into place. "But now," he said, spinning around, "how about some coffee?"

"I don't…"

"Yeah, I forgot you're not big on coffee. Tea'll be fine."

Peter raised himself slowly, thinking of his last cup of coffee during a long storm at sea: instant coffee in a white plastic cup in the lifeguard hut facing the beach. Sharp zigzagged grooves around the top half of the cup but his hand would not hold it. A splash. A stomach turning smell of instant coffee mixed with damp towels and salt, mixed with pain in his head, how his head had hurt then as he listened to the creep of glistening coffee over concrete as the wind howled around the walls of the hut.

In the kitchen Peter stared at the stovetop, forgetting why he was there. Tom had followed him in and was studying the shelves. "You like to cook," Tom said, flicking a stack of nested pans. "A domestic urge, eh? Ever thought of settling down?"

"I'm pretty settled now." Peter's eyes found the kettle.

"You know what I mean—wife, kids..."

Ignoring Tom, he took the kettle to the sink.

"Still looking for the right person, I guess."

Peter filled the kettle and lit the gas.

"You'll find her one of these days—if I can, anyone can...though maybe," Tom added, lifting up a saucepan lid, "she found me." He stared into the pan and dropped the lid back with a cymbal-like clash. "Anyhow," he said, turning to Peter. "Tell me about Friday."

"Friday," Peter repeated, leaning against the stove. He looked out the window. The sky was a deep blue. He felt distinctly unwell. "On Friday," he said, "I sat on a bench and watched the river. It's frozen at the moment. Very flat."

"Come again?"

"The ice. It makes the river look—"

"You're telling me you didn't show?"

Peter gave the slightest nod, although even that much hurt.

"What the—" Tom dug a hand into his hair. "This was the interview of interviews. Might I ask why?"

"I couldn't put on an act." Peter played with a button on the cuff of his shirt. "I mean, I could have said I didn't know the answer yet, or argued like a lawyer knowingly skewing the truth. But I couldn't. The fact is, I just can't lie."

"I'm not following you."

"Everything repeats," Peter said, pulling a loose thread. "The same thing happens every time."

"Jeez, you could at least have given it a chance, let them be the ones to decide!"

"It's hardly their decision, is it?" The button bounced across the floor. He watched, unaccountably helpless, as Tom chased after it and pounced.

"Look, maybe we should go sit down again," Tom said, handing the button back. He turned the burner off. Peter followed him compliantly and dropped back onto the chair he had just left.

"What exactly is going on?" Tom asked, sitting down opposite.

Tom's lack of comprehension was exhausting. "The fact is," Peter said, "I'm thirty-five years old and going nowhere." The smell of sawdust was strong. "What's the point in coming up with cool hypotheses when every good idea I have is wrong?"

"Man," Tom said. "What's gotten into you?"

Peter was starting to wonder whether, like all those other ideas, his latest theory—conceived as he watched the geese walk single file across the snow-flocked ice—would also turn out to be wrong. Even now the logic of his bold decision was starting to slip. He tried to explain:

"I'm tainted," he said. "Last time I dropped out I wasn't even knowingly wrong, and no one wanted me. Now I *am* wrong. I can't vindicate my model, and the overblown vengeance that was driving me no longer matters, so really what's the point? I thought if I could make it to the next rung, to tenure track, then there'd be time to come up with something new that *would* be worthwhile. But it was already set in stone, I guess. Everything has come full circle. It's too late. I've shot myself down again, which only goes to show that it was never meant to be. I'm sorry, Tom—truly I am."

"Sorry about what? About screwing up your future time and time again?" Tom stood up and strode across the room. "After all that work, all that goddamn effort!"

"I know. It's all gone to waste, and that's why I'm really done this time."

"Your brilliant intellect," Tom, yelled. "That's what's gone to waste." He crossed the room again, his unceasing motion causing Peter's head to spin. "Jesus," he said, suddenly close. "You spent half of last week puking. Why didn't you tell them you were sick?"

"I wasn't any longer." Peter closed his eyes. "If you saw the mice yourself, you'd understand."

"You told me—the first lot was contaminated. Though if you'd actually checked the—"

"It wasn't contaminated. I started from scratch the second time and it's the same: They're dropping like flies."

"For Christ's sake, a harmless vector can't be killing the mice. And besides, you saw my data from the first—"

"I don't have to see it to know."

"So you didn't see it. Man, I typed it all up, took me hours. Printed it out and…where the hell did it go? I was going to call you, but what with the grant renewal—"

Peter could feel the waves of Tom's deep concern. "Don't worry," he said. "I know it's a lost cause."

"Not necessarily. If you saw—"

"All those corpses," Peter said. "And the ones that were still breathing, fighting for life, how could I— Oh God," he gasped, opening his eyes. "I should have euthanized them." He had thought he was done, was metaphorically free and clear but he had forgotten about the ones that had not died. "They're still down there," he said. "I should get back—"

"Get a hold of yourself." Tom had come close. "You've gotten it all wrong,"

But Peter knew that. Of course he had gotten it all wrong. They had been right to ignore his model. And his paper. He wished no one had read it, wished it had never been published; then he would not have seen it on that desk, and would not stopped to look, and would never have noticed the woman who had looked so sad today, and he still wished he could have—

"Look, if I'm not deceived," Tom said, and then said something more, but Peter knew he had been deceived. Deceived by his equations and his predictions in the paper on her desk that day; and by that double-crossing Sarah and her sweet earnest smile; and by his cousin and her friend in Wales, because they *had been* yelling for help, whatever they said about him being confused, priming everyone with lies before he recovered enough to defend himself; and even when he did, those girls—front-page heroes of the day before—had insisted that he was still confused, said they had categorically told him to stay on the beach and that he had refused.

"...So at least in that respect it all makes sense."

Peter opened his eyes. His attention was jagged, and Tom's words made no sense. He was definitely confused. And maybe he had been confused then, too, recovering as he was from hypothermia, suspected concussion and an advanced state of shock. Maybe. But then why did he remember it so vividly? It was almost as if it was happening again as he listened to Tom: the wind, the waves, the rain; the weeds blowing inside out along the side of the hut—and he felt again the nausea and the pain.

He had liked the rain. And it had rained every day of that

visit to South Wales. In truth he had been looking forward to visiting monastic ruins and medieval castles on that once-in-a-lifetime trip, but there had been no room in the car. His parents, aunt and uncle, and Eric—who had been too young to care—had driven off and left to himself to explore on foot the lanes and woods and cliff-top trails, amidst nature let loose. Often gales had swept in, sculpting their ever changing moods on the transmigrating clouds, and on that especially tempestuous day he had walked down to the bay for no other reason than to watch the quarrelsome sky and the detonating waves.

They had found him there by chance, or so they maintained. He had been standing on the rocks facing the waves, when he heard the crunch of tires on the gravel behind him. At the slap-slap of car doors, he had turned around and seen Fran—his distant one-year-older cousin, plump and pretty in a soft pale way—and her voluptuous best friend, Kim. Dressed in skin-tight neoprene, they had bounced toward him and he had thought about the night before, when the parents were out and the girls helped themselves—and him—to gin and Vermouth. Two against one: what else could he have done?

His teenage hormones had surged. He had taken a deep breath and looked up at the promontory with its steep limestone sides. And seen someone looking down. My alter ego, he had thought—inexplicably, because it looked like a girl. And a part of him had ached to be up there too, elevated by the cliffs, raised above the surging swell that even down there on the rocks made his adolescent appetite seem sordid and small. His ego, however, was trapped on the beach; he was sixteen years old and male, and so he had stayed where he was.

All the same, he had laughed off Fran's suggestion that he join them in the waves. "Look," she had said, dragging him back

217

to the wagon. "We've brought our mini surf ski too, just for you." Surfing was not his thing, he had said; he was from Massachusetts and not California; and yes, he was a lifeguard, but back home it was warm, and he had no wetsuit, neither there nor here. Fran had called him a wimp, said she would go and fetch her Dad's, and he had told them that if he had been on patrol, he would have kept them ashore. But he was not on patrol—as they had made quite clear—although he had felt he was each time he watched them paddle out, keeping his eyes on their receding forms and listening with trepidation to their shrieks as they washed up, time and time again, far too close to the rocks.

Sometimes a kayak capsized as it came slanting in against a wave—or the semblance of a wave as the surf lost its shape. The clouds thickened, darkening the swell, but the girls remained undeterred even by the deepening troughs that formed between increasingly untidy crests. The rain picked up and Peter climbed the rusted lookout chair, but even from that height he could not always see them as the wave fronts toyed with their small kayaks. He thought of the neat parallel waves Old Cross had generated in class using pulsating propagators, the tidy interference patterns where two sets of waves met. He searched for signs of those patterns but instead saw one of the kayaks too far out and upside down; when the slow swell rose again, the other kayak was over too, and two tiny dark heads bobbed between the upturned hulls.

He held his breath and watched, waiting, hoping they would help each other, right the kayaks, climb back in. Idiots, he thought. Surely now they would give up. He, for one, was getting cold. He waved both arms, and when at last they looked his way kept one arm raised high, the unambiguous signal among lifeguards to come ashore. One of them waved in return. Were they stupid, or what? Or were they just saying farewell? He could leave, of course; he wanted to leave. But his training as a lifeguard obliged him to stay.

A sound slipped by him on the wind, obscured by deafening surf. They were both waving at him now. Farewell, or...they might not be lifeguards, but maybe they knew that one arm waved back and forth was the signal for help. Were they yelling for help, too? The sound rushed past him again, not clear enough to be sure, but also not clear enough to rule anything out. He tried to tell himself that they were fine; they had said they did this all the time, and probably they did. His heart was pounding. He had forgotten to breathe. And he was angry. With them. For doing this to him. For being in distress. And he realized he was scared. He had never dealt with a real life incident, not even back home. And now he was alone. Every decision was up to him. There was no room for doubt or hesitation. Terrified, he grappled for the rubrics and rules they had learned in class. And that, it seemed, was the key: as soon as he had caged the unraveling moment with the secure framework of established theory, his fear disappeared.

Call for help, he had thought, and ran back to the padlocked lifeguard hut and circled its stone walls. He was looking for a pay phone, any phone, but did not know where to look—or even, he realized, what their pay phones looked like. He had to act fast. Safety first, he reminded himself, cupping his hands against smeared window glass. On the far wall inside was a clock, its hands askew, but no sign of a phone. He turned around and saw the car, the enclosed ski, and breathed again—Fran had given him her keys. Flinging open the rear door, he hauled out the ski, hoisted it onto one shoulder, grabbed the paddle and made his way down the rocky tumbling slope.

Stepping into a froth of broken waves, he let the ski fall. The boulder under his right foot tipped, and he was under the ski, thigh grazed by salt-stung pain that was instantly numbed by the needling cold and so he climbed up and on and held the paddle tight—as tight as he held onto the knowledge of what he simply had to do. In a fury he paddled across the liquid corrugations, meeting head on—as he knew he must—the rapidly rising concave wall of an oncoming wave. Momentarily lost, he surfaced—salt-blind, lungs waterlogged, wind sucking life from his limbs and pushing against him like an airless cushion—and fought forward with his paddle against the straightjacket of his soaked long-sleeved shirt. There was no time to breathe before the next wave was upon him; and on it went, on he went—up, down and through—tossed about by a swell that lifted him, abandoned him part way to fall, landing prematurely with a spine-jarring smack as it rose again…until suddenly there was Fran, almost close enough to touch.

"We knew we'd get you out here," Fran shrieked. "Now how about you tow our kayaks back? We're body-surfing in!"

They are laughing, he had thought, wanting to speak but his features would not move. He had watched Kim tie her kayak onto his.

"Don't just sit there or you'll freeze," she had said, and he had looked at his clenched hands, numb and fused with the paddle, knuckles white.

"Come on," Fran had said. "It's all in fun—Whoops! Look out for the…"

And he was in, gasping salt-water, wet denim dragging him down, plastering his limbs that would not move as the sky turned and the world's surface tipped—

"…I reckon you'll be fine."

Peter opened his eyes. Tom was grinning at him. He did not feel fine at all—felt the undertow sucking from below and the thwack of Kim's kayak on his skull as it spun around, and the last thing he saw was the grey sky shrinking in a liquid aperture—

"...I'm telling you, there was nothing," Tom was saying and Peter, too, remembered nothing: nothing to hold, no leverage, nothing to breathe, only darkness, leaden pressure on his limbs, on his torso as the water's surface floated up and away as he sank, lungs compressed and bursting in the panic of impending doom. Until, all of a sudden, there was no need to fight. There was nothing but serenity. It had entered and possessed him and he had felt himself let go. Nothing mattered any more. The weight of water pressed in from all sides, he could not have moved if he had tried, but there was no need to try; all limits had melted, all boundaries gone, he was one with the sea, and it was quiet and calm, and it would all be all right, he was escaping the bonds of time, there was no need to breathe, he was calm and relieved, and he began to understand something, anything, everything if he could only—

Only hands were grasping at him, pulled him back, voices yelling, wave crests churning, skull shattering—

"...So it's just as well you hung onto them," Tom said, shaking his arm amidst the roar of the swell as he broke the surface gasping, head exploding, someone's arm around his neck as he struggled, fought it off, a paddle thrust against his chest, barring the truth once and for all as he was dragged by them, half drowned, toward the shore, feeling cheated and confined by the trivial nature of things corporeal.

"...You'll be fine," he thought he heard Tom say again.

"You'll be fine," they had said then as well. He had lain beached beside a salt-damp crevice and watched a whelk slowly rotate. He would have liked to stay there watching the whelk rotate, but they had made him stand up. "You had us scared for a moment there," Fran had yelled. And with Kim on his other side they had helped him up the rocks that swung wildly with every step because no surface was flat, it was no different from the sea, worsening the queasiness, the pain in his head that seemed unsettlingly real as he watched Tom say again that he knew he would be fine.

"You'll be fine," they had assured him again when he came in from the rain. He had joined them in the porch of the hut into which they fled after, gathering up his last ounce of strength, he had cast off their combined embrace and staggered to its back wall. "Oh lovely," he had heard one of them moan as the contents of his stomach poured through the grating of a drain. He should have felt much better then, but he did not— still did not as he remembered following them around, his head hurting just as it was now. "You went out for the fun of it," Fran had added, filling his line of sight, making him look into her eyes. "You didn't realize it would be so cold. Or else…or else just say it never happened, that you fell in off the rocks and got wet."

But Peter had wanted to watch the rain fall behind her in dense wind-ripped sheets. He was shivering, head splitting in two, and Fran's purple lips were making curious shapes. Lips that only the night before she had offered him so sweetly, so charmingly, so pleasantly. He had watched her teeth come and go between those lips—small yellow plaque-dulled teeth—and wondered why he had not noticed them last night. Then some-one had unlocked the hut, and they had brought him hot coffee. As if the coffee might have helped. A scalding splash and he was curled up on the ground, listening to liquid creep on concrete as the smell of instant coffee and damp salt mingled with confusion and visceral emptiness—

Someone was talking. Tom was still there. He should tell Tom he was sick. Or was he cursed? Fran had cursed him. Later, maybe the next day or the day after, she had thought he was asleep and had said he would rot in hell. She need not have feared; no harm had been done, no one had listened to him anyway. By the time he had told his version, theirs was set in dry black ink on every newsstand in the Vale: *LOCAL GIRLS RESCUE YANKEE BOY.*

"…And that way we'll know what's going on," Tom was saying. But Peter was not sure what was going on. Perhaps the journalist had been right: *An American teenager ran into trouble after paddling out from Llanmaer Bay during yesterday's storm.* That much was true. *He had no life vest, wet suit or knowledge of our notorious tides.* That part was also mostly true. *"He was lucky that the girls were there," head coastguard M. B. told the press*…and Peter was, indeed, lucky they had been there; in the end they had rescued him. Yes, that was true. And what if the girls *had* needed help? Where would they be now? Where would any of them be now?

"…Tomorrow morning, then." Tom stood up. "Peter?" Tom's face had come close. "What's gotten into you?"

"Sorry, I must have drifted off. My head—it's…" Peter winced at the pain in his neck as he rose from his seat.

"Stress. You've been under too much stress. It's clearly gotten to you. Kiddo, you'll be fine." Tom slapped him on the back. "Get some rest now and you'll see what I mean—and we'll run through this again in the morning before you get going. Say nine o'clock?"

Peter grimaced his assent.

"I'll see myself out," Tom said, picking up his bag of untouched dumplings. Peter stood up, slowly following.

"Any light to help me on my way?" Tom inquired from the landing, but he must have found a switch: light exploded behind Peter's eyes and he recoiled in alarm as Tom called out a last farewell. Every step of Tom's hasty descent sent an agonizing tremor up the stairs and Peter's spine. He had never known such stiffness in his neck, such bodily wretchedness. He might have called Tom back—perhaps he did—but heard only a rattle-slam down in the hallway below. Then there was silence. Peter backed inside around his own front door, not quite ready for its easy response to his indifferent weight or the compact snap of the latch.

Chapter Twenty

ALICE WANTED to stay home. She needed time for her hair to grow, or at least time to get used to it—and to her self-imposed fresh start. Worse still, the rain and sleet of the previous evening had frozen overnight and the sidewalks were slick. She had started to bike in again, but when she saw the icy varnish took her bicycle back in, and might have stayed there herself if she had not promised Sage that she would help with his experiment. Buoyed also by the long-awaited prospect of working with LCMV, if only peripherally, she set off cautiously on foot.

When at last she reached her building, tense and tired from the long enforced slow shuffle, she opened the door and then stepped back to make way for someone coming out. That some-one turned out to be Dee. And Dee was not alone. Her hand clasped another hand—a hand Alice had thought she would know anywhere, but did not recognize at all. She had never seen that hand before, or that arm, or that pale young man dressed exclusively in black.

"Thanks, Alice," Dee said, flashing a wide smile. "Hey, you've cut your hair short—that's so cool! And this here is Jed—I was showing him the lab." She turned to look at Jed. "What do you think about me cutting off all *my* hair?" she asked and nudged his thin arm. Jed's heavy-lidded eyes took in Alice and returned to Dee, who pulled him away from the entrance and nuzzling up close, limbs entwined, they promenaded down the salt-strewn steps in a private minuet.

Alice leaned against a pillar of the portico. Interpretations rearranged. Because whatever Dee had been doing in Peter's lab that night, it had nothing to do with love.

Duncan hurried up the steps, not seeing—or perhaps not wanting to see—Alice. She watched the doors close behind him. When he was long gone, she followed him in. Too cold to stay outside but not yet ready to face anyone in this glaring new light, she took advantage of the vacant restroom near the first floor elevators. Locking herself in, she sat down on the cold tiled floor in the dark, her mind a ramifying void without her false conception of Peter Young. For two whole weeks she had interpreted everything he did on the basis of one hasty and insecure assumption, and that assumption was wrong. Groping her way through compounded errors, she saw with shame that time after time she had been hostile to a blameless bystander, while she went to such great lengths to please a cheating fraud like Dan. And still Peter had been kind. She almost cried, thinking of the previous night when he had seemed so concerned even though he had looked so tired and pale himself, so weary and cowed when she shunned him yet again—because even her own senseless actions begot reactions, of course.

Someone tried the handle of the door. Alice leapt to her feet. She switched on the light and ran the tap. The sight of her hair in the mirror startled her anew. It was really very short. And plain. And she had forgotten to put on earrings, distracted as she had been by the braid still lying like a small dead mammal on the edge of the bathroom sink, its severed end unraveling. Leaning closer to the restroom mirror, she thought of the satisfying crunch of steel on hair as she had hacked last night, the satisfaction of liberating the countercurrent that immediately took charge, sweeping back from her hairline like a partly broken wave. Tracing its path now, she understood what Grandma had meant when she had asked, long ago, what she was trying to hide. No wonder it had made no difference when she later grew out that long fringe, carefully cultivated to weigh down and disguise the cowlick—which, long after she first learned its name, she had thought meant she had been licked by a cow. Grandma had been talking about false personas and hiding behind façades.

I'm done with hiding now, she thought, splashing cold water on her face. Though with this haircut, she observed as she dried her hands, there would be nothing to hide from anyway, she looked so ridiculous. No one would look at her twice—not even kind Peter Young—and that was what she deserved.

She opened the door and stepped into the hallway as if nothing were amiss. Except that instead of turning left toward the stairs, she turned right into the dim-lit corridor. Her new and candid self was going to be forthright. And what better place to start than by apologizing to the victim of her cold ingratitude— even if it meant crushing his illusions about her once and for all.

As if by way of punishment, delaying fulfilment of her penance, Peter Young's laboratory was dark. His door was closed. He was not there. Then again, Alice thought, it was still early— barely gone nine. She could try again later. Perhaps. If she could think of what to say. Or perhaps not—perhaps she ought to stay away. Perhaps she had already done him enough harm.

AS ALICE CROSSED the fifth floor landing, the elevator doors slid open and Helen stepped out.

"Hi!" Alice said, abruptly remembering where Helen had been. Their recent conversation seemed a lifetime ago. "How was your trip?" she asked.

"Caught the red-eye—too much to do… But do tell me all about it—I'm delighted! What wonderful news! Of course you're welcome to stay here as long as you wish. I can see the project blossoming in so many ways."

"You like the idea?" Alice's spirits rose.

"Well, of course." Helen touched Alice's arm. "I've made a few discrete inquiries," she said, leaning close, "and there's a real chance that we can publish back-to-back with Zhou if we wrap it up soon."

"Zhou? He's working on Sharden's?" This was a surprise. And Alice was hardly ready to publish anything yet.

"No, no. The receptor-signal studies."

"Wait, I thought we were the only ones—" Alice was having to think fast.

"Same answer, different approach. But Alice, I'm so glad your interests lie over here, you're such an asset to my lab."

"Thanks! In fact, that's sort of what I was hoping to talk to you about: my interests."

"Come along with me then, we'll sit down quickly before I get swamped."

"What I actually have in mind," Alice said as she caught up, "is to pick up the Sharden's hypothesis you don't want. Just as a sideline, of course, while I do what needs doing with Ken's project. That way, I could start carving out my own niche and write my own proposal without encroaching on any of *your* ideas."

Helen had stopped walking. She turned to Alice, quite transformed. "No. No-no-no. I told you I wasn't interested. I do not like to find my lab and its resources being used for other people's gain—beside which, it's not Ken's project any more than it's yours."

"But I would still be—"

"Look, you have no hard evidence, no track record in Sharden's—who's going to take you seriously anyway? You're here to work for me." Helen glared at her, incredulous. "It's a cut-throat world out there. Every person for himself—and especially for *her*self—and that, of course, includes me. Besides, this sudden change of plan dumps responsibility for your future on me—"

"No, I—"

"—and that's something I can't afford to take in these difficult times. You saw what happened with Ken. You came here on the understanding that you were going back, that you more-or-less had a job. I made it clear that I had nothing to give away when this came up with Ken. All my projects and their offshoots are mine, and that's how it's going to stay."

"But that's the whole point. I was trying to explain—"

"Richard is furious. I assume you're aware of that. He was counting on you. Now he's turned the blame on me. However, I am not about to bow to anyone's pressure to start giving out a reagent that I've spent the better part—"

"But I'm not asking you to, I—"

"Incidentally," Helen said with sudden warmth, "I've been meaning to warn you. Funds are looking unexpectedly tight and I'll only be able to keep you on while your fellowship lasts." She began to walk on. Alice stayed where she was, feeling as if she had smashed her head against an invisible brick wall.

Helen stopped and turned back. "Listen," she said, seemingly sincere. "I have to stay afloat. No one's looking out for me, either. Please understand how it has to be." Then her expression changed. "Tell me," she said in mock-confusion. "What did you do to your hair?"

SHORTLY AFTER NOON, Sage shuffled in. Alice had been waiting for him all morning, though she had taken advantage of the delay to tidy her bench, tossing tube after tube of decayed cells into the trash. She had also been wondering whether to cut her losses and go home for the wedding in August and never come back.

"Where've you been?" she asked, peering through the shelves. "If you think Helen has it in for *you*— Wow, you look terrible!" she said, catching sight of him. "What's wrong?"

Sage had slumped into his chair and looked desperately pale. "*Never drink alone*," he said. "That's what my dad always says. I guess he has a point."

"Sage, be careful. What about Bill?"

"Off at some retreat in New York. Learning about substance abuse by high-achieving teens—as if he can't get his fill of that at home. Not back until tomorrow around five."

Alice did not like the edge in his voice. "You should have called," she said.

"It wouldn't have helped. Unless you can wave a magic wand and turn me into a scientist." He snickered unpleasantly.

"We were going to set up the LCMV experiment today. Remember? I'm sure we'll figure out what's going wrong."

"Yeah, right. God, I'm so tired of trying when I know I'm going to fail." Sage let his head fall back and stared up at the maze of pipes and shafts hanging above the lab.

"You're still drunk."

Sage shrugged.

"We could leave it until tomorrow," Alice said. In fact, it

might be better if we did." Better, she thought, if they gave up altogether. Except that here, at least, was a way to get back at Helen, by showing that Sage was capable—and if they were very, very lucky, by generating results that were unambiguously irrelevant to self-tolerance or whatever Helen wanted to show. Except that then they would not vindicate Sage, she realized, reining in her thoughts.

Sage righted himself. "Sorry," he said. "I'm being a jerk. No, let's get it over with for what it's worth. A quick shot of coffee'll set me right—I swear I'm not all that far gone." He rubbed his face vigorously. "By the way, you look great," he said, relaxing into grin. "The hair. It looks really cool. You look like—well, you look like yourself."

TEN MINUTES LATER, Alice and Sage were shrouded head-to-toe, almost indistinguishable in their laundered blue robes, facemasks, shoe-coverings and caps. Before pulling on his gloves, Sage typed four digits on the keypad of the well-secured facility. Then, in silence, they padded down the gleaming corridor and let themselves into the cell-like room assigned to Helen. Alice searched through the cage tags for the mice reserved by Sage, while Sage wiped down the surface of the sterile hood. He flipped the switch of the small water bath in its far corner and then fetched a small white box from the freezer by the door.

"Shit," he said, opening the box. "There's only one tube left. There should be at least three."

"Oh. Then maybe we should wait? I really don't mind."

"Nah, we'll make do. This way you can watch me grow up more and tell me what I'm doing wrong there, too." He stopped and looked at Alice. "Especially since you're such an expert," he said.

"I'm not an expert at all," she said, taken aback. "But I'd like to watch you culture it, learn how it's done."

Sage looked away, making her wonder all the more what Helen had said to him the other night, and why. Then he peered into the hood.

"Man," he said, reaching in with one arm. "The water bath's still eff-ing cold." He flipped the switch again, and back, and checked the outlet in the wall. "Jeez." He tried the other outlet. "Still no sign of frigging life. Here, hold this," he added, handing Alice the tube as he picked up the receiver of the phone on the wall. "Let me just call Dee and see what's going on."

Alice stared at the small tube in her palm.

"Make a fist around it," Sage said, eyes on the tube. "Body heat'll speed up the thaw."

"It has a snap-cap lid," Alice said.

"Yeah.... Yes, I know it's not ideal," Sage added after a short pause. "I do usually use screw cap tubes, but there were none around that day—these were the only ones we found." He dialed the lab, five cheerful electronic beeps. "I know, I know," he said as the phone rang dimply on the other end. "They could pop open. It wasn't the best idea. Just as well we're thawing this one slowly, then. Look, put your hand in the hood if you're worried— Dee? Hi, it's Sage in the virus room. You know, the water bath's not working down here.... You might have said something—that was weeks ago! Anyhow, I thought you never actually set that one up, so what happened to all the tubes? I only have one."

Alice examined the tube in her gloved hand.

"You did?" Sage said. "So why didn't you just inject the mice?"

A thin black *V* was penned on top of each small lid. What

on earth did that mean? Had no one ever told Sage to be explicit when labeling tubes? And especially when it came to actual bio-hazards…

"Who had gone? You mean you left them floating around in some random guy's lab? Didn't I tell you we had to do it all down here?"

Some random guy? Alice stopped breathing.

"Yes, but that's not the point…. Never mind, it's too late now. Just tell me what's going on next time, OK?" Sage set back the phone.

First one simple assumption had been shattered. Now Alice understood exactly what Dee had been doing in Peter's lab. Once more, interpretations rearranged—this time with knife-edge precision. Too late now? Alice was afraid.

"Sage, this causes meningitis and/or encephalitis," she said.

"What?"

"That's what LCMV does to people—Lymphocytic chorio-*meningitis* virus."

"I know. I do know. But only when you lick it or inhale it or whatever. That's why we do the work down here, wear gloves and—" Sage blanched. "She only left them floating around, didn't open them or anything like that." He glanced at the snap-cap tube. "And it's not as if everyone gets symptoms even if they *are* infected." He was speaking hurriedly now, as if his words might forestall anything bad.

"I guess not," Alice said doubtfully. She thought of Peter in the library, head in his hands. "Just a splitting headache," he had said. And the next day, when she collided with him downstairs—

"It's hardly ever fatal," Sage urged with pained enthusiasm. "Less than one percent."

Less than one percent. Half the time there might be several

233

days of remission before the photophobia, the stiff neck or worse. Where was he this morning? Did he always come in late? It might of course have been nothing, the way he pressed his hand to his head last night, looked so pale, washed out and wan. It might have been nothing.

"What's the matter, Alice?"

"Wait here, I just need to make sure that he's OK."

"Who?"

"The guy whose lab she left the tubes in."

"How on earth do you know—?"

"I just know."

THE FIRST FLOOR corridor was empty, until the woman with a snake tattoo who had been reading Sage's palm stepped out of a side-door holding a bucket full of ice.

"Excuse me, do you know where Peter Young is?" Alice asked, feeling herself flush as she said his name out loud.

"In his lab?" The woman seemed to think this obvious.

"It's empty—and dark."

The woman moved with Alice back to his door.

"No idea then. I've not seen him today. Not that that means anything. It's locked?" She tried the handle and peered in. "Go ask Elaine," she said. "The secretary. He's probably at a conference or whatever, I really don't know."

You also don't care, Alice thought. The woman headed through another side-door, looking back before it closed to tell Alice to keep going to the far end of the corridor and turn right. Alice did as she was told, continuing on toward an open doorway in which a woman in blue scrubs stood with a phone to her ear.

"No, he can't be dead!" the woman wailed as Alice drew

near, scattering the words like bullets of despair before spinning around and slamming the door. Alice turned right to the sound of muted sobs and saw a middle-aged woman sitting upright at a desk—portly, comfortable, concerned—looking anxiously her way. She recognized the woman from the parking lot, so cozy in her car.

"Poor Josie," the woman said as Alice approached. "One of her patients again, I think. She cares so very much." She turned for confirmation to a young man standing behind her trying to send a fax. He nodded in sympathy. The office filled with a collective sigh.

Then the woman smiled at Alice. "May I help you?" she asked.

"I'm looking for Peter Young." Alice's face burned again.

"Not in his lab down the hall there?"

"Most likely still at home," said the man at the fax machine. "I called him up earlier—kind of." He smirked at Elaine. "Woke him up, I guess—sounded like someone had a rough night. I still have no clue where he stashed the enzymes that came in last week. Was he incoherent, or what?"

Elaine frowned. "That doesn't sound like Peter." The young man rolled his eyes. Then a door to the right, which had been standing ajar, flew open and Tom Dannet stepped out. Alice was struck dumb. To her immense relief he showed no sign of recognizing her. Slouching amiably against a shelf, he looked from face to face.

"This is Peter we're discussing? He should have been here at nine." His pale eyes homed in on Alice. "What do you want him for, if you don't mind my asking?" His tone was civil, almost warm.

Alice hesitated. It was possible that she was wrong. "It's…it's about some tubes containing a virus," she said. "It's just that someone from my group them in his lab a couple of…"

"Well, I can easily let you in and you can try to find them." He held up a bunch of keys and flipped them over one by one.

"It was over two weeks ago," she said. "The fact is—"

Tom Dannet's eyes narrowed, the keys were still.

"The fact is, she left them in the water bath, and they were snap-cap tubes, and it's an encephalitogenic virus—LCMV. It's often asymptomatic and it's not contagious man to man or anything but—"

"LCMV?" Tom Dannet stared at Alice, his eyes now wide. "Jesus Christ," he said. "Here, give me the phone, Elaine. Peter's number?" Elaine ran her finger down a list pinned to the wall and read off ten digits. Silence all around.

"Peter. Peter, this is Tom." He spoke clearly, as if to a child.

"Damn," Tom said, staring at Elaine. "He's dropped the phone or something. Listen, Peter," he shouted. "Peter, are you listening? You may be very sick. I'll be over there in ten minutes. Can you open the door, Peter? Peter?"

"Jesus Christ," he gasped to Elaine and replaced the receiver clumsily. "Come with me," he said to the young man at the fax machine man, grabbing his sleeve. "Dial 9-1-1, Elaine. Have them meet me over there right now!" Then Tom and the young man were gone.

Chapter Twenty-One

PETER PANICKED, trying to wake up. Someone was knocking. But he was caught between two intersecting phase planes and could not get out. A steady state ran down his spine and disappeared as variables diverged and he was dragged along the wrong trajectory—and then he crashed into an intersect he had not known was there, because someone was still knocking, rattling the door, and Violet was shrieking again, he had to get up, give her food, let them in, make them go, but the pianist's arms were caging him, constraining him, her face far too close so he only saw her teeth, small teeth dulled by yellow plaque as two separate pasts converged and frantic words were drowned out by the sound of shattering glass.

Shattering glass, nausea and pain, this wretched ache in his head, all come full circle again in another loop of repetition, because everything repeats, bad things always reproduce, and someone had his jaw, pain was shooting up his spine, through his neck and it was time to escape, get away from this predictability, and he was burning, so hot, if he could only dive in, sink, melt beneath the leaden pressure, if he could only let go, but they would not let him go, they were circling, confining him, trapping him with words, detaining him with meaning he could not make out except for when they said his name, again and again, as they touched and grabbed his limbs, making him struggle all the more, which only made it more unpleasant and more painful and persistent as he rose on the swell, spinning, lurching, rising, falling, sinking, finally sinking beneath an ocean of glorious weight that compressed him like his chainmail vest that dissolved his body, soothed the heat, quenched the pain in dark calm velvet waves and—

And then he saw an image of the woman with grey eyes, grey like the reassuring sea in which he was sinking and he tried to cling to the image, cling to her, but she was too far away. He tried to call to her, beg her to stay—but then he realized he could not, because he did not know her name.

Chapter Twenty-Two

DUSK FELL. The lab was quiet—far too quiet. Sage was not there and Alice did not know where he was. She had set aside all day for his experiment, but by the time she went back to the animal room he was no longer there and she had not seen him since. Which was probably for the best, she thought. She could not have focused anyway—could barely even think beyond the dead weight of her dread as she watched the lights of the chimney tower pulsate.

Dee walked in, still chattering with someone who had stayed in the corridor. Their laughter sounded incongruous, even obscene. Alice thought about interrupting to tell Dee what she had done. But to put it into words seemed too final and definitive. Alice still held out hope that she was wrong, that Peter Young was fine. There was always hope until you knew the facts for sure.

Soon, though, the useless repartee stoppering the lab felt like a mockery of Alice's ignorance, hermetically sealing her from the truth. She might be worrying about nothing, but might alternatively not be worrying enough. Taking a deep breath, she stood up, crossed the room and, eyes down, plunged through the bond between Dee and her friend. Then she turned into the corridor, heading toward the stairs on her way to find Elaine. However, on her way past the office, she saw none other than Tom Dannet standing in Helen's doorway, arms spread across the frame like Samson trying to raze the walls. Before Alice could collect herself, he had thrust himself back, turned around and stepped into her path.

"Comatose," he said, stopping far too close. "Hooked up to all sorts of drips if that's what you want to know."

"I'm so sorry," Alice said, terrified by his demeanor as well as by his words. She stood there, paralyzed, while he plowed toward the elevator, stared for a moment at the lifeless button, glanced at Alice as if it were her fault, and then dove with abandon for the stairs.

FROM THE COFFEE ROOM, Alice watched the sun setting luminously pink on the windows of downtown. By the time she went back to her desk, Dee had gone and no one else was around. She imagined them all having supper, watching television, doing whatever people did when they went home. There was still no sign of Sage. Outside, the beacons on the chimney tower flashed their solemn vigil over the windows of the wards. Peter Young was somewhere over there.

At the sound of footsteps in the corridor, Alice stood up. The footsteps stopped outside the lab. If it was Sage, she wondered if he knew, if she would have to explain and cement reality once and for all. She was almost relieved when Tom Dannet appeared instead.

"Hi," he said, still near the door. He seemed unusually hesitant, stooping to peer through a gap in the shelves. "I wasn't sure if this was the right lab."

Alice held her breath, fearing the worst.

"You're working late," he said, picking up an empty bottle Dee had left by the sink. He scanned the label, set it down. "Listen, I apologize if I, uh…intimidated you earlier. And," he added with a grin that dispelled any lingering terror, "it finally occurred to me that we've met before. The hair, I guess. I do believe it's changed." He clenched his own grey mane and strode across the lab into Alice's bay.

"Anyhow, I've just been over there again," he said, perching on her desk as if he had known her for years and she took a step back. "They think he'll be all right. Supportive therapy—that's all they can do for now but his condition's stabilizing."

"I'm so glad!" Alice's heart beat was deafening.

"So am I. And you know what? I've forgotten your name."

"Alice—Alice Gaines."

Tom leaned forward and took her hand. His large grip was secure. "You know him well?" he asked, studying her face.

"We've…uh…sort of met." Alice stared at the floor, at a misaligned tile.

"Ah. Well, don't let him put you off. He can be abrupt—asocial, some might say, or even downright rude—"

Alice looked up, astonished by this man. "He's always been pleasant to me," she said, not hiding her disgust.

"I'm glad to hear that," Tom said, hands raised in defense. "I assumed… It's just that not everyone sees beyond that frown. A scar, you know. Right here." Tom pressed his thumb between his own thick eyebrows. "From the chickenpox, he said. Makes him look as if he's brooding even when he's not—though in all honesty he often is these days, because…well that's how he is."

Alice coveted these small personal details, and felt all the more protective of Peter—especially since Tom had no business sharing any of this.

"Man, it's been hell down there all afternoon," Tom said, now dropping into her chair. "My newer postdocs never really warmed to him, and now they're all wracked with guilt. And they're not the only ones. I was so damned sure it was stress, I didn't see the obvious. Just like I was so damned sure that his approach would work... Look, I have a favor to ask you, Alice Gaines. Peter was in the middle of a big experiment involving lymphocytes, and since you're an immunologist and—"

"What?" Alice stared at him, appalled. "Your postdoc's in a coma and you worry about some dumb experiment?"

"Please. Don't get me wrong. It's not dumb at all. Let me back up. He's been working on this for years, conceived his own mathematical model that caused its fair share of suffering at the time, and now, just when he's almost verified its premise experimentally, his goddamn mice start to die when they damn well shouldn't, and he himself gets struck down."

"I'm sorry." Alice fixed her gaze again on the misaligned tile.

"Sorry? If it hadn't been for you, then who knows where he'd be now? In fact, Marion—my wife—I was just telling her what happened here today. She's in the UK right now, by the way." He looked at Alice eagerly.

"Really?" Alice softened a little, but held back from asking exactly where; Britain really was not all that small.

"Yes." Tom looked at her quizzically, and she almost did ask. "Anyhow," he said before she could, "Marion reckons it's fate the way the pieces fell together. She's big on convergence, is Marion—a little too much sometimes, but that's my wife for you." Tom grinned and Alice smiled too; he was missing his wife and she liked him for that.

"But as I was saying," Tom continued, "Peter's gone through a lot for this project. Now, there's only so much anyone can do about whether or not his model holds up, but if I could find a way to help him out meanwhile..." and he told Alice about the premise and the experiments, and the supposedly harmless constructs that were killing the mice. "Obviously we need more data, and of course we can't publish unless we know why the mice are dying. So I thought we could at least make a start by taking inspiration from LCMV."

Alice did not care for this suggested resonance, and tried not to think about Peter's T-lymphocytes killing off his own virus-infected cells. Especially not now that the virus had evidently homed in on his brain. But it did make sense to look at whether his manipulations had somehow changed the way T-cells reacted when they saw the altered construct. "You want to look for T-cell mediated pathology?" she asked.

"Yep. And I'd do it myself, only immunology's not my forte, and I'd hate to screw things up. Anyhow, isn't this what you guys look at the time?"

"Pretty much."

"Can you get something going tonight?"

"Tonight?" Alice was dead tired. "I suppose so—if you know where he keeps his reagents."

"Uh, that's one of the snags. We hadn't exactly anticipated this direction, so if you wouldn't mind..."

"Using our stuff? I'd have to ask Helen. She's really not too keen on us handing out—"

"I don't imagine she is." Tom looked at the clock. "And she'll have gone home by now. But I need this done tonight. Jeez, I have to do something—anything! For pity's sake, don't you? God only knows who could rest easy with him at death's door."

"I thought you said—"

"What does it matter what I said? Look, let's get this started right now—if you can handle a nightshift. I'll talk to Helen myself first thing; and if it comes to it I'll take the blame. Really, this is the least of Helen's problems right now, and I think she'll soon see that she owes Peter this."

Just as I owe him too, Alice thought.

SAGE DID NOT COME IN the next morning and did not pick up his phone. Every couple of hours Helen walked through the lab looking for him. She seemed more annoyed each time he was not there, and did not once meet Alice's eye. Lightheaded from lack of sleep, Alice sustained herself with walks to the coffee room and frequent cups of tea. Rumors reached her in the corridor about labs being closed down, projects placed on hold. In between, she kept herself busy taking care of samples and assays she had set up with Tom, encountering no resistance— or even interest—from Helen. There had been no word from anyone downstairs since the sun rose and Tom disappeared.

At six o'clock, Alice tried Sage again. This time, instead of Sage's answering machine message, she reached an urgent steady beeping. Not sure what else to do, she called Bill's number, which Sage had given her back when she stayed at his place. Bill picked up straight away.

"Is Sage with you?"

"No, but then I only stepped in a few minutes ago." Bill's voice was mellow, his clear elocution calling to mind the word Thespian.

Trying not to sound melodramatic, Alice told him she'd been trying to call to Sage.

"Me too," Bill said. "He hates it when I'm at these off-the-grid retreats. You're sure he's not holed up somewhere at work?"

Bill's tone gave Alice a vicarious glimpse of what it felt like to be loved.

"That's the thing," Alice said. "I haven't seen him since yesterday. Just after lunch."

"You mean he's gone AWOL? Shit. I saw this coming—all that Wild West business. That's why we've been talking about getting away for a couple of weeks. Just as soon as I—"

"Look, I don't know if I should tell you this, but he was already drunk."

"Damn."

"And then something happened here. And I think he might blame himself."

There was a pause. Then Bill spoke in a voice she barely recognized. "He wouldn't go without telling me," he said, sounding like child. "He wouldn't…"

"Maybe we should start by checking his apartment," Alice said, taking control. "I assume you have a key. I'll meet you there right now."

THE HOSPITAL, late at night: Bill pacing the clean floor of the subdued corridor; Alice sitting on a blue plastic chair. Time passed and a kind older nurse came and told them they were doing all they possibly could.

Chapter Twenty-Three

A LARGE VASE of flowers on the windowsill, a closed slatted blind. Twilight or dawn. A hospital. There was a knock on the door. A nurse bringing medication with a "Why, you're awake, hon', how are you feeling? Let me just take your vital signs, check the IVs— yes, that's good, now can I get you anything, hon'?"

Peter looked at her, not sure what he felt, what he was doing there, what was wrong with him, but there were flowers on the windowsill, a card. For him?

"From Elaine," the nurse said, following his gaze. "Your girl?"

He shook his head and a queasy dizziness reminded him of sinking, falling, feeling oh, so sick. He still felt quite sick but in a calm gentle way now in the dim blue light, with the murmur of kind voices in the hall, with the capable bustle of this woman who seemed pleased to see him, there to see to his needs.

"Just press this button here if you want anything," the nurse said cheerily, rearranging the cable of the nurse-call button at his side. Another smile and she was gone. Elaine had sent flowers? He closed his eyes again and slept, and dreamed that he had turned into one of his mice.

*

"FOR TOM DANNET, I presume." Helen sneered at the rack of tubes in front of Alice in the hood.

"No, for your paper," Alice said, telling the truth: various samples for Tom were sticking out of the ice-bucket waiting on her bench.

"I told him it was just this once," Helen said. "You understand that too?"

Alice nodded and then feigned intense concentration as she began to pipette cells. Helen moved off, and was intercepted near the door by a man in a dark suit who shook her hand. The words 'safety committee' traveled across the room. Helen left with the man.

Time passed by the minute. Feeling like an automaton, Alice worked through the remaining steps of the assay, and then went back to staining Tom's chilled cells.

One o'clock. One minute past.

A cup of strong tea, and she started processing the tissue sections Tom had helped her prepare, and then returned to the stained cells. Carefully and systematically back and forth.

Dee arrived. She walked straight over to Alice, who was standing at her desk trying to remember why she had stopped there.

"I was in Maine," Dee said, the whites of her eyes an alarming glassy pink. "I had no idea. I...I'm just so stupid. I'm... Alice, what do we do now?"

Alice had expected to feel only revulsion for Dee. But a lump came to her throat at Dee's use of the plural pronoun. She had not realized how alone she had felt since Tom left at dawn, and the next thing she knew she had put her arms around Dee.

"Thanks," Dee said, hugging her back. "I'm sorry. I really, really am. D'you think he'll be OK?"

"I don't know," Alice said, not sure if Dee meant Peter or Sage, but the answer was the same.

"I'm fired."

"I didn't know that…I'm sorry."

"It's what I deserve." Dee squeezed Alice's arm and left.

Two o'clock.

The telephone rang.

"Alice? It's Tom. Any trouble from your boss?"

"No, not really. How's—"

"Any results yet?"

She was getting used to Tom. "Too soon to say," she said, not entirely lying since she had only ruled out two of five options so far. She wondered if he would have sought her help if he had known her talent for dashing hopes. "How's—"

"Peter? He's looking mighty good—awake and alert, though he's not spoken yet. In fact, if you have a moment," he added, not quite spontaneously, "why not stroll over to the ward with me? It's visiting time."

"Oh, I don't think I should. I mean I really don't know him that well and—"

"I insist. It'll do Peter good,"

In the interest of escaping from Helen, Alice gave in.

TOM LOOKED as if he had not shaved for a week. "I should give you some reprints," he said the moment Alice met him at the bottom of the stairs. "Fill you in on the background to what you're doing for us. Let's stop by my office on our way back." He started to walk.

"Thanks," Alice said, jogging to catch up and wondering if

he had forgotten that this was still Peter's project and not hers. "Though actually, I was going to check on Sage after this."

"Another time, then."

"Sure."

They walked in silence for a while.

"Sage," Tom said with a frown. "How is he?"

"They can't say yet. They think he hit his head quite hard."

"I heard his blood alcohol was astronomically high."

"Well, yes," she said, "but it's still a head injury. He was up on a table trying to take a huge heavy trunk from the top of a closet."

"Still sounds like alcohol to me," Tom said and turned into a windswept alleyway.

Alice bit her lip and followed. Airborne grit hit her face and she raised her hand as a shield.

"I knew he was drunk," she said suddenly. "He had been all weekend. He was miserable. Had been for a while. If I had told someone, done something—I don't know."

"Jeez—cut that out, will you? Who can know everything? It was an accident." He held open a door and she found herself at the back of the hospital lobby. She traipsed behind Tom to the matte steel elevators at the front, where the population density increased, and stood beside him watching the orange glow move haltingly and differentially through each backlit row of numbers.

"He had problems, did he?" Tom asked eventually.

"Only with Helen." Alice turned to look at Tom's expression in case she had said too much. Indeed, his features had stiffened. He seemed about to speak when the elevator doors opened and a flood of passengers spilled out. Alice squeezed in with Tom amidst a blend of visitors and personnel and nothing more was said. The elevator rose, the demographic around them changing drastically, along with the mood, each time the doors opened and closed on a different specialty. Alice's heart raced when they opened on Peter's floor.

A nurse came smiling toward Tom as they walked toward the wards. "I think he's sleeping right now," she said, and murmured something to Tom, who thanked her and then waved at a serious young man wearing scrubs.

"I'll be right back," he said to Alice, "That's my former MD/PhD student."

The nurse, seeing Alice standing abandoned, came back and showed her into Peter's ward.

Peter was, indeed, asleep. Not want to draw attention to herself if he woke up, Alice remained part-hidden behind the open door. She felt awkward being there without his knowledge, as if taking advantage of his compromised position. Yet at the same time it seemed quite natural to watch him sleep, his fine features serene, his thick hair unkempt; and before she knew it, the dark stubble on his chin had kindled something undeniably carnal in her innermost being. Unashamedly she went on watching him.

The back of his lean hand was attached to a drip. Beside his bed, a bag of clear fluid hung at the spiraling top of a shining metal stand. It was attached to a long winding tube that connected to the needle that entered his skin. Pierced by a spindle, Alice found herself thinking. Laid to sleep behind tendrils of tubing, briars of steel that would dissolve into flowers like the ones on the windowsill as she fought her way through to him, casting them aside and—

And Alice froze, startled out of her silly fantasy, wishing she could melt into the door. He had turned his head, and his eyes were wide open and staring into hers. Mortification quenched her delight even before he closed his eyes again. How could she indulge in trifling daydreams, be carried away by inappropriate thoughts when she had no right even to be there, let alone make use of him like that. She took a step back—and bumped up against Tom Dannet, who must have crept up behind her, who knew when.

"Yep, I guess we'd better leave him be," Tom said, making way for her to pass before following her out. She kept her face turned away from him, radiating heat as if caught in an act of extreme indiscretion.

"So you're going on up," Tom said when they reached the elevator. "You know I realize this was not your friend's fault. It's the fault of a growing breed of so-called mentors whose only concern is their own success. Jeez. I don't think Helen gives a damn about what actually happens in her lab as long as you guys get results—I doubt she even thinks of you as people. Mentors like her, they just use you till they have used you up."

Alice turned to him, astonished—and excited, too. She threw propriety to the wind. "Helen asked me to put together a grant proposal," she said. "On Sharden's Syndrome. So I did, and I based it on the most compelling evidence—and she threw it in my face because it didn't fit her preconceived idea."

"She has you write her grants, too? It's worse than I thought." He frowned. "You really think Sharden's is an auto-immune disease?"

"*Helen* does. *I* think it has something to do with bacteria."

"What, virulence factors? Sounds like my kind of thing." Tom pushed back his limp hair.

"Not exactly. More like…well, commensal bacteria that are perfectly benign—if not even advantageous—when they're in the right place. But what if, when they leak into the wrong location, they're not so benign? Such as if gut permeability is compromised as a result of, say—"

The elevator bell pinged, the car going down. "Darn," Tom said. The matte steel doors yawned wide. "I have to go." He stepped inside. "But when you bring me down the data you can tell me more. Sounds like a curious idea."

"OK," Alice said before the doors slid closed, the elevator taking with it the heat of the moment and any chance, Alice thought, of discussing this again.

FROM THE HALLWAY, Alice could see Sage's bed. Bill's face was buried in the blanket, Sage's hand held tight in his. Without announcing herself, she turned around and left.

*

OPENING HIS EYES and seeing again the closed venetian blind and voluptuous flowers, Peter had known straight away that someone was watching him. From over by the door. He had moved his head in that direction—and the room had gone on rushing past his eyes as if his head was still turning. He had closed his eyes again against the dizzying parade. But he had seen her, the woman who was not Welsh. She was clinging to the door, trying to steady his world. Or so it had appeared. The next time he opened his eyes, not sure if he had slept, she had gone and the world no longer seemed to turn.

Part VI

Convalescence

Chapter Twenty-Four

EXACTLY A WEEK after he had been admitted, Peter woke up feeling hungry and substantive. By lunchtime he had signed his discharge papers and Tom had arrived to drive him home.

"So, you should stay at my place first," Tom said. "Until you find your feet again. Convalescence can be slow."

"Thanks, Tom. But really I'll be fine." Peter squatted to tie up his boots.

"Don't be a fool. Besides, your small furry creature's not ready to leave."

Peter smiled. "Yeah, thanks again for taking care of her. But seriously, I'll be fine."

"Suit yourself—the offer still stands."

Peter stood, pausing briefly while his head cleared before going to find the floor staff and make his farewells. By the time he joined Tom at the elevators, he felt strangely bereft, as if he had taken leave of old friends he would never see again.

They had barely reached the lobby downstairs before he had to sit down.

"Marion's not back for another couple of weeks," Tom said, squinting at the ceiling. "You'll have the place to yourself except when I'm home."

Peter acknowledged defeat. He was feeling like a child on his first day of school, overwhelmed by the enormity, the speed, the industriousness of ordinary life. The feeling of vulnerability increased as Tom drove him through lunchtime traffic and pedestrian-filled streets. He missed acutely the ministrations of the nurses, the unconditional care, the buffered peace of the microcosm he had just left. And he still felt so tired, so ready to sleep, so incapable of thinking about even the little things required to make it through the day.

"Schofield called this morning," Tom said, turning into his street. "He's more than happy to reschedule. They fully understand."

"Understand what?"

"Don't start that again."

"I didn't start it."

Tom said no more until he had ushered Peter into his cluttered red-brick home. "It's a goddamn prestigious job," he said, opening the door to the spare room and guiding him past the piles of fabric, tubes of paint, a large stretched canvas and partly clothes mannequin, toward a piercing welcome from his pet.

Peter leaned down and stroked Violet's back. "What about BLAI?" he said. "Or was I still delirious when you said they wanted me?"

"Our local Liberal Arts Institute has, indeed, offered you their job. However…you might as well know that it was only after their first choice dumped them at the eleventh hour. You're their goddamned fallback, Peter! Is that what you want?"

Peter shrugged. "It happens to be the job I want most, so what does the rest matter?" He lifted Violet with both hands.

"Come now, with a very real possibility of Schofield's department?"

"It's a subjective thing, I guess." Peter lowered Violet back into her cage and sat down on the bed.

Tom shook his head. "Your mind's not clear yet."

Peter rubbed his face, wishing it had been when he saw the woman at his door. "It's perfectly clear," he said. "And what I tried to explain that night, however sick I was, still stands. Look, it's not as if I'm not ambitious," he said before Tom could interrupt. "But I'd rather have a job that lets me risk original ideas that may well not pan out—even if I have to pay for it with extra teaching—than spend the rest of my life scrambling and rushing for the next big breakthrough before someone else gets there first. It's like the way I run and swim," he added, swinging his legs onto the bed. "I may be fit and reasonably fast, but I know my limitations and they're not all under my control. I'd never want to be an Olympic athlete at the mercy of coaches, trainers and stop-clocks, and it's the same with my science."

"As I said, your mind's not yet clear. When it is, I'll share the good news about your experiments."

"Let me guess. Those expiring mice were just a bad dream?"

"No such luck there…but I found the viral titers—they'd gotten in among some papers I'd left with Elaine. Anyhow, I know it's not conclusive since we've only looked at one point in time, but for that one time point they're showing exactly what you predicted."

"Snap shots deceive. My predictions change—in fact, flip completely—on an arbitrary time scale. How on earth would you know yet which day corresponds to—"

"OK, I believe you now: your mind is quite clear. Let's just say that, twice now, the data fits the predicted pattern for that time point. How it changes in more detail over time will, of course, be critical."

"As with all things in life." Peter leaned back and closed his eyes.

"Let's look on the bright side for once?"

"When most of the mice die?"

"We're working on that."

"What's your theory then? Over-active defenses?"

"I doubt it."

"We should still check."

"As it happens, we already did."

Peter opened his eyes. "Who's *we*?"

"I had a little help from a friend."

Peter stiffened. "What friend?"

"Alice Gaines."

"Jeez, Tom. You know I wanted to do this myself. I don't even know who she is—though I'm really very, very grateful that she saved my life," he added with remorse as the implications of the name sank in.

"She knows who you are," Tom said.

"Does she? Look, it was incredibly good of her to help you out—especially after everything else; it's not that I'm not grateful. But to come to it blind—how would she know what to do? It's hardly surprising that she didn't see anything."

"And it's hardly her fault that there was nothing to see. And she likely knows a darn sight more about immunology than you. I've never come across such thorough results. Trust her, Peter. Trust *someone* for a goddamned change. By the way I think you'll get along with her, if you don't mind my saying."

"I do mind. It was really good of her to help, but that's no reason to get ideas. Besides, I'm all set on that front," he added, looking away. "And the bottom line is that we still don't know why those mice end up sick or dead. Though I'm guessing my manipulations exposed some kind of latent virulence factor—which could actually be quite interesting, don't you think?"

"Wouldn't that be novel? Meanwhile she's saved all sorts of samples in case you want to—"

"What, in case I want to step aside?"

"To look at them yourself, kiddo. Which I'm sure you do."

"Of course. Only there's so much else to think about first." There was, but he was starting to lose track of the argument, and which side he was on. "Man, suppose the virulence factor jumps and inserts itself into other microbes the way these factors sometimes do? We really should have been more careful. Have you told them over in Public Health? This already rules out any kind of vaccination plan—"

"Relax, will you? First of all, we don't even know if there *is* a virulence factor. But yes, I've stepped up precautions, and once you're well there's a whole new world out there waiting to be explored."

Peter leaned forward, knees to his chest. "What a goddamned mess," he said, staring at his socks. "Wouldn't it be poetic justice if I'd caught whatever it is that I've created from the mice?"

"Don't be an idiot. You had a *bona fide* case of LCMV. And quit being so negative. Be grateful to Alice—and no, don't look at me like that. She's ruled out the obvious, which means we can get straight down to the business of thinking outside the box."

"I guess." Peter's grasp of science was slipping fast. "You know, I really am amazingly tired," he said, rubbing his eyes.

"Yep, you should sleep. And I suggest you keep your hands off your face from here on. Meanwhile," Tom added from the door, "you can forget about making another melodramatic exit, if that's what's on your mind."

"BLAI will do just fine, nothing melodramatic about that," Peter said, letting go of his knees and leaning back on the bed to give in to the tide of somnolence already carrying him away.

Chapter Twenty-Five

ALICE HEARD nothing more from Tom. Not even after she took down the data and left it with Elaine, who interrupted a tense phone-call to say she would pass them on to Tom. Then again, Alice had never intended to be more than a pair of hands, and what was there to say anyway about her lackluster results? Except that in the course of running all those assays, she had come to feel she had a stake in what they did or did not show. Just as she had come to feel—every time she locked or unlocked her bike, or saw the doorway to the first floor corridor, or hid herself in the library stacks—that she had a stake in Peter's health.

After several more days of hearing nothing from downstairs, she called the hospital herself. When they told her that Peter had been discharged, her relief was tarnished somewhat by the self-ish realization that the episode was over and her role in it was done. Done, that is, beyond an ongoing discomfort around Helen, who was facing disciplinary action for what she claimed was not her fault and would jeopardize everything. "*Everything,*" she told Alice far too often, still not meeting her eye. Soon those few highly charged days gained an illusionary quality as if they had never been quite real, or belonged to the distant past.

DIANE CALLED, interrupting Alice's limbo with a lengthy and dramatic monologue. Since this whole engagement thing, she said, all anyone did was offer unsolicited advice, fuss over stupid details, and insinuate themselves into supposedly official roles she had not even known existed—she had always wanted a simple wedding. Two of her friends were begging to be bridesmaids but had fallen out with each other, and another had taken it upon herself to give tips on how to run a marriage and even how to handle Ian. "As if he'd ever need handling, sweetheart that he is! Good Lord," Diane said, almost in tears. "She barely even knows him! I'm ready to call the whole thing off."

"Just stop listening," Alice said, her mind still elsewhere. "It's your wedding; do whatever you want." This was the downside, Alice thought, to having so many friends. However, after she had put down the phone, she wondered if she had been too harsh—and what she would do if the wedding was indeed called off. She had started to view the event as a pivot, a defined point of escape, an obvious deadline if her options here fell through.

AFTER THREE WEEKS of silence, Elaine appeared at Alice's desk. Tom had been up to his neck, she said, what with Peter—who was doing well now—and with his wife being away. "But he wants to show you something," she added without a pause. "So he's hoping you'll stop by—say, tomorrow at ten—and you can see where it leads." Then she had hurried off to take care of other business she apparently had on the fifth floor.

Alice was mystified. There was no way that the data she had given Tom could lead anyone anywhere. All the same, she set off for work that Tuesday in a more than usually hopeful mood, giving herself time to start staining cells before meeting Tom. It was in any case a beautiful day, a prelude to spring, though snow still lingered in odd corners and the grass was not yet green.

The walk signal beckoned on Beacon Street. As Alice left the curb, a sunbeam fanned out from the gap between two buildings like a searchlight breaking through the fog of the past few weeks. She felt a rush of anticipation, as if something momentous were about to happen. A train pulled up at the T stop just as she reached the median, and opened its doors. Pounding footsteps closed in behind her and she let herself pretend that, rather than running for the train, someone was trying to catch up with her.

"Hello," said Peter Young, gasping for breath as he drew up on her left.

She looked over her shoulder to make sure he meant her; there was no one else around. "Hi," she managed to say. "You're OK again!"

"Kind of." He was still panting pitiably. "It's my first day back." He looked at her questioningly. "I'm sorry," he said, "but how did you know that I wasn't...OK, that is?"

"Well, because I...Tom...I was the one—"

His clear brown eyes studied her as if weighing up evidence. "You're Alice," he said, shaking his head. "It never occurred to me."

Alice shrugged. "Why would it?" She watched a large plane rise above the buildings and crawl too slowly across sky. No one ever knew who she was.

"I'm Peter, of course," he said and held out a hand.

She felt his warm palm on hers, pulling every shred of her perception toward him alone.

"I've been thinking of you as two separate people all this time," he said, his features alight.

"Me too," she answered, finding herself compelled to speak her mind though she must sound insane.

"Well, I'm glad you're both you," he said.

"Thank you." Her smile matched his.

"But I should thank *you*," he said, suddenly earnest. "I owe you my life."

Alice's sense of wellbeing fell apart. "It was nothing," she said. "I'm glad you're OK." Gratitude: too easily confused with something more. She pictured the faded note above her kitchen door: *Forbidden…DO NOT VIOLATE.*

"Don't be ridiculous," Peter was saying as the train moved on. "It was not remotely nothing. And then you ran all those assays for us—"

"Tom was desperate and I was there. Anyhow, I didn't exactly make any great breakthroughs."

"And I probably wouldn't have thanked you if you had." He laughed, apparently to himself. "But you've ruled out more possibilities than I knew were there."

"Ruling out possibilities is my forte." Alice glanced at his kind eyes and her heart seemed to break.

"Shall we walk?" he asked. The lights changed again.

She fell into step with him. "So I guess it's still a matter of figuring out the right questions," she said for want of anything else.

"And deciding which ones to pursue." He paused. "Ultimately science is a gamble, don't you think? And usually I'm out of luck."

"Same here." Alice wondered if her luck was worse when it came to science or to love.

"Well then," he said, stooping to pick up something from the ground, "maybe this will help."

Alice held out her hand, thinking again of her landlord, this time with the woman on the beach. Instead of a shining shell, a tarnished penny dropped onto her palm—and she noticed that Peter was not wearing a ring. "Thank you," she said, unable to contain a smile. "But doesn't the luck go to whoever picks it up?"

"Maybe so," he said, smiling as well. Rather beautifully, she thought.

"Maybe," he said, "maybe…if you have time…maybe you'd join me for a cup of tea?"

"That would be lovely!" Alice clenched the coin tight. But no, she thought in alarm. He had caught her off guard. He was overcome by gratitude and would register this soon. There was no point in leading him on; she would only end up hurting him and getting hurt herself. "Only I'm pretty busy at the moment," she added. "So I really don't—"

"This is all I need," Peter cut in, and Alice looked askance at him. Did it matter so much? Surely not enough to make him veer toward a nearby tree and, leaning back against its trunk, lower himself to its dirt base.

"Are you all right?" she asked.

Peter shook his head, face hidden between his knees.

"Should I get help or something?"

He shook his head again.

Not sure what else to do, Alice stood sentinel. Occasional passers-by veered in a cautious arc about them. She looked at Peter's hiking boots, not made for running fast; and the whorl of his crown, glinting copper in the sun. Wayward tufts on the nape of his neck shied away from his plaid collar. She tried not to think about how it would feel to run her fingers through his hair by wondering how many dogs had stopped to mark that smooth-barked tree.

At last he uncurled. "You're still here," he said.

"Are you OK?" She crouched down beside him.

"I am now. I still get dizzy sometimes—but it passes." He looked sidelong at her. "You know, I caught up to ask if *you* were all right. That night in the rain."

"Thanks for asking. But it was nothing."

"You keep on saying that."

She supposed he was right. Then again, it *was* nothing. "I thought I'd lost my bike lights," she said, rolling her eyes. "But it turned out I hadn't. Stupid, isn't it?"

"Not especially."

He was gazing at her in a way she should discourage. "Anyway, I should be getting on," she said rather too heartily and jumped to her feet. "Here, let me." She reached for his elbow as he struggled to stand up. She had braced herself against his weight but not against the fact of it being *his* weight, and was momentarily paralyzed.

He had started to back away. "Are you coming?"

"Yes…sure." Alice was still dazed. She expended every shred of concentration on maintaining at least some distance in body and mind as they walked side by side talking about work.

"You're sure you won't join me for a cup of tea?" he asked again inside their building at the turn-off to the stairs.

"No, I really—"

"You've cut your hair," he said.

"I have." Alice tried not to laugh.

"It's short," he added as if still taking it in.

"It is." Alice did laugh. If he was really that oblivious to her appearance, then things were surely not so bad. "Oh all right," she said. "Perhaps a quick cup of tea. And then I really will have to get on."

Chapter Twenty-Six

WHEN PETER SET OFF that morning, he had been dreading his return, harboring no illusions about having been missed. He had expected to feel out of place in a new status quo, his inevitably unfamiliar presence the only indication to the others that he had been gone. But when he turned into his corridor, his trepidation was lost in the overwhelming novelty of walking in with Alice. Besides which, his presumptions were quite wrong.

"Hey, Peter," Stace said, looking up from her clip-board as they passed the main lab. "Welcome back."

"Thank you," he said, hearing his surprise.

"Sure—and hi there," Stace added, waving at Alice. A new vine trailed the snake on Stace's arm. Just then, two of Tom's graduate students joined Stace at the door and, more surprising to him still, he stopped to ask them what he had missed.

"I'm sorry," he told Alice when they had moved on. "It's not usually like this."

"It's fine!"

And it was, he thought. He showed her through the inert lab into his office, where the desk drawer was still open, the bottle of ibuprofen on the desk. Stowing the bottle in the drawer, he turned his chair around—and heard Alice gasp.

"My earring," she said, head bent to one side. "It's caught on my scarf."

"Let me," he said, fingers guiding the thin wire from the hole in her flesh while she held up her scarf.

"Isn't that from *The Concise British Flora in Colour*?" she said, folded under his arm and facing the thistles on the wall.

"Yup. Colour with a *u*," he said, trying to sound matter-of-fact, as if her knowing the source was unremarkable—as if her downy lobe was unremarkable too. He gave the released earring back. He was not going to delude himself: she did not hate him anymore—that much was clear—but she had hardly fallen into his circumstantial embrace.

"What's a book about British flowers doing over here?" she asked, blindly hooking back the earring.

Peter shrugged. "Though we do have some of the same. Take lesser celandines—they're in the book and…well, you should see the patch of woodland just off Beacon Street. Right around the middle of April you can almost see them pushing through the leaf mold as you watch, and the next thing you know, the ground's carpeted in a field of yellow on lush green."

He stopped, afraid that he was boring her, but she told him how she used to resent lesser celandines for not being buttercups until she saw that book. "It turns out that they're both *Ranunculaceae*," she said, "and on the same page."

Like you and me, he thought, but kept his mouth shut and prepared two large mugs of tea. When he pushed hers over to her, their eyes met and blood rushed to his head, at which point she frowned and studied the side of her mug. It advertised a brand of restriction enzyme, and they talked about molecular biology for a while. Then she said she liked the tea and asked what type it was, and they compared preferences: Chinese versus

Indian, green versus black, brands of tea bag and loose leaf. She told him about some of the more obscure types she had tried, such as cherry blossom and mango, and the glass carafe she had owned in which she watched the tea leaves swirl as their smoke-like trails diffused. Soon she started to relax, still showing interest in whatever he said and offering up connected ideas. She even laughed at his jokes—once, until she very nearly cried—although every such meeting of minds was followed by a period of forced reticence, as if she had caught herself being led dangerously astray. Whenever this happened, he had the feeling she was not talking to him as such; he was more like that glass carafe, simply making her thoughts visible.

And then, after what seemed like no time at all, she glanced at the clock.

"I have to be somewhere in less than two minutes," she said, wide-eyed in alarm. "Thanks so much for the tea—but I really must rush." Springing to her feet, she grabbed her coat and bag and fled.

Slowly, Peter stood up too. He walked toward the door, in the process stepping on something soft: one of Alice's gloves. He picked it up and stroked the soft black fleece. There was no point in following her out; he knew she had gone.

ALICE BARELY had time to drop off her bag, let alone start the assay she had planned. She returned to the first floor via the fire stairwell, coming out through the red door so as to bypass Peter's lab. She had not told him about her meeting with Tom, and was not sure why not.

Tom, however, was not in his office, and even Elaine was not there. Alice hovered at the notice board, reading fliers she had already seen on the board upstairs. Now and then someone walked past behind her, and she waited a few seconds before turning to see one of Peter's colleagues checking a mailbox, grabbing a pen from the shelf or laying something on Elaine's neat desk. Each time her irritation increased at the thought of how much longer she could have spent in Peter's office—and at the knowledge that it would not have done her any good. It was always the best men that were out of bounds. He would make a decent friend though, she thought. More than decent. She had rarely known anyone, male or female, she could talk to like that. She needed a good friend.

"Well hello there!" Elaine said, bustling in and hanging up her coat. "Waiting for Tom? Why don't you sit yourself down? He's just talking to Peter—did you know it's his first day back? Ah—here's Tom now…"

"Come on in," Tom said, frowning at the clock before unlocking his office door. "Take a seat," he added. "Yeah, dump them on the floor," he told her, gesturing to the pile of papers on the only other chair besides his.

"So," he said, sitting himself down and looking abnormally kempt. "As I may have said, the data's just great—even Peter's impressed."

"Thanks." Alice avoided his gaze.

"No need to blush."

Alice blushed still more.

Tom grinned. "Meanwhile," he said, leaning back, "what's up with your commensal work?"

Alice sat up straight. He had actually remembered. "Nothing," she said with a tight smile. "Helen is not interested."

"And presumably she wouldn't be even if she wasn't dealing with the safety committee and worrying about potential law suits and the like." Tom crossed his arms. "From what you told me in the hospital, I am guessing all is not well on floor five—even beyond the obvious. How is he, by the way?" he added in a more somber tone.

"No change. They're making long term arrangements."

"Jeez." Presumably out of reverence to Sage, Tom was quiet for a while.

"But tell me what happened," he said, brightening again. "You sounded decently content that, uh, first time we sat down and talked."

"Yes, well. I suppose things change." Alice stared at a photograph on the wall behind Tom—a slightly leaner dark-haired Tom, and a woman with large thighs and two plump little girls, all of whom looked heartwarmingly happy. Then, startled by her own candor, she found herself pouring out her woes to this man she barely knew. She told him of the first impossible-to-repeat result, the all-too-reproducible project she had inherited from Ken, Ken's fate, her Sharden's epiphany, Richard's job and Helen's turncoat response. "So as you can see," she concluded, "in a matter of weeks I've completely wrecked my career."

Tom pressed his fingertips together, forming an open cage. Eventually he spoke. "Helen's a fool," he said. "Even if this messy business doesn't destroy her, which knowing sod's law it won't, what she fails to see is that she's killing off her legacy. It's all very well churning out papers, but how many of them will anyone be reading in ten or fifteen years' time? Science moves on. The only chance most of us have of a lasting legacy is the success of our trainees—a branch of intellectual offspring that we've influenced in some way. Helen's totally missed the point. All she wants from you guys is instant gratification: the data you churn out, the grants you write, your good ideas."

"She didn't want my idea," Alice pointed out.

"No. But she doesn't want you to have it either. Look, it's not just that she depends on you. From her skewed point of view, your interest in becoming independent means not only that you'll abandon her, but you'll become her competition. Friend becomes foe, she turns on her defenses and you're dead meat." His fingers burst apart.

"Dead meat?" Alice had been hoping for encouragement.

"But if she goes on like this," Tom said, "she'll get what she deserves: The line will terminate with her. The fact is, Alice, you've come to the end of a trajectory that was going nowhere anyway."

"I know." Alice pressed her hands to her cheeks. "I never meant to stay. Only now I've burned my bridges back home too, except for going to my sister's wedding which also might not happen, and even my landlord needs me out by the fall, and I don't have my own furniture or anything, and…" Alice was only just realizing quite how much was wrong—and quite how silly she must sound.

"Don't let yourself get worked up. As you've just illustrated, circumstances change. Maybe it's time to start again somewhere new. You see, I reckon your hunch about commensals may pay off." Tom leaned forward and grinned. "What if I called you down to let you know that I can help?"

Alice lowered her hands. "How?"

"Well first of all, I have this old friend." Tom reached for a yellow envelope on one side of his desk. "Joe sends me his thoughts now and then," he said, emptying it out. "As a tribute to the good old days of share and share alike. So a few weeks back this lot arrives." He rummaged among the papers and pushed a page toward Alice—a photographic plate covered in many shades of grey. "Muscle contraction's his thing," Tom said. "He's been looking at gut contraction in the presence of neuro-chemicals linked with stress. When he looked at this one molecule, NGF—nerve growth factor, that is—well, take a look at this." He pointed to several regions of the magnified tissue section. "These guys show up all over the place."

Alice stared at the data. "Granulocytes?" There was no mistaking those granular white blood cells, a primary line of host defense also involved in—dare she even think it?—inflammation and permeability. "It's too good to be true," she murmured in awe.

"Interesting, isn't it? NGF levels rise in response to all kinds of stress—including early stage romantic love, ha ha! Bet you didn't know that…"

His eyes met hers and she ignored his grin, her mind racing, trying to take it all in. She focused on the photograph. And maybe it was too good to be true, she realized. "If he's already working on it," she said, tempering her hopes, "then there's really no point in—"

Tom held up a hand. "Joe is about to retire and says his few remaining postdocs all have minds of their own, won't come near his ideas. However, he figures this is something big and wants to see it in good hands before he bows out. Knowing that chance favors the prepared mind, he's hoping my mind might be more prepared than his—and what *I'm* hoping is that yours is more prepared than mine. Reckon it's a piece in your puzzle?"

"It's just got to be." The data took her breath away.

"Good." Tom stuffed the papers back into the envelope. "There's potential here, I'm willing to bet—whether or not it ties in with your Sharden's grant. Which brings us back to that little issue of jobs. You said you've wrecked your career and burned your bridges back home. Well, how about starting afresh down here with me?"

"With you?" The possibility had never crossed Alice's mind—at least not consciously—but she could not have come up with a better solution. Possibilities opened up, hurdles fell away like water from a duck's back; she and Peter would be colleagues, one step more than friends, and it was just as well now that they were only friends—

"—because as it happens there's going to be a whole lot of space in my group when our friend Peter moves on—"

Moves on? Alice shook her head slowly as her mood took another dive—into a bottomless pit this time. Why had he not told her himself?

"Indeed there is," Tom said. "So, if you're willing to put in time on my projects while you gather your preliminary data, you can take up here where he's leaving off."

Emotions collided and crashed. It was all so perfect, and yet so calamitous. She could not argue with a fate that promised security and at the same time set her free—what more could she ask? She tried to thank Tom, but managed only a wordless sob before her tears erupted in a cataclysm as violent and chaotic as her anger and relief.

"I'm sorry," she said when she had calmed down.

Tom had his back to her and was typing at a large computer behind his desk. He spun his chair around. "No sweat, you're hardly the first—grab some facial tissues from Elaine on your way through. Meanwhile I'll take that as a yes—wait, I was just kidding," he said as Alice started to cry again at the thought of the handkerchief upstairs in her bag, and of Peter giving it to her. She wiped her face with her sleeve and stood up.

"Really, there's no great rush," Tom said, following her out. "Think it over and we'll talk again soon. And if you're in need furniture, by the way, talk to my wife—she'll know exactly where to look. Won't she, Elaine?"

"Marion? You bet—speaking of which, did she have a good flight back?"

"Until next time," Tom called after Alice as she started for the corridor—and almost collided with Peter, who was just coming in.

"What's wrong?" he asked in evident alarm.

"Nothing." Alice looked to one side, feeling raw.

"Your glove," he said. "You dropped one of your gloves—"

"Hello Peter. Settling in OK?" Tom intervened, robust and hearty between them. "I've just been having a talk with your possible replacement. Speaking of which," he continued relentlessly, "what did you decide?"

"I told you—I've accepted their offer." Peter sounded confused.

"What, from BLAI?" With one hand, Tom steered him toward Elaine's desk.

"Of course."

Every muscle in Alice's body went limp. She backed away, still looking at Peter even when his eyes met hers over his shoulder and his look of distress collapsed into a penetrating smile—and she realized she was smiling too.

"It's open," he called over to her. "My lab."

"Thanks," she said and hurried to pick up her glove before he returned.

Chapter Twenty-Seven

IN MAY, Peter took up his faculty position at BLAI and Alice moved into his space. She could not have endured another day in Helen's lab, where she was constantly reminded of the absence of Sage, who continued to lie inert in a small suburban nursing home. Alice visited him sometimes, often accompanied by Dee, who had lined up a new job in the Performing Arts department; Dee and Alice were now friends. Alice could not have stayed with Helen anyway. Soon after the imposition of tight restrictions by the disciplinary committee—including termination of the LCMV project—Helen had announced that she had accepted the proposal of a long-time gentleman friend and was moving to Maine. Helen said little more about her future spouse or her wedding plans, and no one in the department was invited to attend. In the intervening months, Alice glimpsed passing looks of resignation as Helen disassembled the lab and tied up loose ends, but saw no signs of sorrow, and Helen seemed more or less at peace. It did not seem fair.

Meanwhile, Diane phoned again. All was well, she said, but in the interest of simplicity she was having just one bridesmaid now—"You, of course!"—and in the interest of practicality suggested Alice find a dress. "I'll pay you back," she said, "but aim for maroon. Simple lines, no frills. One you'll want to wear again." All Alice had come up with so far was the fancy boutique filled with outfits she would not want to wear at all, let alone again, and had made no progress beyond wishing that some kind of fairy godmother would appear out of nowhere and take care of it for her—until Tom's wife Marion came to her aid.

Alice had gone into the lab one sunny Saturday to meet Tom's friend Joe, who had stopped by on his way to Vermont and was eager to see what Alice was doing with his work. After an energetic morning in Tom's office going through data and ideas, Marion had joined them, bringing along a large box of homemade sandwiches from which they picnicked outside in a small park behind the building. After Joe drove off and Tom went back inside to revise a rejected manuscript, Marion said she was off to look for baby clothes—among other random things—and asked Alice if she would like to come.

Alice leapt at the chance. She told Marion about the wedding and her needs, and how she had no idea where to begin. Marion said she knew exactly where.

"Just on the off-chance," she explained, pulling into a crowded parking lot in a rundown part of town. "Because thrift shops are all about chance. There's no one telling you what to like, subliminally influencing your tastes. You might find nothing at all, but I can't count the times I've found exactly what I wanted without even knowing I was looking—as if *it* had found *me*…know what I mean?"

Alice laughed, not sure that she did know. But it turned out to be true. A couple of hours later she crossed the sunbaked asphalt back to the car, not with a bridesmaid dress, but with a large remnant of deep maroon raw silk and a dusty old sewing machine that still seemed to work. Within a week she had sketched out a design, and deconstructed it into flat shapes that she cut out from the silk and re-built to create a simple and yet elegant gown that would offset the bride and not distract or detract. She had also found an Indian bedspread, a wooden chair and matching bookcase carved with small hearts, and a sundress much like one she had wanted in her teens and had tried on just for fun but—having stepped out of the changing room to show Marion—realized, when she held down the flounces and raised the hem, really looked quite good; she had done the alterations that first night with her new sewing machine.

*

JUNE PASSED, the sun shining down day after day, radiating from the sidewalks and roads. The humidity soared. Alice had never known such heat, had never thought of summer as a time to stay indoors—except when it rained or was unseasonably cold. From the air-conditioned bubble of her first-floor laboratory, the placid blue skies looked inviting and innocuous, and she longed to be outside.

One hot morning late in the month, she took advantage of a three-hour incubation period—after which she would be busy well into the night—and, with her swimsuit and towel rolled up in her bag, jumped on her bike. Marion had pointed out an outdoor pool on their way home that recent Saturday, reminiscing how she had taken her girls there often when they were small. Alice had always loved to swim outdoors, and during her first summer in Cambridge had often biked to the pool on Jesus Green to swim long vigorous laps in frigid ecstasy—though that was before she met Ben, who had told her she was crazy to go near a place like that with all those little kids and bodily fluids and weirdos and the like. She had been crazy, she thought now, to have listened to Ben.

This pool—also in Cambridge, although not the same one—was not as long and not as cold, but just as invigorating. After swimming countless laps, she climbed out and sat on the side with her ankles submerged and the sun on her back. Basking in the tranquil pre-noon glare, she barely noticed the scattering of other patrons—some bobbing alone or in pairs, others gliding back and forth in rhythmic solitude—until one of the rigorous single-minded lap-swimmer veered directly toward her and stopped near her feet. And, to her astonishment, stood up in front of her, rising like a stunning virile Venus from a turquoise lagoon.

"Hi," Peter said, pulling off his goggles with a glistening hand. "I didn't realize it was you."

"Me neither," Alice said, dazzled by his grin as she shaded her eyes. She had not seen him since he moved out of the lab—not for three weeks and two days. "How's BLAI?" she asked.

"Good—very good," he said. "And how is Tom's lab?"

"Good!"

Before the move, she had seen Peter often—especially at the lunchtime meetings Tom had called to ease the transition, during which Tom always had to rush off elsewhere before she and Peter had finished their food. She tried not to stare, had not expected his lean torso to be so sculpted and smooth—though the goggle imprint around his eyes made him look prematurely old. She asked about his teaching preparations. All-consuming, he said as wavelets lapped his pelvic girdle, Speedos only just submerged. He should be working on it now, he added, but had needed a break. Had she found a new apartment yet? Going slowly, she said. But she was getting to know the neighborhoods and figuring out what she was looking for. And soon they were talking about all sorts of things as if they had met up in the grocery store—until Peter started shivering and Alice realized that her back was burnt. So they said their farewells and Alice left him swimming a few last laps as she went off to shower and change.

While she soaped and rinsed, she thought about how much she liked him as a friend. For one thing it meant she could think about his fine physique without investment or greed—and his physique was indeed rather fine. Too bad that she had been likewise barely dressed, her wide thighs flattened even wider on the concrete ledge on which she had been perched—she could still feel the dents in her flesh. She wrapped herself in her large towel, thinking it was just as well that he had gone back to swimming laps as she skirted the pool, allowing her one last lingering glance at his wide strong shoulders on her way toward the changing room. And just as well it would not have mattered if he *had* seen the dents in her thighs. It was also just as well, she affirmed, looking in the dingy mirror in the even dingier changing room, that she had not known that the goggle imprint around her eyes was even deeper than his; or that her hair had been slicked down in the silliest possible way. Otherwise she would never have been able to sit there chattering to him happily as if she had known him all her life.

*

IN AUGUST, Alice saw many people she had known all her life. Yet more often than not she had the feeling that she was getting to know them for the first time—even Diane, she might almost have said. Alice and Diane had always been companionably close, but not in an especially confiding way.

"You were always too busy thinking your deep thoughts," Diane teased as they wrapped homemade favors in ribbon and gauze.

"Silly daydreams, more like," Alice replied. "Whereas you were always out there actually living your life. All those boy-friends, Diane!"

"A chapter that has, happily, now closed. Be glad, Alice—your pickiness has saved you a lot of heartache."

"Believe me,' Alice said, "that is a myth on both counts."

THE DAY BEFORE the wedding, Alice went down to the church. The western wall of the graveyard was curtained by a cascade of brambles that had climbed the other side, weighed down by fistfuls of not-quite-ripe blackberries. Alice knew which veiled spot she had come to find, and with a skill refined over many childhood seasons of gathering out-of-reach fruit, soon made short work of the tangle of thorns.

Here lieth the body, she read, crouching down to touch the stone tenderly. But wait…*the body of Captain William Severs, a brave and courageous man, and his second mate John Bow, and a nameless drowned youth, washed ashore…* Alice stood up and frowned. Had she really remembered only one part, and blocked out the rest? She liked her version more—but it was wrong…or perhaps not wrong, just incomplete? She tried to re-equilibrate.

"Well, if it isn't our hero!" a woman's voice exclaimed.

Alice jumped from the thicket and stood aside.

"No, not on the gravestone, silly—you!" It was Valerie, an old family friend Alice had not seen for years.

Alice embraced her almost-aunt. "Me?"

"Of course! For calming Diane down when it seemed all was

281

lost. A watershed moment, I hear—she almost called the whole thing off!"

"Seriously?" Alice barely remembered what she had told Diane that day—though she did remember that she had barely been listening.

"Oh yes—it was all quite alarming. But then she's always looked up to you—her reliable big sister. Clearly you said just the right thing."

That was a first, Alice thought. She had always liked Valerie, who had always seemed so fashionable and sophisticated, and fascinated by whatever Alice and Diane said or did. On one visit, she had brought with her a well-dressed man who looked like Gregory Peck, and he had spent long hours reading quietly in the living room, which had meant no television for Alice and Diane. The next time, though, she had come on her own and spent long hours whispering with Alice's mother behind closed bedroom doors, and not played with them at all. Later, she had married someone else—someone not quite as good-looking or well dressed, but far more friendly and fun.

"Do you have time to walk?" Valerie asked, linking arms with Alice. "Let's stretch our legs and see what has changed."

THE WEDDING took place in the cool damp shadows of the old stone church lush now with freshly gathered flowers. Afterwards, the bride and groom and guests mingled among the generations of graves in a sea of summer sunlight and good cheer. Then they processed up the tree-lined slope, and strolled through terraced gardens overflowing with color before dining in simple rustic splendor on the wide smooth green lawn beneath the castle's crenellated walls. In her subtle and well-fitting dress, Alice felt thoroughly at ease among uncles, aunts, cousins and Diane's myriad friends. No one seemed sorry for her—least of all herself.

As the ribbon of reflected sun began to spread across the Bristol Channel, a small jazz band struck up their first cool cords and the dancing began. Alice danced all night with Diane's childhood friends and the parents of those friends. Those once-annoying little kids and faceless grown-ups were now charming individuals, age differences compressed by time. She even found herself flirting with some of the men. But she did no more than flirt, because although she half-wished all this had happened before she left for the States, she knew that it would not have been the same, and had a strong suspicion that her very distance made the flirting more fun—for herself as well as for the men. And so, when Diane tossed her bouquet just before she and Ian squeezed into their small car and drove off into the night, Alice stood back and let the bunch of wildflowers land in the hands of one of Diane's closest friends.

"Ever the hero," Valerie said in her ear.

"No point in letting it go to waste!" Alice had not realized Valerie was near.

"Oh come now, you could well be next—you've met someone, haven't you?"

Alice flushed. "I wish." She tried to sound more flippant than she felt.

"Oh, I know you have. It's written all over you. Believe me, he's the one." Valerie patted Alice's arm and hurried off to join her husband, who was smiling on a nearby bench.

Alice looked across the warm dark night at the tapering edge of Devon, at the tiny lights of scattered coastal towns spread like a row of land-bound stars. She might have immersed herself then in the fantasy, only the guests were beginning to depart, seemingly all at once, leaving behind them compressed crumbs of wedding cake and decimated flowers, and—to Valerie's cries of alarm—a pair of strong prescription spectacles that someone must have missed.

BEFORE SHE LEFT her green and pleasant home, Alice revisited her not-so-solitary youth. She gathered the first few ripened blackberries, dangling like drops of glistening tar over the drowned sailors' grave. One day she walked along the clifftop, circling back through overgrown woodland carpeted thickly with ferns; another morning she went down to the bay before low tide and hiked back over the temporarily exposed limestone layers that revealed the fossilized remains of two hundred million years. For the first time she noticed the billowing firmness of the ever-present clouds, as if they had been nourished and groomed during their transatlantic passage; and how quickly the sky cleared after rain; and how beautifully the evening sun cast long shadows on the fields. But the sun rose a little lower than she remembered, and the shadows were longer even at high noon. And when she looked down at her beloved coastline as she was carried west again, her regret at leaving home was sublimated by the prospect of great change in store, of undefined options waiting up ahead as time inevitably moved forward—even as the plane raced hard against the sun and the day rewound. She touched down in Boston one evening in late August, renewed and refreshed, knowing she was ready to move on.

*

IN SEPTEMBER, Alice moved into a new apartment. She had found somewhere with more light, and unfurnished this time.

She savored the vast potential of her small rooms, and spent many pleasurable hours rediscovering the joys of solitude, embellishing her space as need and chance ordained.

The evening before she moved out, she went to see her landlord. He had already said many times that he was sorry she must leave, that he hoped she understood. He led her into his dining room and offered her a chair—and said so again. "But I am sure it was meant," he added, "that I was sent such a sweet and charming English girl as you."

"Actually, I'm not exactly English," she told him at last.

"Ah." He grinned knowingly. "I remember. You told me that you came from Wales. I should have said British—I know how sensitive these things can be!"

"Well, it's not really that. You see my father's parents were German. They changed their name to Gaines when they came to Britain—it used to be Ganz, though even that was an assumed name. They left Germany just before the war."

"Is that so?" The landlord frowned. "I would never have guessed. You look so very British, remind me so very much of— Ach, but of course now that you tell me, it is plain to see. You are Jewish too?"

"Well, not exactly. They assimilated. Two generations ago. And it's only on my grandfather's side. And my mother's neither German nor Jewish, so it's pretty much diluted out…" Alice was stopped by the landlord's severe glare.

"Why diluted out?" he asked. "Mixing enriches, makes a thing more complex. Now take an old man's advice," he said more kindly. "There you sit, telling me what you are not. Yet who cares about these labels anyway? Labels change. Often. We scientists, for example—"

"You're a scientist? I had no idea."

"You see—even your landlord is made up of more than you think! Professor of Biochemistry, once upon a time... But yes, we scientists, we are always redefining, inventing of new names and terminologies for what we already know—and even for what we don't know."

"That's true." Alice smiled.

"Now in the first place, these labels mean nothing if you don't keep track of them, know what they're for. Many times they're just words or strings of letters that someone makes up. And in the second place—you, with your family history, should know this as well as I do—the weight, the meaning, the significance of a label can altogether change. My dear Miss Ganz or Gaines or what you will, never mind about classifying yourself with words. Don't you know that Ganz means complete? Your pieces still make up a complete whole—a unique whole, which exempts you from that most dreaded of labels: cliché."

Alice remembered Sage saying something similar about wanting to be exempt. She missed him acutely.

"Come and visit me sometimes," the landlord said when he showed her back downstairs—after weaving first through various memories to talk again about the woman on the beach that fine summer before the war. "Will you promise me that?"

Alice promised. And she visited him sometimes, and together they drank tea with lemon from his gilt-edged china cups. She told him many things about herself during those visits, and he told her more about his life before the war. He also talked about the woman on the beach, and Alice wondered what had happened to the woman in real life—and in real time, because how real was anything confined to just one point in time? It would have been so easy to find out, she thought, to use searches and modern technology to tie up those loose ends. However, the old man had already told her he did not want to know—neither what he had missed, nor what he had falsely dreamed. And Alice understood. It was better that way; the open question never closed, the possibilities there for looking at and giving back untouched. As her other grandmother, Oma, had liked to say: *Have a good look. But please, do not touch.*

Part VII

Recovery

Chapter Twenty-Eight

IT WAS A MONDAY in April—Patriot's Day, a public holiday—and a little over a year since the business with the virus. Peter had settled in well at BLAI, and though his first semester lecture schedule had felt like an accelerating treadmill, he had managed to keep up and had gained a cult following among the students, who came to his office in droves—if only to see his chainmail vest, which he had hung on the wall to fill a large empty space. His first week there, someone had changed his name on the department photo-board to read Young Peter instead of Peter Young, so he had taken to wearing the tweed jacket he had bought the previous summer—bought one Saturday when he had seen Alice trying on dresses with Marion after he had dropped off some plates.

He had not made himself known to them that day, not wanting to spoil their fun. He had not even been looking for a jacket—one dark suit served his few formal needs—but as he turned away from watching them laugh, he had knocked it from its hanger on the rail. Since it looked to be his size, had tried it on, its classic cut and superior quality at once emphasizing and softening his realization that he was a solitary academic on the cusp of middle age. His male colleagues like it too: a week ago, he had walked in on three of them, and they had broken off their laughter to tell him they had been joking about needing a jacket like his—something to do with a skit at the recent departmental retreat, when a student playing a prince, wearing a jacket and plaid shirt, had been pecked by a princess and turned into a frog.

Peter had not quite understood their laughter or the skit, but in both cases the tone had been benign. He liked his colleagues, and, as he had anticipated, enjoyed teaching. Especially now that, midway through the second semester, his preparations were two weeks ahead, thanks in no small part to having woken before dawn in a state of strangled anxiety from another half-remembered dream in which he very nearly drowned.

The meteoric roar of a military jet filled up the living room, followed by a cataclysmic silence. Sunlight filtered through un-furling leaves on the branches outside; the sky was a clean blue. Stepping over, Peter raised the window sash and broke the pro-longed moment, letting in the cool air and a jumble of partially recalled quotes about adolescent yearnings and heartfelt long-ings for not-quite defined things—though he knew exactly what he wanted, and whom.

He had stopped by the week before to borrow a text book from Tom and she had not been there. His disappointment had been sufficiently eviscerating that Tom had asked, more than once, if he felt all right—Tom was evidently still traumatized from having misread the signs before. Peter wished there were more signs to read in relation to Alice. Though at least they were now friends—and he refused to diminish what he had by con-ceding the word *just*. Absence makes the heart grow fonder, he thought, resting his forehead on the trellised glass, feeling like a lovelorn poet or thwarted beaux—and a feeble-minded idiot. Pushing himself back from the window, he grabbed his grown-up jacket from the back of his chair and went out.

After twenty minutes, he reached the patch of woodland he had extolled to Alice—not because of her, but because it was April and the time of year when those celandines were due to appear. Indeed, even from afar he had seen their yellow haze spread like a buttery ocean under the trees. Up close, the myriad petals sparkled and glowed, each stellate flower like a tiny shining sun. Here and there a small patch of violets broke through, or the brand new fronds of uncurling ferns. For the first time in years, he felt compelled to draw—even if all he had on him was a narrow-ruled notebook and a blue ballpoint pen—and sat down on a wooden bench in the shade just off the path. He had just completed a sketch of pale feathery fiddleheads when he looked up and saw Alice on the far side of the trees. She seemed to be watching him. He stowed his notebook and stood up.

"You're right," she called, circling the bed of ferns, her short hair golden in the light. "The lesser celandines are beautiful!"

And so are you, he thought—as he did every time he saw her. She was wearing a dress. He wondered if it was the one she had been trying on that day with Marion; he had no memory for these things—though if it was, it looked still more perfect now. He recognized her earrings, though, made from two lozenges of chainmail he had linked the week before and left on her desk when he did not find her there. On the envelope he had written that he had no use for them but hoped that she did.

"Off to watch the marathon?" she asked as she approached. In twenty minutes, the front-runners of the annual race were expected on Beacon Street, on the far side of the park.

Peter shook his head. "I should get back to work."

"Me too." Alice looked up at the treetops, seeming to inhale loveliness. Faint sounds of anticipation wafted from the street.

"But I might stop for a cup of tea first," Peter said, surprising himself.

Alice turned to him. "May I join you then?" she asked, surprising him even more. It was a fine day indeed.

They found a small side-street tearoom and a vacant table near a man with two little girls waiting patiently for food. Peter went up to the counter, ordering Oolong for himself and Earl Grey for Alice. Alice was looking at the girls when he returned.

"Hello Peter!" A hand tapped his shoulder as he reached his chair, and he turned to see the ebullient wife of one his colleagues. "I thought you'd be out there racing today," Joan added with a quick embrace.

"Not me," Peter said. "I only ever run alone."

"That's too bad. But meet my good friend, Lois. Lois, this is our resident eccentric bachel— Ah Peter, you have company!"

"This is Alice," Peter said. "From my old department."

Alice stood up and exchanged easy pleasantries.

"Well, we're very pleased to meet you, Alice," Joan said, patting Alice's hand. "Have a fun afternoon." She raised her eyebrows at Peter and tugged Lois away.

Peter was mortified. "I'm sorry," he said, dropping onto his chair. "She means well." He rubbed the handle of his fork, and wondered why it mattered what Joan thought. Why did it matter what any of them thought? What mattered was what Alice thought. And what if she thought the same thing? What if she, too, thought he was just an eccentric bachelor?

ALICE THOUGHT, as she watched Peter's fingertip move back and forth on his fork, that he bore all the marks of her idea of a bachelor. Not single, that was too trivial a word. He was definitely a bachelor. She had always thought of bachelors as so romantic, linked by long-lost association with quiet, intelligent men who needed to be saved. Something like the perfect youth of her teenage dreams, she supposed. Or maybe not; maybe she was thinking of the man who had come once with Valerie, half-heard hushed words behind closed doors about not needing to be saved, not wanting to be saved.

And that was the thing, she realized. Her idealized bachelor—personified right here—might not want to be saved. And after all, who was she to save anyone? She had tried to save her idealized youth long ago, and fixated on the wrong victim, her solitary specter—who had not even been solitary in the first place—while a real-life boy almost drowned. Besides, hadn't she already paid the price of Peter's judgement-clouding gratitude for saving him once?

At the thought of gratitude, she touched her ear. "I almost forgot," she said. "Thank you so, so much for these!"

"It's nothing," Peter said, eyes on his fork, adding with a parenthetic smile that they'd only have gone to waste. "I'm glad you could use them," he murmured, eyes still on the fork. "They look really good on you."

Alice wished she could wrap those slivers of chainmail around her heart; she needed armor to protect herself. Whichever way she looked at it, she was doomed. *Bachelor*, she thought, still surveying at him. So much more romantic than *spinster* or *old maid*. So much more romantic—and so far out of reach.

"Acshully, I've changed my mind," one of the girls at the next door table announced as a plate of food was placed in front of her.

Actually, I've changed my mind, Alice wanted to say to Peter as he turned toward the voice. I've changed my mind about not wanting to get involved. It sounded too childish for words. As childish as *Let's just be friends*, which she had never had to say either, he had already understood. Only now she had changed her mind.

"Peter," she began.

His eyes met hers again, so brown.

"Excuse me." Two ceramic cups and pots of tea were set down between them.

"Any progress on the model?" she asked him instead. The last time she saw him, he had offered to mathematically model the equilibrium between intestinal T-cells and commensals.

"Yes," he said indifferently. "And it's impossibly stable so it can't be right. Nothing perturbs the balance long-term, and that's obviously not what you see."

"Well then, next time you come by let's—"

"I came by last week. As you know. You weren't around." He sounded annoyed.

"No, I don't suppose I was." Alice concentrated on filling her cup with too-weak tea. "Did Tom tell you?" she asked.

"Tell me what?"

"It was his idea," she said, rotating her cup on the circle of its footprint. "They're interested in gut immunity. Tom said now was the time to apply, what with the papers coming out…and given that my virulence project doesn't really have a future—"

"It was an interview?"

Alice poured cold milk into her cup. "A second one," she said. Light bounced off the cup's rim into a fine looped cusp on the surface of her tea.

"They want you, then."

Alice shrugged.

"Where?"

"San Diego."

ALICE MIGHT AS WELL have slapped Peter's face. She was going to leave. He had not seen it coming. *Doesn't really have a future*, her words echoed back.

"That's great," he said, feigning enthusiasm as he gripped the handle of his fork. "I assume you're considering it?"

"I suppose I should."

With his other fist he bore down on the tines as if trying to press them flat. "That sort of thing doesn't happen every day," he said.

"I know."

"Take them up on it, then." The pain was intense. But who was he to hold her back? Who was he to interfere?

"Ow! You're bleeding!" Alice was staring at his hands that he realized were now clasped.

"I'm sorry," he said, squeezing his palm as the blood began to spread.

A moment later her hand was on his; she had reached across the table and pressed soft fabric on the wound. Her hand, like that first time, was cold. He took charge of the makeshift dressing without looking up.

"Thanks," he said and pulled the bandage tight. "I'll wash it and—"

"No need," Alice said as he recognized the green bandana.

It's come full circle, he thought. Another loop has closed. The girl at the next table launched a brokenhearted wail and he turned to see a teardrop hit the side of her plate.

Conversation dissipated after that as if by mutual consent. Peter drained his cup.

"Well, I'd better go," he said eventually, rewrapping his hand.

Alice concurred and took one last gulp of tea. As he followed her into the sunshine, a festive cheer erupted not far off: the runners had arrived. Alice and Peter went their separate ways with little more than a sigh.

PETER KEPT to the back streets to avoid the applause. He had nothing to feel good about. The bleeding had stopped but the side of his hand still hurt. Whenever he reached a cross-street the jubilation swelled, each time more than before. It was impossible to ignore—especially when he reached an elevated intersection from which he could see, one block south, a rapid trickle of bobbing heads beyond a wall of static backs. He had never seen the point of running *en masse*, or of manically watching a stream of strangers run past. He stood on the corner and stared, the looming prospect of an empty future only adding to the vacuum he sensed between himself and the world. Eventually, he felt so thoroughly alone that he walked toward the race.

The strange thing was that as he came closer, the mania down there seemed less irrational. He was drawn not only by a longing to lose himself in the crowd, but by a not-quite-comprehending curiosity—and the almost physical tug of the steady one-way flow. He felt a glimmer of excitement. And yet it seemed so arbitrary, this bulk enthusiasm of one group of for another. Arbitrary and infectious: soon even he was mesmerized. The trickle swelled, became a stream, a rising tide confined by solid human banks of which he was now a part—though at the same time he still saw each separate runner, each discrete spectator, each not only a part of but creating the whole.

A salt-caked athlete stopped nearby, clutching his calf. Runners flowed around him and merged again in front. The man raised his salt-caked face, seeking a way out and in obvious pain, but he was trapped by that living moving ectoplasm, hemmed in place. Peter watched him with sympathy, holding his breath. The man closed his eyes and looked ready to give up. But then, as Peter's heart started to pound, he drew himself up and limped on through a crowd that cheered as if he had just won. Peter let go his held breath, but his cheer caught in his throat. It was his dream: he had remembered something more, something crucial, from his dream.

"Go for it!" the man beside him yelled, and Peter realized he was right. He ripped his gaze from the race, tore himself from the crowd, crossed the train tracks to the far side of the street and ran.

ALICE WALKED FAST. As if Peter's attitude had not been enough, when she tried to cross the street a race official had barred her way.

"No one's crossing here for the next two hours," he had said although the road just then was clear. "Rules are rules," he had interjected when she pointed that out, waving an arm toward the Citgo sign and telling her to use the underpass up there.

Setting off as bidden, she had not gone far when she noticed she was walking in step to a beat—to the beat of dance music coming from a roadside stand. Immediately she broke her pace, but was moved almost to tears by the opening chords of the next song, which she instantly recognized—a song she had hated with a vengeance in her teens when it hit the charts and laden now with all the hopes and dreams of those lost halcyon days. She had waited out the song, barely seeing the blur of runners, until she noticed how often one or other of them smiled as he or she ran through the song.

Twenty-four miles and these people still smiled, she had thought and wished that she could too. Then again, that was what exercise did for you: *The simple shifting of a lighted candle from the normal atmosphere into one of oxygen.* She wished that she could run—wished she could feel.

Her eyes had fallen on a small man weaving briskly through the pack. *What's your dream?* he had written on his chest. He had caught her reading it, and met her eye and grinned—a brief and seemingly all-knowing grin—and as she watched him pass by and disappear again, she had seen the words *Then live it!* scrawled across his back. Yes! a voice inside her had urged. Live your dream! For a moment this had seemed painfully obvious, painfully right. Then she had remembered, and smarted again at Peter's thoughtless remarks. What dream was that, anyway?

She had left off watching and walked fast along the empty sidewalk on the far side of the street. She needed to be alone. Now and then an augmented cheer traveled wave-like down the lines. Often, the urgent cries of a name burst for a moment through the vague white noise of gaiety. All along the broad straight boulevard, trees were coming into bud against the brilliant sky, branches softened by the ghost-green promise of leaves soon to come. Alice loved these first signs of spring, these wide tree-lined avenues, this city in which she now lived. She would miss them if she left—when she left.

She would especially miss Peter, she acknowledged. Peter, who saw no reason for her to stay. Perhaps he was right. Perhaps she should take what she could get. She had to think of her career, the reason she had come, and the reason she should leave; she had to think of all that she would gain.

She thought of all that she would lose—of Peter.

Yet this was a job any of her colleagues would have died for.

I am not any of my colleagues, she reminded herself. Surely there would be other jobs. Would there be other men like Peter?

Peter, who saw no reason for her to stay—she had to keep reminding herself of that. He had told her to go. In which case what did he matter?

Did he matter? She knew it mattered that whenever he was there her surroundings seemed to fade, and a cool shower of joy soaked her senses and awakened her dreams—her very own dreams, not other people's hoped-for realities. And it mattered that whenever he smiled between his dimpled parentheses, his canines pricked her heart anew. He mattered to her, even if she didn't to him. Did he not want her anymore?

What mattered now, though, was what *she* wanted. She had to focus on her own desires.

Her own desires? She desired Peter. She ached with desire for him. So much so that that she felt like kicking something hard by the time she reached the underpass, and almost pushed back in anger when a group of wild male teens knocked her aside as they poured down the steps, their echoing yells fading as the tunnel engulfed her and blocked out the sunlight and exuberance above. Far below a train groaned to a halt. And Alice had the strangest sensation that she was walking into anonymity. The half-light reeked of anonymity—and of urine and stale beer. Of anonymity, and of trying and failing to live up to expectation. Red brick walls rose around her on all sides; she looked for the door but there was no door, only darkness and a stench of urine and stale beer.

She pulled herself back to the present. Nothing much changed. The red brick walls of the underpass loomed close, the stench was stronger than before. This was reality through which she was walking, and that was a stain of something nasty running down the wall. And through the rank odor and gloom, the sense of anonymity clung. At least it numbed the crippling grief that was trying to stake its claim and made it easier somehow. Anonymity was really not so bad.

Yet it was all so very sad, she thought. Peter knew who she was. She had always been herself with him—her unedited self. Even at her worst. Perhaps especially at her worst. And he had put up with her even at her worst. She was sure he had felt something for her during those wintry days when his eyes had said so much, when she was too cold—or maybe too confused—to care, when she was cruel enough to stop him in his tracks with an explicit stare. So it was her fault if he felt nothing for her now.

Did he really feel nothing anymore? Alice stopped walking. Did he? She thought of his fist on the fork's tines, his self-inflicted pain. Could there be more to that pain than a puncturing wound? She had no idea. And there was no point in guessing or speculating or assuming or hoping or dreaming. To find answers you had to ask questions, and ask the *right* questions—and Alice knew exactly which question she had to ask. *Live your dream*, the words flashed, screamed through her mind. She simply had to know. She swung around. And walked straight into Peter.

For Peter had run fast. Peter, who had remembered his entire dream, had at last understood. It always started out the same with the darkness and the panic, the leaden pressure that dissolved all boundaries between him and the sea. The calm enlightenment of which he was always robbed had begun—as always—to dawn out of nowhere and everywhere at once in intense pleasure and pain combined. Only this time it was different: he had seen Alice. She was standing on the shore. And knowing he would not see her again, he had felt tragically sad, consumed by the exquisite agony of sacrifice. Exquisite, that is, until he saw that she was crying, and that she was crying for him. His agony had changed. It was no longer exquisite; there was no pleasure in that pain at all. He had to get back. All balance was lost, all serenity gone. With a colossal burst of willpower, he had forced himself to move. He had struggled to regain his limbs, fill his lungs, because he could not hurt her in this way however much he hurt himself, and it had hurt so very much as he searched for the surface that was somewhere out of reach, impossible to find—and he had woken in the dark, gasping horribly, on his own. Knowing as he ran that it was only a dream; knowing also—fearing too—that dreams might yet come true.

"Hey, the race is over there!" someone yelled from a balcony as he passed by.

Alongside but apart, Peter thought. Eccentric—and so much the better if it meant he could be like Old Cross's cam with its off-center axis which, even as it went full circle, transformed rotary motion to linear—movement back and forth. Reciprocating. Could it be true here? He had to find out. He ran down the steps into the underpass and daylight disappeared, replaced by blinding darkness and a stench of urine and stale beer, and—

Live your dream, a voice whispered inside Alice as her body fused with Peter's. And before Peter said a word she reached up around his shoulders, slid her fingers through his hair, pulled his face down close to hers and kissed his mouth. The biggest question—the biggest risk. And in an instant he was kissing her. He was kissing her and nobody else. And stars were flowing through her body, from her soles of her feet, and she was rising from the ground as if propelled by those stars—though in reality it was only Peter who was lifting her up.

And as Peter held Alice and Alice held Peter, time disappeared. And in that timelessness a resonance welled up and spread out around them, so that every object, every sense, every sensation reconnected and synergized, became saturated with a vividness, a fundamental oneness that had been absent for too long. And no longer an endpoint, the future was a beginning and that beginning was now—and that was all that either Alice or Peter cared to know.

At that moment, Tom, who for no particular reason was taking a stroll, walked past the oblivious pair and breathed a sigh of relief; Bill, who was reading beside Sage's bed, felt the pressure of Sage's hand as it closed around his; the landlord, staring out of his front window, was struck by a sudden feeling that his life had not quite gone to waste. And far away across the ocean, Ben approached a London restaurant and knew he truly loved the woman waiting for him there.

Meanwhile, on the south coast of Wales, a man chuckled suddenly and told his curious wife that he had just remembered a kiss he misplaced one stormy late-spring day. On the other side of that same rural town, a not-unhappily-married mother of three held a match to an old newspaper clipping she had found in a drawer, and watched a glorified lie of which she had long been ashamed curl and blacken and crumble into ash.

Acknowledgements & Author's Note

I AM GRATEFUL to the many kind and patient people—including Richard Gallagher, Alex McAdam, Dayo Forster, Judith Rees, Lynda Morgenroth and Patrick, Michael and Deirdre Schweitzer—who read versions of this story in part or in full over the years. Thank you for the words left unsaid as well as spoken out loud. I am especially grateful to Yoshie Rice and Dora Schweitzer, as well as Jenna Blum at Grub Street and Chris and colleagues at Writers Services, for their invaluable detailed critiques. I owe a heartfelt thank you to my daughters Anna and Nelly for putting up with this for quite so long and for their intense and targeted advice during the final stages, and of course to my husband Jen-Wei Lin for just about everything else.

EARLY INSPIRATION for this novel sprang from my reading of Bruno Bettelheim's "The Uses of Enchantment: The Meaning and Importance of Fairytales." (Vintage Books, 1989).

For historical details, I am grateful for the privately published compilation, "The Twelve Grandchildren of Eugen & Algunde Hollaender Schweitzer: The Impact of Nazi Racial Policies on One Family," edited by Christoph E. Schweitzer in collaboration with Wolfgang and Carl-Christoph Schweitzer.

The two old manuscripts that recur throughout the novel actually exist. Their full references are: "The Influence of Exercise on Growth," by H. G. Beyer, *Journal of Experimental Medicine*, Volume 1, page 546 (1896) and "Sur un foetus humain à trois têtes," by Doctors Reina et Galvagni, *Annales des Sciences Naturelles* second series, Volume 10 (Zoology), page 349 (1838). The specific edition of "Kiss in the Hotel Joseph Conrad," by Howard Norman was published by Summit Books (1989), and "The Concise British Flora in Colour," by W. Keble Martin by Holt, Rinehart & Winston (1965).

For background details of life in the lab, I have drawn from my own experience at a number of institutions—including having heard seminar speakers introduce talks on the immune system by referencing Jenner's development of a smallpox vaccine and the role played by milkmaids. I am grateful to my many former colleagues and mentors whose diverse influences and even throw-away comments provided much food for thought.

The infectious virus, Lymphocytic Choriomeningitic Virus, also known as LCMV, is valued by immunologists as a versatile tool for studying immune responses in mice. The idea for its role in this novel came from my general knowledge of the works of R. M. Zinkernagel and colleagues, and from a casual conversation with Alex McAdam. Details of human symptoms were drawn from an amalgam of mutually consistent medical references, and I have tried to adhere as closely as possible to both the properties of, and symptoms associated with the virus. Indeed, the novel's subtitled parts correspond to the distinct phases associated with symptomatic infection and recovery. I am grateful to Alex and to Iain Fraser for answering my questions, and for providing additional anecdotal information. I apologize for any inaccuracies that may have occurred while shaping this information to the fictional narrative.

The specific fields—mucosal immunity, self-tolerance and autoimmunity, host defense against pathogens, microbial virulence and host-microbe interplay—were chosen for practical and metaphorical purposes related to the story being told. The scientists and their projects are wholly fabricated, though I have tried to keep the fictional science more or less plausible. For those interested in the corresponding areas of real science, the mathematical model was loosely based on by my own published—though never tried and tested—foray into modeling, and although Sharden's Syndrome and Tom's avirulent virus and the studies connected to them were made up, the concepts underlying them were inspired by the following articles:

H. Ochman & N. A. Moran, (2001), "Genes lost and genes found: evolution of bacterial pathogenesis and symbiosis," *Science* 292, 1096

L. V. Hooper & J. I. Gordon (2001), "Commensal host-bacterial relationships in the gut," *Science* 292:1115

F. Barreau et al. (2004), "Neonatal maternal deprivation triggers long term alterations in colonic epithelial barrier and mucosal immunity in rats," *Gut*, 53:501

F. Barreau et al. (2004), "Nerve growth factor mediates alterations of colonic sensitivity and mucosal barrier induced by neonatal stress in rats." *Gastroenterology*, 127: 524

A. J. Macpherson & T. Uhr (2004), "Induction of protective IgA.by intestinal dendritic cells carrying commensal bacteria," *Science* 303:662

K. J. Rhee et al. (2004), "Role of commensal bacteria in development of gut-associated lymphoid tissues and preimmune antibody repertoire," *J. Immunol.* 172:1118

www.ingramcontent.com/pod-product-compliance
Lightning Source LLC
Chambersburg PA
CBHW070725280626
47159CB00023B/2665